Lotte Hansen

PAUL AUSTER is the bestselling author of *Sunset Park,*
Invisible, The Book of Illusions, and *The New York Tril-*
ogy, among many other works. In 2006 he was awarded
the Prince of Asturias Award for Literature. Among his
other honors are the Prix Médicis étranger for *Levia-*
than, the Independent Spirit Award for the screenplay of
Smoke, and the Premio Napoli for *Sunset Park.* In 2012
he was the first recipient of the NYC Literary Honors in
the category of fiction. He has also been a finalist for the
International IMPAC Dublin Literary Award (*The Book*
of Illusions), the PEN/Faulkner Award for Fiction (*The*
Music of Chance), and the Edgar Award (*City of Glass*).
He is a member of the American Academy of Arts and
Letters, the American Academy of Arts and Sciences,
and a Commandeur de l'Ordre des Arts et des Lettres.
His work has been translated into forty-three languages.
He lives in Brooklyn, New York.

Also by Paul Auster

NOVELS

*The New York Trilogy (City of Glass • Ghosts • The Locked Room) •
In the Country of Last Things • Moon Palace • The Music of Chance •
Leviathan • Mr. Vertigo • Timbuktu • The Book of Illusions •
Oracle Night • The Brooklyn Follies • Invisible • Sunset Park*

NONFICTION

*The Invention of Solitude • The Art of Hunger • Why Write? •
Hand to Mouth • The Red Notebook • Collected Prose • Winter Journal •
Here and Now* (with J. M. Coetzee) • *Report from the Interior*

SCREENPLAYS

*Three Films: Smoke, Blue in the Face, Lulu on the Bridge
The Inner Life of Martin Frost*

POETRY

Collected Poems

ILLUSTRATED BOOKS

The Story of My Typewriter (with Sam Messer)
Auggie Wren's Christmas Story (with Isol)
City of Glass (adapted by Paul Karasik and David Mazzucchelli)

EDITOR

*The Random House Book of Twentieth-Century French Poetry •
I Thought My Father Was God and Other True Tales
from NPR's National Story Project •
Samuel Beckett: The Grove Centenary Edition*

Praise for Paul Auster

"Auster really does possess the wand of the enchanter."
—The New York Review of Books

"One of America's greats." *—Time Out* (Chicago)

"A genuine American original." *—The Boston Globe*

"One of America's greatest living novelists."
—The Observer (London)

"Contemporary American writing at its best . . . It has the illusion of effortlessness." *—The New York Times Book Review*

"Paul Auster is definitely a genius." —Haruki Murakami

"One of the great writers of our time." *—San Francisco Chronicle*

"A literary original who is perfecting a hybrid genre of his own."
—The Wall Street Journal

"One of America's most inventive and original writers."
—The Seattle Times

"Auster is unquestionably a literary genius."
—Deseret Morning News

Praise for *Travels in the Scriptorium*

"This is a chilling story of isolation. . . . All of this refracting inventiveness is why Auster is often referred to as a master of the metaphysical detective story. . . . The reader is kept on edge, guessing until the very end."   —*The Washington Post*

"The writing is as tight as ever."

—Jonathan Messinger, *Time Out* (Chicago)

"This brief work radiates in so many directions . . . that there must be involved in it some sort of magic or wizardry."

—*Rain Taxi*

"Auster's lean, poker-faced prose creates a satisfyingly claustrophobic allegory."   —*Publishers Weekly*

"Archly playful and shrewdly philosophical . . . Celebrates the power of the imagination . . . The labyrinthine nature of the mind . . . [A] tribute to the transcendence of stories."

—Donna Seaman, *Booklist*

Praise for *Man in the Dark*

A *Washington Post* Best Book of the Year
Longlisted for the International IMPAC Dublin Literary Award

"An undoubted pleasure to read."
—Michael Dirda, *The New York Review of Books*

"The narrative juxtapositions and the riddling starkness of Auster's prose create an absorbing . . . effect, breathing life into a meditation on the difference between the stories we want to tell and the stories we end up telling."　—*The New Yorker*

"Works beautifully . . . This is perhaps Auster's best book. Like Vonnegut's classic antiwar novel [*Slaughterhouse Five*], Auster's book leaves one with a depth of feeling much larger than might be expected from such a small and concise work of art."　—*San Francisco Chronicle*

"*Man in the Dark* is at once haunting, thought-provoking, emotional, and compellingly readable." —*The Philadelphia Inquirer*

"Remarkable . . . *Man in the Dark* possesses a grand and generous heart."　—*The Boston Globe*

"A novel that kept my attention from the first page all the way to the last. Frankly, it hypnotized me."
—Alan Cheuse, NPR's *All Things Considered*

"[Auster's] magic has never flourished more fully than it does in *Man in the Dark*. . . . The novel delivers intense reading pleasure from start to finish." —*The Orlando Sentinel*

"Provoking and entertaining in brilliant fashion . . . [Auster] draws you into a literary maze and sets you marveling at how he will get you out." —*The Seattle Times*

"Intricately layered, playful with the notions of 'real' and 'unreal' . . . *Man in the Dark* is the work of a master, confident of his powers to move readers smoothly between worlds, totally in control of setting, pace, and dialogue. . . . A deep, fraught book." —*Daily Kos*

"Auster has crafted a stirring, politically charged portrait of the power of fiction." —*The Newark Star-Ledger*

"Auster's latest astute and mesmerizing metaphysical fiction . . . A master of the matter-of-factly fantastic, Auster tells an utterly authentic story of culpability and survival, the vortex of loss, and our endless struggle to translate terror into understanding." —*Booklist* (starred review)

"Another wild fictive device that demolishes the walls separating author, character, and reader, leading to that familiar through-the-looking-glass feeling . . . The man is a magician." —Jeff Turrentine, *The Washington Post*

DAY/NIGHT

Travels in the Scriptorium

and

Man in the Dark

PAUL AUSTER

PICADOR

Henry Holt and Company
New York

These novels are works of fiction. All of the characters, organizations, and events portrayed in these novels are either products of the author's imagination or are used fictitiously.

DAY/NIGHT. Copyright © 2013 by Paul Auster. *Travels in the Scriptorium* copyright © 2006 by Paul Auster. *Man in the Dark* copyright © 2008 by Paul Auster. All rights reserved. Printed in the United States of America. For information, address Picador, 175 Fifth Avenue, New York, N.Y. 10010.

www.picadorusa.com
www.twitter.com/picadorusa • www.facebook.com/picadorusa
picadorbookroom.tumblr.com

Picador® is a U.S. registered trademark and is used by Henry Holt and Company under license from Pan Books Limited.

For book club information, please visit www.facebook.com/picadorbookclub or e-mail marketing@picadorusa.com.

Library of Congress Cataloging-in-Publication Data is available upon request.

ISBN 978-1-250-03787-9 (trade paperback)
ISBN 978-1-250-04504-1 (e-book)

Picador books may be purchased for educational, business, or promotional use. For information on bulk purchases, please contact Macmillan Corporate and Premium Sales Department at 1-800-221-7945, extension 5442, or write specialmarkets@macmillan.com.

First Edition: November 2013

10 9 8 7 6 5 4 3 2 1

CONTENTS

TRAVELS IN THE SCRIPTORIUM

for Lloyd Hustvedt
(in memory)

The old man sits on the edge of the narrow bed, palms spread out on his knees, head down, staring at the floor. He has no idea that a camera is planted in the ceiling directly above him. The shutter clicks silently once every second, producing eighty-six thousand four hundred still photos with each revolution of the earth. Even if he knew he was being watched, it wouldn't make any difference. His mind is elsewhere, stranded among the figments in his head as he searches for an answer to the question that haunts him.

Who is he? What is he doing here? When did he arrive and how long will he remain? With any luck, time will tell us all. For the moment, our only task is to study the pictures as attentively as we can and refrain from drawing any premature conclusions.

There are a number of objects in the room, and on each one

a strip of white tape has been affixed to the surface, bearing a single word written out in block letters. On the bedside table, for example, the word is TABLE. On the lamp, the word is LAMP. Even on the wall, which is not strictly speaking an object, there is a strip of tape that reads WALL. The old man looks up for a moment, sees the wall, sees the strip of tape attached to the wall, and pronounces the word *wall* in a soft voice. What cannot be known at this point is whether he is reading the word on the strip of tape or simply referring to the wall itself. It could be that he has forgotten how to read but still recognizes things for what they are and can call them by their names, or, conversely, that he has lost the ability to recognize things for what they are but still knows how to read.

He is dressed in blue-and-yellow striped cotton pajamas, and his feet are encased in a pair of black leather slippers. It is unclear to him exactly where he is. In the room, yes, but in what building is the room located? In a house? In a hospital? In a prison? He can't remember how long he has been here or the nature of the circumstances that precipitated his removal to this place. Perhaps he has always been here; perhaps this is where he has lived since the day he was born. What he knows is that his heart is filled with an implacable sense of guilt. At the same time, he can't escape the feeling that he is the victim of a terrible injustice.

There is one window in the room, but the shade is drawn, and as far as he can remember he has not yet looked out of it. Likewise with the door and its white porcelain knob. Is he locked in, or is he free to come and go as he wishes? He has yet to investigate this matter—for, as stated in the first paragraph above, his mind is elsewhere, adrift in the past as he wanders among the phantom beings that clutter his head, struggling to answer the question that haunts him.

The pictures do not lie, but neither do they tell the whole story. They are merely a record of time passing, the outward evidence. The old man's age, for example, is difficult to determine from the slightly out-of-focus black-and-white images. The only fact that can be set down with any certainty is that he is not young, but the word *old* is a flexible term and can be used to describe a person anywhere between sixty and a hundred. We will therefore drop the epithet *old man* and henceforth refer to the person in the room as Mr. Blank. For the time being, no first name will be necessary.

Mr. Blank stands up from the bed at last, pauses briefly to steady his balance, and then shuffles over to the desk at the other end of the room. He feels tired, as if he has just woken from a fitful, too short night of sleep, and as the soles of his slippers scrape along the bare wood floor, he is reminded of the sound of sandpaper. Far off in the distance, beyond the room, beyond the building in which the room is located, he hears the faint cry of a bird—perhaps a crow, perhaps a seagull, he can't tell which.

Mr. Blank lowers his body into the chair at the desk. It is an exceedingly comfortable chair, he decides, made of soft brown leather and equipped with broad armrests to accommodate his elbows and forearms, not to speak of an invisible spring mechanism that allows him to rock back and forth at will, which is precisely what he begins to do the moment he sits down. Rocking back and forth has a soothing effect on him, and as Mr. Blank continues to indulge in these pleasurable oscillations, he remembers the rocking horse that sat in his bedroom when he was a small boy, and then he begins to relive some of the imaginary journeys he used to take on that horse, whose name was Whitey and who, in the young Mr. Blank's mind, was not a wooden object adorned with white paint but a living being, a true horse.

After this brief excursion into his early boyhood, anguish rises up into Mr. Blank's throat again. He says out loud in a weary voice: I mustn't allow this to happen. Then he leans forward to examine the piles of papers and photographs stacked neatly on the surface of the mahogany desk. He takes hold of the pictures first, three dozen eight-by-ten black-and-white portraits of men and women of various ages and races. The photo on top shows a young woman in her early twenties. Her dark hair is cropped short, and there is an intense, troubled look in her eyes as she gazes into the lens. She is standing outdoors in some city, perhaps an Italian or French city, because she happens to be positioned in front of a medieval church, and because the woman is wearing a scarf and a woolen coat, it is safe to assume the picture was taken in winter. Mr. Blank stares into the eyes of the young woman and strains to remember who she is. After twenty seconds or so, he hears himself whisper a single word: Anna. A feeling of overpowering love washes through him. He wonders if Anna isn't someone he was once married to, or if, perhaps, he isn't looking at a picture of his daughter. An instant after thinking these thoughts, he is attacked by a fresh wave of guilt, and he knows that Anna is dead. Even worse, he suspects that he is responsible for her death. It might even be, he tells himself, that he was the person who killed her.

Mr. Blank groans in pain. Looking at the pictures is too much for him, so he pushes them aside and turns his attention to the papers. There are four piles in all, each about six inches high. For no particular reason that he is aware of, he reaches for the top page on the pile farthest to the left. The handwritten words, printed out in block letters similar to the ones on the strips of white tape, read as follows:

Viewed from the outermost reaches of space, the earth is no larger than a speck of dust. Remember that the next time you write the word "humanity."

From the look of disgust that comes over his face as he scans these sentences, we can be fairly confident that Mr. Blank has not lost the ability to read. But who the author of these sentences might be is still open to question.

Mr. Blank reaches out for the next page on the pile and discovers that it is a typed manuscript of some sort. The first paragraph reads:

The moment I started to tell my story, they knocked me down and kicked me in the head. When I climbed to my feet and started to talk again, one of them hit me across the mouth, and then another one punched me in the stomach. I fell down. I managed to get up again, but just as I was about to begin the story for the third time, the Colonel threw me against the wall and I passed out.

There are two more paragraphs on the page, but before Mr. Blank can begin reading the second one, the telephone rings. It is a black rotary model from the late forties or early fifties of the past century, and since it is located on the bedside table, Mr. Blank is forced to stand up from the soft leather chair and shuffle over to the other side of the room. He picks up the receiver on the fourth ring.

Hello, says Mr. Blank.

Mr. Blank? asks the voice on the other end.

If you say so.

Are you sure? I can't take any chances.

I'm not sure of anything. If you want to call me Mr. Blank, I'm happy to answer to that name. Who am I talking to?

James.

I don't know any James.

James P. Flood.

Refresh my memory.

I came to visit you yesterday. We spent two hours together.

Ah. The policeman.

Ex-policeman.

Right. The ex-policeman. What can I do for you?

I want to see you again.

Wasn't one conversation enough?

Not really. I know I'm just a minor character in this business, but they said I was allowed to see you twice.

You're telling me I have no choice.

I'm afraid so. But we don't have to talk in the room if you don't want to. We can go out and sit in the park if you'd prefer that.

I don't have anything to wear. I'm standing here dressed in pajamas and slippers.

Look in the closet. You have all the clothes you need.

Ah. The closet. Thank you.

Have you had your breakfast, Mr. Blank?

I don't think so. Am I allowed to eat?

Three meals a day. It's still a bit early, but Anna should be coming around pretty soon.

Anna? Did you say Anna?

She's the person who takes care of you.

I thought she was dead.

Hardly.

Maybe it's a different Anna.

I doubt it. Of all the people involved in this story, she's the only one who's completely on your side.

And the others?

Let's just say there's a lot of resentment, and we'll leave it at that.

It should be noted that in addition to the camera a microphone is embedded in one of the walls, and every sound Mr. Blank makes is being reproduced and preserved by a highly sensitive digital tape recorder. The least groan or sniffle, the least cough or fleeting flatulence that emerges from his body is therefore an integral part of our account as well. It goes without saying that this aural data also includes the words that are variously mumbled, uttered, or shouted by Mr. Blank, as with, for example, the telephone call from James P. Flood recorded above. The conversation ends with Mr. Blank reluctantly giving in to the ex-policeman's

demand to pay him a visit sometime that morning. After Mr.
Blank hangs up the phone, he sits down on the edge of the narrow bed, assuming a position identical to the one described in
the first sentence of this report: palms spread out on his knees,
head down, staring at the floor. He ponders whether he should
stand up and begin looking for the closet Flood referred to, and
if that closet exists, whether he should change out of his pajamas and put on some clothes, assuming there are clothes in the
closet—if indeed that closet exists. But Mr. Blank is in no rush to
engage in such mundane chores. He wants to go back to the
typescript he started reading before he was interrupted by
the telephone. He therefore stands up from the bed and takes a
first tentative step toward the other side of the room, feeling a
sudden rush of dizziness as he does so. He realizes that he will
fall down if he remains standing any longer, but rather than
return to the bed and sit there until the crisis passes, he puts his
right hand against the wall, leans the full brunt of his weight
against it, and gradually lowers himself to the floor. Now on his
knees, Mr. Blank pitches himself forward and plants his palms
on the floor as well. Dizzy or not, such is his determination to
reach the desk that he crawls there on all fours.

Once he manages to climb into the leather chair, he rocks
back and forth for several moments to steady his nerves. In
spite of his physical efforts, he understands that he is afraid to
go on reading the typescript. Why this fear should have taken
hold of him is something he cannot account for. It's only words,
he tells himself, and since when have words had the power to
frighten a man half to death? It won't do, he mutters in a low,

barely audible voice. Then, to reassure himself, he repeats the same sentence, shouting at the top of his lungs: IT WON'T DO!

Inexplicably, this sudden burst of sound gives him the courage to continue. He takes a deep breath, fixes his eyes on the words in front of him, and reads the following two paragraphs:

They have kept me in this room ever since. From all I can gather, it is not a typical cell, and it does not seem to be part of the military stockade or the territorial house of detention. It is a small, bare enclosure, measuring roughly twelve feet by fifteen feet, and because of the simplicity of its design (dirt floor, thick stone walls), I suspect that it once served as a storehouse for food supplies, perhaps for sacks of flour and grain. There is a single barred window at the top of the western wall, but it is too far off the ground for me to get my hands on it. I sleep on a straw mat in one corner, and two meals are given to me every day: cold porridge in the morning, tepid soup and hard bread in the evening. According to my calculations, I have been here for forty-seven nights. This tally could be wrong, however. My first days in the cell were interrupted by numerous beatings, and because I can't remember how many times I lost consciousness— nor how long the oblivions lasted when I did—it is possible that I lost count somewhere and failed to notice when a particular sun might have risen or another might have set.

The desert begins just outside my window. Each time the wind blows from the west, I can smell the sage and juniper bushes, the minima of those dry distances. I lived out there on my own for close to four months, wandering freely from one place to another, sleeping outdoors in all kinds of weather, and to return from the

openness of that country to the narrow confines of this room has
not been easy for me. I can bear up to the enforced solitude, to
the absence of conversation and human contact, but I long to be
in the air and the light again, and I spend my days hungering
for something to look at besides these jagged stone walls. Every
now and then, soldiers walk below my window. I can hear their
boots crunching on the ground, the irregular bursts of their
voices, the clatter of carts and horses in the heat of the unat-
tainable day. This is the garrison at Ultima: the westernmost tip
of the Confederation, the place that stands at the edge of the
known world. We are more than two thousand miles from the
capital here, overlooking the unmapped expanses of the Alien
Territories. The law says that no one is allowed to go out there.
I went because I was ordered to go, and now I have returned to
give my report. They will listen to me or they won't listen to me,
and then I will be taken outside and shot. I am fairly certain of
that now. The important thing is not to delude myself, to resist
the temptation of hope. When they finally put me up against the
wall and aim their rifles at my body, the only thing I will ask of
them is to remove the blindfold. It's not that I have any interest
in seeing the men who kill me, but I want to be able to look at
the sky again. That is the extent of what I want now. To stand
out in the open and look up at the immense blue sky above me,
to gaze at the howling infinite one last time.

Mr. Blank stops reading. His fear has been replaced by confusion, and while he has grasped every word of the text so far, he

has no idea what to make of it. Is it an actual report, he wonders, and what is this place called the Confederation, with its garrison at Ultima and its mysterious Alien Territories, and why does the prose sound like something written in the nineteenth century? Mr. Blank is well aware of the fact that his mind is not all it should be, that he is entirely in the dark about where he is and why he is there, but he is reasonably certain that the present moment can be situated sometime in the early twenty-first century and that he lives in a country called the United States of America. This last thought reminds him of the window, or, to be more precise, of the window shade, on which a strip of white tape has been attached bearing the word SHADE. With the soles of his feet pressing against the floor and his arms pressing against the armrests of the leather chair, he swivels right by ninety to a hundred degrees in order to have a look at said window shade—for not only is this chair endowed with the ability to rock back and forth, it can turn in circles as well. This last discovery is so pleasing to Mr. Blank that he momentarily forgets why he wanted to look at the window shade, exulting instead in this hitherto unknown property of the chair. He spins around once, then twice, then three times, and as he does so he remembers sitting in the chair at the barbershop as a young boy and being spun around in a similar fashion by Rocco the barber both before and after his hair was cut. Fortunately, when Mr. Blank comes to rest again, the chair is more or less in the same position as when he started going around in circles, which means that he is once again looking at the window shade, and again, after this enjoyable interlude, Mr. Blank wonders if he shouldn't walk over to the window, pull up the shade, and have a look outside to see where he is. Perhaps he's no longer in America, he says to himself, but in some other country, abducted in the dead of night by secret agents working for a foreign power.

His triple revolution in the chair has left him somewhat dizzy, however, and he hesitates to budge from his spot, fearing a recurrence of the episode that forced him to travel across the room on all fours some minutes ago. What Mr. Blank is still unaware of at this point is that in addition to being able to rock back and forth and turn around in circles, the leather chair is further equipped with a set of four small wheels, which would make it possible for him to journey over to the window shade without having to stand up. Not knowing that other means of propulsion are available to him besides his legs, Mr. Blank therefore stays where he is, sitting in the chair with his back to the desk, looking at the once white but now yellowing window shade, trying to remember his conversation the previous afternoon with the ex-policeman James P. Flood. He casts about in his mind for an image, some hint as to what the man looks like, but rather than conjure forth any clear pictures, his mind is once again overwhelmed by a paralyzing sensation of guilt. Before this fresh bout of torments and terrors can build into a full-blown panic, however, Mr. Blank hears someone rapping on the door, and then the sound of a key entering the lock. Does this mean that Mr. Blank is imprisoned in the room, unable to leave except through the grace and good will of others? Not necessarily. It could be that Mr. Blank has locked the door from within and that the person now trying to enter the room must undo that lock in order to cross the threshold, thus sparing Mr. Blank the trouble of having to stand up and open the door himself.

One way or the other, the door now opens, and in walks a small woman of indeterminate age—anywhere between forty-five and sixty, Mr. Blank thinks, but it is difficult to be certain. Her gray hair is cut short, she is dressed in a pair of dark blue slacks and a light blue cotton blouse, and the first thing she does after entering the room is smile at Mr. Blank. This smile, which seems to combine both tenderness and affection, banishes his fears and puts him in a state of calm equilibrium. He has no idea who she is, but he is nevertheless happy to see her.

Did you sleep well? the woman asks.

I'm not sure, Mr. Blank replies. To be perfectly honest, I can't remember if I slept or not.

That's good. It means the treatment is working.

Rather than comment on this enigmatic pronouncement, Mr. Blank studies the woman for several moments in silence, then asks: Forgive me for being such a fool, but your name wouldn't be Anna, would it?

Once again, the woman gives him a tender and affectionate smile. I'm glad you remembered it, she says. Yesterday, it kept slipping out of your mind.

Suddenly perplexed and agitated, Mr. Blank swivels around in the leather chair until he is facing the desk, then removes the portrait of the young woman from the pile of black-and-white photographs. Before he can turn around again to look at the woman, whose name appears to be Anna, she is standing beside him with her hand poised gently on his right shoulder, looking down at the picture as well.

If your name is Anna, Mr. Blank says, his voice quivering with emotion, then who is this? Her name is Anna, too, isn't it?

Yes, the woman says, studying the portrait closely, as if remembering something with equal but opposite feelings of revulsion and nostalgia. This is Anna. And I'm Anna, too. This is a picture of me.

But, Mr. Blank stammers, but . . . the girl in the picture is young. And you . . . you have gray hair.

Time, Mr. Blank, Anna says. You understand the meaning of time, don't you? This is me thirty-five years ago.

Before Mr. Blank has a chance to respond, Anna puts the portrait of her younger self back on the pile of photographs.

Your breakfast is getting cold, she says, and without another word she leaves the room, only to return a moment later, wheeling in a stainless steel cart with a platter of food on it, which she positions alongside the bed.

The meal consists of a glass of orange juice, a slice of buttered toast, two poached eggs in a small white bowl, and a pot of Earl Grey tea. In due course, Anna will help Mr. Blank out of the chair and lead him over to the bed, but first she hands him a glass of water and three pills—one green, one white, and one purple.

What's wrong with me? Mr. Blank asks. Am I sick?

No, not at all, Anna says. The pills are part of the treatment.

I don't feel sick. A little tired and dizzy, maybe, but otherwise nothing too terrible. Considering my age, not too terrible at all.

Swallow the pills, Mr. Blank. Then you can eat your breakfast. I'm sure you're very hungry.

But I don't want the pills, Mr. Blank replies, stubbornly holding his ground. If I'm not sick, I'm not going to swallow these wretched pills.

Rather than snap back at Mr. Blank after his rude and aggressive statement, Anna bends over and kisses him on the forehead. Dear Mr. Blank, she says. I know how you feel, but you promised to take the pills every day. That was the bargain. If you don't take the pills, the treatment won't work.

I promised? says Mr. Blank. How do I know you're telling the truth?

Because it's me, Anna, and I would never lie to you. I love you too much for that.

The mention of the word *love* softens Mr. Blank's resolve, and he impulsively decides to back down. All right, he says, I'll take the pills. But only if you kiss me again. Agreed? But it has to be a real kiss this time. On the lips.

Anna smiles, then bends over once more and kisses Mr. Blank squarely on the lips. In that it lasts for a good three seconds, the kiss qualifies as more than just a peck, and even though no tongues are involved, this intimate contact sends a tingle of arousal coursing through Mr. Blank's body. By the time Anna straightens up, he has already begun to swallow the pills.

Now they are sitting beside each other on the edge of the bed. The food cart is in front of them, and as Mr. Blank drinks down his orange juice, takes a bite of his toast and a first sip of the tea, Anna softly rubs his back with her left hand, humming

a tune that he is unable to identify but which he knows is familiar to him, or was once familiar to him. Then he begins to attack the poached eggs, piercing one of the yolks with the tip of
the spoon and gathering up a modest combination of yellow and
white in the hollow of the utensil, but when he tries to lift the
spoon toward his mouth, he is bewildered to discover that his
hand is shaking. Not just some mild tremor, but a pronounced
and convulsive twitching that he is powerless to control. By the
time the spoon has traveled six inches from the bowl, the spasm
is so extreme that the better part of the yellow-and-white mix-
ture has splattered onto the tray.

Would you like me to feed you? Anna asks.

What's wrong with me?

It's nothing to worry about, she answers, patting his back in
an attempt to reassure him. A natural reaction to the pills. It
will pass in a few minutes.

That's some treatment you've cooked up for me, Mr. Blank
mutters in a self-pitying, sullen tone of voice.

It's all for the best, Anna says. And it's not going to last forever. Believe me.

So Mr. Blank allows Anna to feed him, and as she calmly
goes about the business of scooping out portions of the poached
eggs, holding the teacup to his lips, and wiping his mouth with
a paper napkin, Mr. Blank begins to think that Anna is not a
woman so much as an angel, or, if you will, an angel in the form
of a woman.

Why are you so kind to me? he asks.

Because I love you, Anna says. It's that simple.

Now that the meal is finished, the time has come for excretions, ablutions, and the putting on of clothes. Anna pushes the cart away from the bed and then extends her hand to Mr. Blank to help him to his feet. To his immense astonishment, he finds himself standing in front of a door, a door that until now has escaped his notice, and attached to the surface of this door is yet another strip of white tape, marked with the word BATH-ROOM. Mr. Blank wonders how he could have missed it, since it is no more than a few steps from the bed, but, as the reader has already learned, his thoughts have largely been elsewhere, lost in a fogland of ghostlike beings and broken memories as he searches for an answer to the question that haunts him.

Do you have to go? Anna asks.

Go? he replies. Go where?

To the bathroom. Do you need to use the toilet?

Ah. The toilet. Yes. Now that you mention it, I think that would be a good idea.

Do you want me to help you, or can you manage on your own?

I'm not sure. Let me give it a try, and we'll see what happens.

Anna turns the white porcelain knob for him, and the door opens. As Mr. Blank shuffles into the white, windowless room with the black-and-white tile floor, Anna shuts the door behind him, and for several moments Mr. Blank just stands there, looking at the white toilet against the far wall, suddenly feeling bereft, aching to be with Anna again. Finally, he whispers to himself: Get a grip, old man. You're acting like a child. Nevertheless, even as he shuffles over to the toilet and begins lowering his pajama bottoms, he feels an overpowering urge to cry.

The pajama bottoms fall to his ankles; he sits down on the toilet seat; his bladder and bowels prepare to evacuate their pent-up liquids and solids. Urine flows from his penis, first one stool and then a second stool slide from his anus, and so good does it feel to be relieving himself in this manner that he forgets the sorrow that took hold of him just moments before. Of course he can manage on his own, he tells himself. He's been doing it ever since he was a little boy, and when it comes to pissing and shitting, he's as capable as any person in the world. Not only that, but he's an expert at wiping his ass as well.

Let Mr. Blank have his little moment of hubris, for successful as he is in completing the first part of the operation, the second part does not go nearly as well. He has no trouble lifting himself off the seat and flushing the toilet, but once he does so he realizes that his pajama bottoms are still gathered around his ankles and in order to pull them up he must either bend over or crouch down and grab hold of the waist with his hands. Neither bending nor crouching is an activity he feels particularly comfortable with today, but of the two he is somewhat more fearful of bending, since he understands the potential for losing his balance once he lowers his head, and he is apprehensive that if he should indeed lose his balance, he might fall to the floor and crack his skull against the black-and-white tiles. He therefore concludes that crouching is the lesser of the two evils, although he is far from confident that his knees can bear the strain that will be put upon them. We will never know if they can or can't. Alerted by the sound of the flushing toilet, Anna, no doubt assuming that Mr. Blank has finished the job he set out to do, opens the door and enters the bathroom.

One might think that Mr. Blank would be embarrassed to find himself in such a compromising position (standing there with his pants down, his limp penis dangling between his naked, scrawny legs), but such is not the case. Mr. Blank feels no false modesty in front of Anna. If anything, he is more than glad to let her see whatever there is to see, and instead of hastily crouching down to pull up his pajama bottoms, he begins undoing the buttons of his pajama top in order to remove the shirt as well.

I'd like to have my bath now, he says.

A real bath in the tub, she asks, or just a sponge bath?

It doesn't matter. You decide.

Anna looks at her watch and says, Maybe just a sponge bath. It's getting a bit late now, and I still have to dress you and make the bed.

By now, Mr. Blank has removed both the top and the bottoms of his pajamas as well as his slippers. Unperturbed by the sight of the old man's naked body, Anna walks over to the toilet and lowers the seat cover, which she pats a couple of times with the palm of her hand as an invitation for Mr. Blank to sit down. Mr. Blank sits, and Anna then perches herself beside him on the edge of the bathtub, turns on the hot water, and begins soaking a white washcloth under the spigot.

The moment Anna begins touching Mr. Blank's body with the warm, soapy cloth, he falls into a trance of languid submission, luxuriating in the feel of her gentle hands upon him. She starts at the top and works her way slowly downward, washing his ears and behind his ears, the front and back of his neck, has him turn on the toilet seat in order to move the cloth up and down his back, then turn again in order to do the same to his chest, pausing every fifteen seconds or so to douse the cloth under the spigot, alternately adding more soap to it and rinsing the soap out of it, depending on whether she is about to wash a particular part of Mr. Blank's body or remove the soap from an area that has just been cleaned. Mr. Blank shuts his eyes, his head suddenly emptied of the shadow-beings and terrors that have haunted him since the first paragraph of this report. By the time the washcloth has descended to his belly, his penis has begun to alter its shape, growing longer and thicker and becoming partially erect, and Mr. Blank marvels that even at his advanced age his penis continues to act as it always did, never once modifying its behavior since his earliest adolescence. So much has changed for him since then, but not that, not that one thing, and now that Anna has brought the washcloth into direct contact with that part of his body, he can feel it stiffening to full extension, and as she goes on rubbing and stroking it with the warm sudsy water, it is all he can do not to cry out and beg her to finish the job.

We're feeling frisky today, Mr. Blank, Anna says.

I'm afraid so, Mr. Blank whispers, his eyes still shut. I can't help it.

If I were you, I'd feel proud of myself. Not every man your age is still . . . still capable of this.

It has nothing to do with me. The thing has a life of its own.

Suddenly, the cloth moves over to his right leg. Before Mr. Blank can register his disappointment, he feels Anna's bare hand sliding up and down the well-lubricated erection. Her right hand is continuing to wash him with the cloth, but her left hand is now engaged in this other task for him, and even as he succumbs to the practiced ministrations of that left hand, he wonders what he has done to deserve such generous treatment.

He gasps when the semen comes spurting out of him, and it is only then, after the deed has been done, that he opens his eyes and turns to Anna. She is no longer sitting on the edge of the tub but kneeling on the floor in front of him, wiping up the ejaculation with the washcloth. Her head is down, and therefore he cannot see her eyes, but nevertheless he leans forward and touches her left cheek with his right hand. Anna looks up then, and as their eyes meet she gives him another one of her tender and affectionate smiles.

You're so good to me, he says.

I want you to be happy, she answers. This is a hard time for you, and if you can find some moments of pleasure in all this, I'm glad to help.

I've done something terrible to you. I don't know what it is, but something terrible . . . unspeakable . . . beyond forgiveness. And here you are, taking care of me like a saint.

It wasn't your fault. You did what you had to do, and I don't hold it against you.

But you suffered. I made you suffer, didn't I?

Yes, very badly. I almost didn't make it.

What did I do?

You sent me off to a dangerous place, a desperate place, a place of destruction and death.

What was it? Some kind of mission?

I guess you could call it that.

You were young then, weren't you? The girl in the photo.

Yes.

You were very pretty, Anna. You're older now, but I still find you pretty. Just about perfect, if you know what I mean.

You don't have to exaggerate, Mr. Blank.

I'm not. If someone told me that I had to look at you twenty-four hours a day for the rest of my life, I wouldn't have any objections.

Once again, Anna smiles, and once again Mr. Blank touches her left cheek with his right hand.

How long were you in that place? he asks.

A few years. Much longer than I was expecting to be.

But you managed to get out.

Eventually, yes.

I feel so ashamed.

You mustn't. The fact is, Mr. Blank, without you I wouldn't be anyone.

Still . . .

No *still*. You're not like other men. You've sacrificed your life to something bigger than yourself, and whatever you've done or haven't done, it's never been for selfish reasons.

Have you ever been in love, Anna?

Several times.

Are you married?

I was.

Was?

My husband died three years ago.

What was his name?

David. David Zimmer.

What happened?

He had a bad heart.

I'm responsible for that, too, aren't I?

Not really . . . Only indirectly.

I'm so sorry.

Don't be. Without you, I never would have met David in the first place. Believe me, Mr. Blank, it isn't your fault. You do what you have to do, and then things happen. Good things and bad things both. That's the way it is. We might be the ones who suffer, but there's a reason for it, a good reason, and anyone who complains about it doesn't understand what it means to be alive.

It should be noted that a second camera and a second tape recorder have been planted in the bathroom ceiling, making it possible for all activities in that space to be recorded as well, and because the word *all* is an absolute term, the transcription of the dialogue between Anna and Mr. Blank can be verified in every one of its details.

The sponge bath goes on for several more minutes, and when Anna has finished washing and rinsing the remaining areas of Mr. Blank's body (legs, front and back; ankles, feet, and toes;

arms, hands, and fingers; scrotum, buttocks, and anus), she fetches a black terry-cloth robe from a hook on the door and helps Mr. Blank put it on. Then she picks up the blue-and-yellow striped pajamas and walks into the other room, making sure to leave the door open. While Mr. Blank stands in front of the small mirror above the sink, shaving with a battery-operated electric razor (for obvious reasons, traditional razor blades are forbidden), Anna folds the pajamas, makes the bed, and opens the closet to select Mr. Blank's clothes for the day. She moves quickly and efficiently, as if trying to make up for lost time. So rapid is her completion of these tasks that when Mr. Blank finishes shaving with the electric razor and walks into the other room, he is startled to see that his clothes have already been laid out on the bed. Remembering his conversation with James P. Flood and the mention of the word *closet*, he was hoping to catch Anna in the act of opening the closet door, if indeed the closet exists, in order to determine where it is located. Now, as his eyes scan the room, he sees no sign of it, and another mystery remains unsolved.

He could, of course, ask Anna where it is, but once he sees Anna herself, sitting on the bed and smiling up at him, he is so moved to be in her presence again that the question escapes his mind.

I'm beginning to remember you now, he says. Not everything, but little flashes, bits and pieces here and there. I was very young the first time I saw you, wasn't I?

About twenty-one, I think, Anna says.

But I kept losing you. You'd be there for a few days, and then you'd vanish. A year would go by, two years, four years, and then you'd suddenly pop up again.

You didn't know what to do with me, that's why. It took you a long time to figure it out.

And then I sent you on your . . . your mission. I remember being frightened for you. But you were a real battler back in those days, weren't you?

A tough and feisty girl, Mr. Blank.

Exactly. And that's what gave me hope. If you hadn't been a resourceful person, you never would have made it.

Let me help you with your clothes, Anna says, glancing down at her watch. Time is marching on.

The word *marching* induces Mr. Blank to think about his dizzy spells and earlier difficulties with walking, but now, as he travels the short distance from the threshold of the bathroom to the bed, he is encouraged to note that his brain is clear and that he feels in no danger of falling. With nothing to support the hypothesis, he attributes this improvement to the beneficent Anna, to the mere fact that she has been there with him for the past twenty or thirty minutes, radiating the affection he so desperately longs for.

The clothes turn out to be all white: white cotton trousers, white button-down shirt, white boxer shorts, white nylon socks, and a pair of white tennis shoes.

An odd choice, Mr. Blank says. I'm going to look like the Good Humor man.

It was a special request, Anna replies. From Peter Stillman. Not the father, the son. Peter Stillman, Junior.

Who's he?

You don't remember?

I'm afraid not.

He's another one of your charges. When you sent him out on his mission, he had to dress all in white.

How many people have I sent out?

Hundreds, Mr. Blank. More people than I can count.

All right. Let's get on with it. I don't suppose it makes any difference.

Without further ado, he unties the belt of the robe and lets the robe fall to the floor. Once again, he is standing naked in front of Anna, feeling not the slightest hint of embarrassment or modesty. Glancing down and pointing to his penis, he says: Look how small it is. Mr. Bigshot isn't so big now, is he?

Anna smiles and then pats the bed with the palm of her hand, beckoning him to sit down next to her. As he does so, Mr. Blank is once more thrust back into his early childhood, back to the days of Whitey the rocking horse and their long journeys together through the deserts and mountains of the Far West. He thinks about his mother and how she used to dress him like this in his upstairs bedroom with the morning sun slanting through the venetian blinds, and all at once, realizing that his mother is dead, probably long dead, he wonders if Anna somehow hasn't become a new mother for him, even at his advanced age, for why else would he feel so comfortable with her, he who is generally so shy and self-conscious about his body in front of others?

Anna climbs off the bed and crouches down in front of Mr. Blank. She begins with the socks, slipping one over his left foot and then the other one over his right foot, moves on to the undershorts, which she slides up his legs and, as Mr. Blank stands to accommodate her, farther up to his waist, thus concealing the former Mr. Bigshot, who no doubt will rise again to assert his dominance over Mr. Blank before too many hours have passed.

Mr. Blank sits down on the bed a second time, and the process is repeated with the trousers. When Mr. Blank sits down for the third time, Anna puts the sneakers on his feet, first the left one, then the right one, and immediately begins to tie the laces, first on the left shoe, then on the right shoe. After that, she emerges from her crouch and sits down on the bed beside Mr. Blank to help him with the shirt, first guiding his left arm through the left sleeve, then his right arm through the right sleeve, and finally buttoning the buttons from the bottom up, and all during this slow and laborious procedure, Mr. Blank's thoughts are elsewhere, back in his boyhood room with Whitey and his mother, remembering how she used to do these same things for him with the same loving patience, so many years ago now, in the long-ago beginning of his life.

Now Anna is gone. The stainless steel cart has vanished, the door has been shut, and once again Mr. Blank is alone in the room. The questions he was meaning to ask her—about the closet, about the typescript concerning the so-called Confederation, about whether the door is locked from the outside or not—have all gone unasked, and therefore Mr. Blank is as much in the dark about what he is doing in this place as he was before

Anna's arrival. For the time being, he is sitting on the edge of the narrow bed, palms spread out on his knees, head down, staring at the floor, but soon, as soon as he feels the strength of will to do so, he will stand up from the bed and once more make his way over to the desk to look through the pile of photographs (if he can summon the courage to face those images again) and continue his reading of the typescript about the man trapped in the room in Ultima. For the time being, however, he does nothing more than sit on the bed and pine for Anna, wishing she were still there with him, wishing he could take her in his arms and hold her.

Now he is on his feet again. He tries to shuffle toward the desk, but he forgets that he is no longer wearing his slippers, and the rubber sole of his left tennis shoe sticks on the wood floor—in such an abrupt and unforeseen way that Mr. Blank loses his balance and nearly falls. Damn, he says, damn these stupid little white fucks. He longs to change out of the tennis shoes and put on the slippers again, but the slippers are black, and if he put them on he would no longer be dressed all in white, which was something Anna explicitly asked of him—as per the demand of one Peter Stillman, Junior, whoever on earth he might be.

Mr. Blank therefore abandons the shuffling strides he used with the slippers and travels toward the desk with something that resembles an ordinary walk. Not quite the brisk heel-to-toe step one sees in the young and the vigorous, but a slow and heavy gait whereby Mr. Blank lifts one foot an inch or two off the ground, propels the leg attached to that foot approximately six inches forward, and then plants the entire sole of the shoe on the floor, heel and toe together. A slight pause follows, and then he repeats the process with the other foot. It might not be beautiful to watch, but it is sufficient to his purpose, and before long he finds himself standing in front of the desk.

The chair has been pushed in, which means that in order to sit down, Mr. Blank is obliged to pull it out. In so doing, he finally discovers that the chair is equipped with wheels, for instead of scraping along the floor as he is expecting it will, the chair rolls out smoothly, with scarcely any effort on his part. Mr. Blank sits down, astonished that he could have overlooked this feature of the chair during his earlier visits to the desk. He presses his feet against the floor, gives a little shove, and back he goes, covering a distance of some three or four feet. He considers this an important discovery, for pleasant as rocking back and forth and turning around in circles might be, the fact that the chair can move about the room is potentially of great therapeutic value—as, for example, when his legs are feeling especially tired, or when he is attacked by another one of his dizzy spells. Instead of having to stand up and walk at those times, he will be able to use the chair to travel from place to place in a sitting position, thus conserving his strength for more urgent matters. He feels comforted by this thought, and yet, as he inches the chair back toward the desk, the crushing sense of guilt that largely disappeared during Anna's visit suddenly returns, and by the time he makes it to the desk he understands that the desk itself is responsible for these oppressive thoughts—not the desk as desk, perhaps, but the photographs and papers piled on its surface, which no doubt contain the answer to the question that haunts him. They are the source of his anguish, and even though it would be simple enough to return to the bed and ignore them, he feels compelled to go on with his investigations, tortuous and painful as they might be.

He glances down and notices a pad of paper and a ballpoint pen—objects he does not remember having been there during his last visit to the desk. No matter, he says to himself, and without another thought he picks up the pen with his right hand and opens the pad to the first page with his left. In order not to forget what has happened so far today—for Mr. Blank is nothing if not forgetful—he writes down the following list of names:

> James P. Flood
> Anna
> David Zimmer
> Peter Stillman, Jr.
> Peter Stillman, Sr.

This small task accomplished, he closes the pad, puts down the pen, and pushes them aside. Then, reaching for the top pages on the pile farthest to the left, he discovers that they have been stapled together, perhaps twenty to twenty-five pages in all, and when he puts down the sheaf in front of him, he further discovers that it is the typescript he was reading before Anna's arrival. He assumes that she was the one who stapled the pages together—to make things easier for him—and then, realizing that the typescript is not terribly long, he wonders if he will have time to finish it before James P. Flood comes knocking at the door.

He turns to the fourth paragraph on the second page and begins reading:

For the past forty days, there have been no beatings, and neither the Colonel nor any members of his staff have shown their faces to me. The only person I have seen is the sergeant who delivers my food and changes the slop bucket. I have tried to act in a civil manner with him, always making some small remark when he comes in, but he is apparently under orders to remain silent, and not once have I extracted a single word from this giant in the brown uniform. Then, less than an hour ago, an extraordinary event took place. The sergeant unlocked the door, and in walked two young privates carrying a small wooden table and a straight-backed chair. They set them down in the middle of the room, and then the sergeant came in and put a tall stack of blank paper on the table along with a bottle of ink and a pen.

—You're allowed to write, he said.

—Is that your way of making conversation, I asked, or are you trying to give me an order?

—The Colonel says you're allowed to write. You can take that in any way you choose.

—What if I choose not to write?

—You're free to do what you want, but the Colonel says it's unlikely that a man in your position would pass up the opportunity to defend himself in writing.

—I assume he's planning to read what I write.

—It would be logical to assume that, yes.

—Will he be sending it to the capital afterward?

—He didn't speak of his intentions. He simply said that you were allowed to write.

—How much time do I have?

—The subject wasn't discussed.

—And what if I run out of paper?

—You'll be given as much ink and paper as you need. The Colonel wanted me to tell you that.

—Thank the Colonel for me, and tell him I understand what he's doing. He's giving me a chance to lie about what happened in order to save my neck. That's very sporting of him. Please tell him that I appreciate the gesture.

—I will convey your message to the Colonel.

—Good. Now leave me in peace. If he wants me to write, I'll write, but in order to do that, I have to be alone.

I was only guessing, of course. The truth is that I have no idea why the Colonel did what he did. I would like to think he's begun to pity me, but I doubt it can be as simple as that. Colonel De Vega is hardly a compassionate man, and if he suddenly wants to make my life less uncomfortable, giving me a pen is surely an odd way to go about it. A manuscript of lies would serve him well, but he can't possibly think that I'd be willing to change my story at this late date. He has already tried to make me recant, and if I didn't do it when I was nearly beaten to death, why would I do it now? What it comes down to is a matter of caution, I think, a way of preparing himself for whatever might happen next. Too many people know that I'm here for him to execute me without a trial. On the other hand, a trial is something that must be avoided at all costs—for once the case is taken to court, my story will become public knowledge. By allowing me to put the story in writing, he is gathering evidence, irrefutable evidence that will justify any action he decides to take against me. Assume, for example, that he goes ahead and has me shot without a trial. Once the military command in the capital gets wind of my death, they will be obliged by law to open an official inquiry, but at that point he will only have to give them the pages I've written, and he will be exonerated. No doubt they will reward him with a medal for resolving the dilemma so neatly. It could be that he has already written to them about me, in fact, and that I am holding this pen in my hand now because they instructed him to put it there. Under normal circumstances, it takes about three weeks for a letter to reach the capital from Ultima. If I have been here for a month and a half, then perhaps he received his answer today. Let the traitor put his story in writing, they probably said, and then we'll be free to dispose of him in any way we like.

That is one possibility. It could be that I'm exaggerating my importance, however, and that the Colonel is merely playing with me. Who knows if he hasn't decided to amuse himself with the spectacle of my suffering? Distractions are scarce in a town like Ultima, and unless you're resourceful enough to invent your own, you could easily lose your mind from the boredom. I can imagine the Colonel reading my words out loud to his mistress, the two of them sitting up in bed at night and laughing at my pathetic little phrases. That would be amusing, wouldn't it? Such a welcome diversion, such unholy mirth. If I keep him sufficiently entertained, perhaps he'll let me go on writing forever, and bit by bit I'll be turned into his personal clown, his own jester-scribe scribbling forth my pratfalls in endless streams of ink. And even if he should tire of my stories and have me killed, the manuscript will remain, won't it? That will be his trophy—one more skull to add to his collection.

Still, it is difficult for me to suppress the joy I am feeling at this moment. Whatever Colonel De Vega's motives might have been, whatever traps and humiliations he might have in store for me, I can honestly say that I am happier now than at any time since my arrest. I am sitting at the table, listening to the pen as it scratches along the surface of the paper. I stop. I dip the pen into the inkwell, then watch the black shapes form as I move my hand slowly from left to right. I come to the edge and then return to the other side, and as the shapes thin out, I stop once more and dip the pen into the inkwell. So it goes as I work my way down the page, and each cluster of marks is a word, and each word is a sound in my head, and each time I write another word, I hear the sound of my own voice, even though my lips are silent.

Immediately after the sergeant locked the door, I picked up the table and carried it to the western wall, placing it directly below the window. Then I went back for the chair, put the chair on top of the table, and hoisted myself up—first onto the table, then onto the chair. I wanted to see if I could get my fingers around the bars of the window, hoping I might be able to pull myself up and hang there long enough to catch a glimpse of the outside. No matter how hard I strained, however, the tips of my fingers fell short of the goal. Not wanting to abandon the effort,

I removed my shirt and tried flinging it up toward the bars, thinking I might be able to thread it through, then grab hold of the dangling sleeves, and in that way manage to haul myself up. But the shirt wasn't quite long enough, and without a tool of some sort to guide the cloth around the metal posts (a stick, a broom handle, even a twig), I could do no more than wave the shirt back and forth, like a white flag of surrender.

In the end, it is probably just as well to put those dreams behind me. If I can't spend my days looking out the window, then I will be forced to concentrate on the task at hand. The essential thing is to stop worrying about the Colonel, to push all thoughts of him out of my mind and set down the facts as I know them. What he chooses to do with this report is strictly his business, and there is nothing I can do to influence his decision. The only thing I can do is tell the story. Given the story I have to tell, that will be difficult enough.

Mr. Blank pauses for a moment to rest his eyes, to run his fingers through his hair, to ponder the meaning of the words he has just read. When he thinks about the narrator's failed attempt to climb up and look out the window, he suddenly remembers his own window, or, more precisely, the window shade that covers the window, and now that he has a means of traveling over there without having to stand up, he decides that this is the moment to lift the shade and have a peek outdoors. If he can take stock of his surroundings, perhaps some memory will come back to him to help explain what he is doing in this room; perhaps the mere glimpse of a tree or the cornice of a building or a random patch of sky will furnish him with an insight into his predicament. He therefore temporarily abandons his reading of the typescript to journey toward the wall in which the window is located. When he reaches his destination, he thrusts out his right hand, takes hold of the bottom of the shade, and gives it a quick tug, hoping to engage the spring that will send the shade flying upward. It is an old shade, however, and much of its bounce has been lost, and rather than ascend to reveal the window behind it, it sags down several inches below the sill. Frustrated by this botched attempt, Mr. Blank tugs harder and longer the second time, and just like that, the shade decides to act like a proper shade and goes rolling up to the top of the window.

Imagine Mr. Blank's disappointment when he peers through the window and sees that the shutters have been closed, blocking any possibility of looking out to discover where he is. Nor are these the classic wooden shutters with movable slats that allow a bit of light to filter through; they are industrial-strength metal panels with no apertures of any kind, painted a dull shade of gray, with areas of rust showing through that have begun to corrode the surface. Once Mr. Blank rebounds from his shock, he understands that the situation is not as dire as he supposed. The shutters lock from within, and in order to get his fingers on the lock, all he has to do is raise the window sash to its maximum height. Then, once the latch has been unhooked, he will be able to push the shutters open and look out at the world around him. He knows that he will have to stand up from the chair to gain the leverage necessary for such an operation, but that is a small price to pay, and so he lifts his body out of the seat, checks to make sure the window is unlocked (it is), places the heels of his two hands firmly under the top bar of the sash, pauses for a moment to prepare for the exertions ahead, and then pushes for all he is worth. Unexpectedly, the window does not budge. Mr. Blank stops to catch his breath, then tries again—with the same negative result. He suspects that the window has jammed somehow—either because of excess moisture in the air or an excess of paint that has inadvertently glued the upper and lower halves of the window together—but then, as he examines the top bar of the sash more closely, he discovers something that previously eluded his notice. Two large construction nails, almost invisible because the heads of the nails are painted over, have been hammered into the bar. One large nail to the left, one large nail to the right, and because Mr. Blank knows it will be impossible for him to extract those nails from the wood, the window cannot be opened—not now, he realizes, not later, not ever under any circumstances at all.

Proof has been given at last. Someone, perhaps several someones, has or have locked Mr. Blank in this room and is or are holding him prisoner against his will. At least that is what he concludes from the evidence of the two nails hammered into the window sash, but damning as that evidence might be, there is still the question of the door, and until Mr. Blank determines whether the door is locked from the outside, if indeed it is locked at all, the conclusion he has drawn could well be false. If he were thinking clearly, his next step would be to walk or wheel himself over to the door and investigate the matter at once. But Mr. Blank does not move from his spot by the window, for the simple reason that he is afraid, so afraid of what he might learn from the door that he cannot bring himself to risk a confrontation with the truth. Instead, he sits back down in the chair and decides to break the window. For whether he is locked in or not, he is above all desperate to find out where he is. He thinks about the man in the typescript he has been reading, and then he wonders if he, too, won't eventually be taken outside and shot. Or, even more sinister to his imagination, if he won't be murdered right here in the room, strangled to death by the powerful hands of some thug.

There are no blunt objects in the vicinity. No hammers, for example, no broom handles or shovels, no pickaxes or battering rams, and thus even before he begins, Mr. Blank knows his effort is doomed to defeat. Nevertheless, he gives it a try, for not only is he afraid, he is angry, and in his anger he slips off his right tennis shoe, grips the toe firmly in his right hand, and starts pounding the heel against the glass. A normal window might give way under such an assault, but this is a double-paned thermal window of the strongest quality, and it scarcely trembles as the old man strikes it with his feeble weapon of rubber and canvas. After twenty-one consecutive blows, Mr. Blank gives up and lets the shoe drop to the floor. Now, both angry and frustrated, he pounds his fist against the glass several times, not wanting to let the window have the last word, but flesh and bone are no more effective in cracking the pane than the shoe was. He wonders if smashing his head against the window might not do the trick, but even though his mind is not all it should be, Mr. Blank is still lucid enough to understand the folly of inflicting grave physical harm upon himself in what is no doubt a hopeless cause. With a heavy heart, therefore, he slumps back in the chair and closes his eyes—not only afraid, not only angry, but exhausted as well.

The moment he shuts his eyes, he sees the shadow-beings marching through his head. It is a long, dimly lit procession composed of scores if not hundreds of figures, and among them are included both men and women, both children and old people, and while some are short, others are tall, and while some are round, others are lean, and as Mr. Blank strains to listen in on them, he hears not only the sound of their footsteps but something he would liken to a groan, a barely audible collective groan rising from their midst. Where they are and where they are going he cannot say, but they seem to be tramping through a forgotten pasture somewhere, a no-man's-land of scrawny weeds and barren earth, and because it is so dark, and because each figure is moving forward with his or her head down, Mr. Blank cannot distinguish anyone's face. All he knows is that the mere sight of these figments fills him with dread, and once again he is overwhelmed by an implacable sense of guilt. He speculates that these people are the ones he sent off on various missions over the years, and, as was the case with Anna, perhaps some of them, or many of them, or all of them did not fare so terribly well, even to the point of being subjected to unbearable suffering and/or death.

Mr. Blank can't be sure of anything, but it strikes him as possible that there is a connection between these shadow-beings and the photographs on the desk. What if the pictures represent the same people whose faces he is unable to identify in the scene that is playing itself out in his head? If that is so, then the phantoms he is observing are not figments so much as memories, memories of actual people—for when was the last time anyone took a photograph of a person who did not exist? Mr. Blank knows there is nothing to support his theory, that it is only the wildest of wild conjectures, but there has to be some reason, he tells himself, some cause, some principle to explain what is happening to him, to account for the fact that he is in this room with these photographs and these four piles of manuscripts, and why not investigate a little further to see if there is any truth to this blind stab in the dark?

Forgetting about the two nails hammered into the window, forgetting about the door and whether it is locked from the outside or not, Mr. Blank wheels himself over to the desk, picks up the photographs, and then puts them down directly in front of him. Anna is on top, of course, and he spends a few moments looking at her again, studying her unhappy but beautiful young face, gazing deep into the gaze of her dark, burning eyes. No, he says to himself, we were never married. Her husband was a man named David Zimmer, and now Zimmer is dead.

He puts the photograph of Anna aside and looks at the next one. It is another woman, perhaps in her mid-twenties, with light brown hair and steady, watchful eyes. The bottom half of her body is obscured, since she is standing in the doorway of what looks like a New York apartment with the door only partially open, as if in fact she has just opened it to welcome a visitor, and in spite of the cautious look in her eyes, a small smile is creasing the corners of her mouth. Mr. Blank feels a momentary twinge of recognition, but as he struggles to recall her name, nothing comes to him—not after twenty seconds, not after forty seconds, not after a minute. Given that he found Anna's name so quickly, he assumed he would be able to do it with the others as well. But such, apparently, is not the case.

He looks at another ten pictures with the same disappointing results. An old man in a wheelchair, as thin and delicate as a sparrow, wearing the dark glasses of the blind. A grinning woman with a drink in one hand and a cigarette in the other, wearing a 1920s flapper dress and a cloche hat. A frighteningly obese man with an immense hairless head and a cigar jutting from his mouth. Another young woman, this one Chinese, dressed in a dancer's leotard. A dark-haired man with a waxed mustache, decked out in tails and a top hat. A young man sleeping on the grass in what looks like a public park. An older man, perhaps in his mid-fifties, lying on a sofa with his legs propped up on a pile of pillows. A bearded, scraggly-looking homeless person sitting on a sidewalk with his arms around a large mutt. A chubby black man in his sixties holding up a Warsaw telephone book from 1937–38. A slender young man sitting at a table with five cards in his hand and a stack of poker chips in front of him.

With each successive failure, Mr. Blank grows that much more discouraged, that much more doubtful about his chances with the next one—until, muttering something under his breath in such a low voice that the tape recorder cannot pick up the words, he abandons the effort and pushes the photographs aside.

He rocks back and forth in the chair for close to a minute, doing what he can to regain his mental equilibrium and put the defeat behind him. Then, without giving the matter another thought, he picks up the typescript and begins reading again:

My name is Sigmund Graf. I was born forty-one years ago in the town of Luz, a textile center in the northwestern part of Faux-Lieu Province, and until my arrest by Colonel De Vega, I worked in the demographics division of the Bureau of Internal Affairs. As a young man I earned a bachelor's degree in classical literature from All Souls University and then served as an army intelligence officer in the Southeast Border Wars, taking part in the battle that led to the unification of the Petit-Lieu and Merveil principalities. I was honorably discharged with the rank of captain and received a distinguished service medal for my work in intercepting and decoding enemy messages. On returning to the capital after my demobilization, I entered the Bureau as a field coordinator and researcher. At the time of my departure for the Alien Territories, I had been a member of the staff for twelve years. My last official title was that of Deputy Assistant Director.

Like every citizen of the Confederation, I have known my share of suffering, have lived through prolonged moments of violence and upheaval, and have borne the marks of loss upon my soul. I was not yet fourteen when the riots at the Sanctus Academy in Beauchamp led to the outbreak of the Faux-Lieu Language Wars, and two months after the invasion I saw my mother and younger brother burn to death during the Sacking of Luz. My father and I were among the seven thousand who took part in the exodus to the neighboring province of Neue Welt. The journey covered some six hundred miles and took more than two months to complete, and by the time we reached our destination, our number had been reduced by a third. For the last hundred miles, my father was so weak from illness that I had to carry him on my back, staggering half-blind through the mud and winter rains until we came to the outskirts of Nachtburg. For six months we begged in the streets of that gray city to keep ourselves alive, and when we were finally rescued by a loan from relatives in the north, we were on the point of starvation. Life improved for us after that, but no matter how prosperous my father became in the years that followed, he never fully recovered from those months of hardship. When he died ten summers ago at the age of fifty-six, the toll of his experiences had aged him so much that he looked like a man of seventy.

There have been other pains as well. A year and a half ago, the Bureau sent me on an expedition to the Independent Communities of Tierra Blanca Province. Less than a month after my departure, the cholera epidemic swept through the capital. Many now refer to this plague as the Blight of History, and considering that it struck just as the long and elaborately planned Unification ceremonies were about to begin, one can understand how it could be interpreted as an evil sign, a judgment on the very nature and purpose of the Confederation itself. I am not personally of that opinion, but my own life was nevertheless permanently altered by the epidemic. Cut off from all news of the city, I went about my work for the next four and a half months, traveling back and forth among the remote, mountainous communities to the south, pursuing my investigations into the various religious sects that had taken root in the area. When I returned in August, the crisis was already over—but not before my wife and fifteen-year-old daughter had disappeared. The majority of our neighbors in the Closterham District had either fled the city or succumbed to the illness themselves, but among those who had remained, not a single person could remember having seen them. The house was untouched, and nowhere in it could I find any evidence to suggest that the disease had infiltrated its walls. I made a thorough search of every room, but no secret was unveiled to me as to how or when they might have abandoned the premises. No missing clothes or jewels, no hastily discarded objects lying about the floor. The house was just as I had left it five months earlier, except that my wife and daughter were no longer in it.

I spent several weeks combing the city for clues of their whereabouts, growing increasingly desperate with each failed attempt to uncover information that would put me on their trail. I began by talking to friends and colleagues, and once I had exhausted the circle of familiars (in which I include my wife's female acquaintances, the parents of my daughter's classmates, as well as the shopkeepers and merchants of our district), I started reaching out to strangers. Armed with portraits of my wife and daughter, I questioned countless doctors, nurses, and volunteers who had worked in the makeshift hospitals and schoolrooms where the sick and dying had been cared for, but among all the hundreds of people who looked at those miniatures, not one could recognize the faces I held in my hand. In the end, there was only one conclusion to be drawn. My darlings had been carried off by the scourge. Along with thousands of other victims, they were lying in one of the mass graves on Viaticum Bluff, the burial ground of the anonymous dead.

I do not mention these things in order to put myself in a sympathetic light. No one has to feel sorry for me, and no one has to make excuses for the errors I committed in the aftermath of these events. I am a man, not an angel, and if the grief that overtook me occasionally blurred my vision and led to certain lapses of conduct, that in no way should cast doubt on the truth of my story. Before anyone tries to discredit me by pointing to those stains on my record, I come forward of my own free will and openly pronounce my guilt to the world. These are treacherous times, and I know how easily perceptions can be twisted by a single word spoken into the wrong ear. Impugn a man's character, and everything that man does is made to seem underhanded, suspect, fraught with double motives. In my own case, the flaws in question stemmed from pain, not malice; confusion, not cunning. I lost my way, and for several months I sought comfort in the obliterating powers of alcohol. Most nights I drank alone, sitting in the darkness of my empty house, but some nights were worse than others. Whenever I encountered one of those bad turns, my thoughts would begin to sabotage me, and before long I would be choking on my own breath. My head would fill with images of my wife and daughter, and again and again I would see their mud-splattered bodies being lowered into the ground, again and again I would see their naked limbs entwined among the limbs of other corpses in the hole, and suddenly the darkness of the house would become too much to bear. I would venture out into public places, hoping to break the spell of those images in the noise and tumult of crowds. I frequented taverns and alehouses, and it was in one of those establishments that I did the most damage to myself and my reputation. The incident occurred on a Friday night in November when a man named Giles McNaughton picked a quarrel with me in the Auberge des Vents. McNaughton claimed that I attacked him first, but eleven witnesses testified otherwise in court, and I was acquitted of all charges. It was no more than a small victory, however, for the fact remained that I had broken the man's arm and shattered his nose, and I never would have responded with such vehemence if I hadn't been going to hell by way of drink. The jury found me innocent, judging that I had acted in legitimate self-defense, but that did not remove the stigma of the trial itself—nor the scandal that broke out when it was discovered that a ranking member of the Bureau of Internal Affairs had been engaged in a bloody barroom brawl. Within hours of the verdict, rumors began circulating that officials from the Bureau had bribed certain members of the jury to vote in my favor. I have no knowledge of any corrupt dealings on my behalf, but I would tend to dismiss those accusations as mere gossip. What I do know for certain is that I had never seen McNaughton before that night. He, on the other hand, knew enough about me to address me by name, and when he approached my table and began to talk about my wife, suggesting that he was privy to information that would help solve the mystery of her disappearance, I told him to go away. The man was after money, and one look at his mottled, unhealthy face convinced me that he was a fraud, an opportunist who had got wind of my tragedy and meant to turn a profit from it. McNaughton apparently didn't like being dismissed in such a perfunctory manner. Instead of excusing himself, he sat down in the chair next to mine and angrily grabbed hold of my vest. Then, pulling me forward until our faces were almost touching, he leaned into me and said, What's the matter, citizen? Are you afraid of the truth? His eyes were full of rage and contempt, and because we were so close to each other, those eyes were the only objects in my field of vision. I could feel the hostility flowing through his body, and an instant later I felt it pass directly into mine. That was when I went after him. Yes, he had touched me first, but the moment I started to fight back, I wanted to hurt him, to hurt him as badly as I could.

That was my crime. Take it for what it was, but don't let it interfere with the reading of this report. Trouble comes to all men, and each man makes his peace with the world in his own way. If the force I used against McNaughton that night was unwarranted, the greater wrong was the pleasure I took in using that force. I do not pardon my actions, but considering my state of mind during that period, it is remarkable that the incident in the Auberge des Vents was the only one in which I did harm to another person. All the other harm was inflicted upon myself, and until I learned to curb my desire for drink (which was in fact a desire for death), I ran the risk of utter annihilation. In the course of time, I managed to take hold of myself again, but

I confess that I am no longer the man I used to be. If I have gone on living, it is largely because my work at the Bureau has given me a reason to live. Such is the irony of my predicament. I am accused of being an enemy of the Confederation, and yet for the past nineteen years there has been no servant more loyal to the Confederation than myself. My record shows that, and I am proud to have lived in an age that allowed me to participate in such a vast human endeavor. My work in the field has taught me to love the truth above all else, and therefore I have cleared the air pertaining to my sins and transgressions, but that does not mean I can accept guilt for a crime I did not commit. I believe in what the Confederation stands for, and I have passionately defended it with my words, my deeds, and my blood. If the Confederation has turned against me, it can only mean that the Confederation has turned against itself. I cannot hope for life anymore, but if these pages should fall into the hands of someone with sufficient strength of heart to read them in the spirit with which they were written, then perhaps my murder will not have been an entirely useless act.

Far off in the distance, beyond the room, beyond the building in which the room is located, Mr. Blank again hears the faint cry of a bird. Distracted by the sound, he looks up from the page in front of him, temporarily abandoning the dolorous confessions of Sigmund Graf. A sudden feeling of pressure invades his stomach, and before Mr. Blank can decide whether to call that feeling one of pain or simple discomfort, his intestinal tract bugles forth an ample, resonant fart. Ho ho, he says out loud, grunting with pleasure. Hopalong Cassidy rides again! Then he tips back in the chair, closes his eyes, and begins to rock, soon lapsing into one of those dull, trancelike states in which the mind is emptied of all thoughts, all emotions, all connection to the self. Thus trapped in his reptilian stupor, Mr. Blank is, as it were, absent, or at least momentarily cut off from his surroundings, which means that he does not hear the hand that has begun knocking on the door. Worse than that, he does not hear the door open, and therefore, even though someone has entered the room, he is still in the dark as to whether the door is locked from the outside or not. Or soon will be still in the dark, once he emerges from his trance.

Someone taps him on the shoulder, but before Mr. Blank can open his eyes and swivel around in the chair to see who it is, that person has already begun to speak. From the timbre and intonation of the voice, Mr. Blank instantly recognizes that it belongs to a man, but he is perplexed by the fact that it is talking to him in what sounds like a Cockney accent.

I'm sorry, Mr. Blank, the man says to him. I knocked and knocked, and when you didn't open the door, I thought I should come in and see if anything was wrong.

Mr. Blank now swivels around in the chair and takes a close look at his visitor. The man appears to be in his early fifties, with neatly combed hair and a small brown mustache with flecks of gray in it. Neither short nor tall, Mr. Blank says to himself, but more on the short side than the tall, and from his erect, almost ramrod posture as he stands there in his tweed suit, he looks like a military man of some kind, or perhaps a lower-level civil servant.

And you are? Mr. Blank asks.

Flood, sir. First name James. Middle name Patrick. James P. Flood. Don't you remember me?

Dimly, only dimly.

The ex-policeman.

Ah. Flood, the ex-policeman. You were going to pay me a visit, weren't you?

Yes, sir. Exactly, sir. That's why I'm here. I'm paying you the visit now.

Mr. Blank casts his eyes about the room, looking for a chair so he can offer Flood a place to sit, but apparently the only chair in the room is the one he now occupies himself.

Something wrong? Flood asks.

No, no, Mr. Blank replies. I'm just looking for another chair, that's all.

I can always sit on the bed, Flood answers, gesturing to the bed. Or, if you're feeling up to it, we could go to the park across the way. No shortage of benches there.

Mr. Blank points down at his right foot and says: I'm missing a shoe. I can't go outside with only one shoe.

Flood turns around and immediately spots the white tennis shoe on the floor below the window. There's the other one, sir. We could get it back on you in two shakes of a cat.

A cat? What are you talking about?

Just an expression, Mr. Blank. No harm intended. Flood

pauses for a moment, looks back at the shoe on the floor, and then says: Well, what about it? Should we put it on or not?

Mr. Blank lets out a long, weary sigh. No, he says, with a tinge of sarcasm in his voice, I don't want to put it on. I'm sick of these goddamned shoes. If anything, I'd rather take the other one off, too.

The moment these words escape his mouth, Mr. Blank is heartened to realize that such an act falls within the realm of possibility, that in this one trifling instance he can take matters into his own hands. Without a moment's hesitation, he therefore bends down and removes the sneaker from his left foot.

Ah, that's better, he says, lifting his legs and wiggling his toes in the air. Much better. And I'm still dressed all in white, aren't I?

Of course you are, Flood says. What's so important about that?

Never mind, says Mr. Blank, waving off Flood's question as of no account. Just sit down on the bed and tell me what you want, Mr. Flood.

The former inspector from Scotland Yard lowers himself onto the foot of the mattress, positioning his body in the left-hand quadrant in order to align his face with the face of the old man, who is sitting in the chair with his back to the desk, roughly six feet away. Flood clears his throat, as if searching for the appropriate words to start with, and then, in a low voice trembling with anxiety, he says: It's about the dream, sir.

The dream? Mr. Blank asks, confounded by Flood's statement. What dream?

My dream, Mr. Blank. The one you mentioned in your report on Fanshawe.

Who's Fanshawe?

You don't remember?

No, Mr. Blank declares in a loud, irritable voice. No, I don't remember Fanshawe. I can hardly remember anything. They're pumping me full of pills, and nearly everything is gone now. Most of the time, I don't even know who I am. And if I can't remember myself, how do you expect me to remember this . . . this . . .

Fanshawe.

Fanshawe . . . And who, pray tell, is he?

One of your operatives, sir.

You mean someone I sent out on a mission?

An extremely perilous mission.

Did he survive?

No one is sure. But the prevailing opinion is that he's no longer with us.

Groaning softly to himself, Mr. Blank covers his face with his hands and whispers: Another one of the damned.

Excuse me, Flood interjects, I didn't catch what you said.

Nothing, Mr. Blank replies in a louder voice. I said nothing.

At that point, the conversation stops for several moments. Silence reigns, and in that silence Mr. Blank imagines that he hears the sound of wind, a powerful wind blowing through a stand of trees somewhere near, quite near, but whether that wind is real or not he cannot say. All the while, Flood's eyes remain fixed on the old man's face. When the silence has become un-

bearable, he at last makes a timid venture to resume the dialogue. Well? he says.

Well what? Mr. Blank replies.

The dream. Can we talk about the dream now?

How can I talk about another man's dream if I don't know
what it is?

That's just the problem, Mr. Blank. I have no memory of it
myself.

Then I can't do anything for you, can I? If neither one of us
knows what happened in your dream, there's nothing to talk about.

It's more complicated than that.

Hardly, Mr. Flood. It's very simple.

That's only because you don't remember writing the report.
If you concentrate now, I mean really focus your mind on it,
maybe it will come back to you.

I doubt it.

Listen. In the report you wrote on Fanshawe, you mention
that he was the author of several unpublished books. One of
them was entitled *Neverland.* Unfortunately, except for concluding that certain events in the book were inspired by similar
events in Fanshawe's life, you say nothing about the subject,
nothing about the plot, nothing about the book at all. Only one
brief aside—written in parentheses, I might add—which reads
as follows. I quote from memory: *(Montag's house in chapter
seven; Flood's dream in chapter thirty).* The point being, Mr.
Blank, that you must have read *Neverland* yourself, and in that
you're one of the only people in the world to have done so, I
would deeply appreciate it, appreciate it from the very bottom of

my miserable heart, if you would make an effort to recall the content of that dream.

From the way you talk about it, *Neverland* must be a novel.

Yes, sir. A work of fiction.

And Fanshawe used you as a character?

Apparently so. There's nothing strange about that. From what I understand, writers do it all the time.

Maybe they do, but I don't see why you should get so worked up about it. The dream never really happened. It's nothing but words on a page—pure invention. Forget about it, Mr. Flood. It's not important.

It's important to me, Mr. Blank. My whole life depends on it. Without that dream, I'm nothing, literally nothing.

The passion with which the normally reserved ex-policeman delivers this last remark—a passion provoked by the sting of a genuine, soul-rending despair—strikes Mr. Blank as nothing short of hilarious, and for the first time since the opening words of this account, he bursts out laughing. As one might expect, Flood takes offense, for no one enjoys having his feelings trampled upon in such a heartless manner, least of all someone as fragile as Flood is at this moment.

I resent that, Mr. Blank, he says. You have no right to laugh at me.

Maybe not, Mr. Blank says, once the spasm in his chest has subsided, but I couldn't help it. You take yourself so damned seriously, Flood. It makes you look ridiculous.

I might be ridiculous, Flood says, with anger rising in his voice, but you, Mr. Blank . . . you're cruel . . . cruel and indifferent to the pain of others. You play with people's lives and take no responsibility for what you've done. I'm not going to sit here and bore you with my troubles, but I blame you for what's happened to me. I most sincerely blame you, and I despise you for it.

Troubles? Mr. Blank says, suddenly softening his tone, doing his best to show some sympathy. What kind of troubles?

The headaches, for one thing. Being forced into early retirement for another. Bankruptcy for yet another. And then there's the business with my wife, or rather my ex-wife, not to speak of my children, who no longer want anything to do with me. My life is in ruins, Mr. Blank. I walk around the world like a ghost, and sometimes I question whether I even exist. Whether I've ever existed at all.

And you think learning about that dream is going to solve all this? It's highly doubtful, you know.

The dream is my only chance. It's like a missing part of me, and until I find it, I'll never really be myself again.

I don't remember Fanshawe. I don't remember reading his novel. I don't remember writing the report. I wish I could help you, Flood, but the treatment they're giving me has turned my brain into a lump of rusty iron.

Try to remember. That's all I ask of you. Try.

As Mr. Blank looks into the eyes of the shattered ex-policeman, he notices that tears have begun to roll down his cheeks. Poor devil, Mr. Blank says to himself. For a moment or two he considers whether to ask Flood to help him locate the closet, for he remembers now that Flood was the one who mentioned it on the phone earlier that morning, but in the end, after weighing the pros and cons of making such a request, he decides against it. Instead he says: Please forgive me, Mr. Flood. I'm sorry I laughed at you.

Now Flood is gone, and once again Mr. Blank is alone in the room. In the aftermath of their disturbing encounter, the old man feels grumpy and out of sorts, wounded by the unjust and belligerent accusations he was subjected to. Still, not wanting to squander any opportunity to increase his knowledge of his present circumstances, he swivels around in the chair until he is facing the desk, then reaches out for the pad and the ballpoint pen. He understands enough at this point to know that unless he writes it down at once, the name will soon fly out of his head, and he doesn't want to run the risk of forgetting it. He therefore opens the pad to the first page, picks up the pen, and adds another entry to his list:

> James P. Flood
> Anna
> David Zimmer
> Peter Stillman, Jr.
> Peter Stillman, Sr.
> Fanshawe

In writing Fanshawe's name, it occurs to him that a second name was mentioned during Flood's visit as well, a name he heard in association with the reference to Flood's dream in chapter thirty of the book, but grapple as he does to recall what it was, he cannot come up with the answer. Something to do with chapter seven, he says to himself, something to do with a house, but the rest is a blank in Mr. Blank's mind. Galled by his own inadequacy, he nevertheless decides to put down something, hoping the name will come back to him at some future moment. The list now reads as follows:

> James P. Flood
> Anna
> David Zimmer
> Peter Stillman, Jr.
> Peter Stillman, Sr.
> Fanshawe
> Man with house

As Mr. Blank puts down the pen, a word begins resounding in his head, and for several moments after that, as the word continues to echo within him, he senses that he is on the brink of a serious breakthrough, a crucial turning point that will help clarify something about what the future has in store for him. The word is *park*. He remembers now that shortly after entering the room, Flood suggested they hold their conversation in *the park across the way*. If nothing else, that would seem to contradict Mr. Blank's previous assertion that he is being held captive, confined to the space in which these four walls surround him, blocked forever from sallying forth into the world. He is somewhat encouraged by this thought, but he also knows that even if he is allowed to visit the park, that does not necessarily prove he is free. Perhaps such visits are possible only under strict supervision, and once Mr. Blank has savored a welcome dose of sunlight and fresh air, he is promptly led back to the room, whereupon he is again held prisoner against his will. He finds it a pity that he did not have the presence of mind to question Flood about the park—in order to determine whether it is a public park, for example, or merely some wooded or grassy area that belongs to the building or institution or asylum in which he is now living. More important, he realizes for what must be the umpteenth time in the past several hours that it all comes down to the nature of the door, and whether it is locked from the outside or not. He closes his eyes and strains to recall the sounds he heard after Flood left the room. Was it the sound of a bolt sliding shut, the sound of a key turning in a cylinder plug, or simply the click of a latch? Mr. Blank cannot remember. By the time the conversation with Flood came to an end, he was so agitated by that disagreeable little man and his whining recriminations that he was too distracted to be paying attention to such petty concerns as locks and bolts and doors.

Mr. Blank wonders if the moment hasn't finally come to investigate the matter for himself. Afraid though he might be, would it not be better to learn the truth once and for all instead of living in a state of perpetual uncertainty? Perhaps, he says to himself. And then again, perhaps not. Before Mr. Blank can decide whether he has the courage to travel over to the door at last, a new and more urgent problem suddenly asserts itself—

what might most accurately be called an *urgent urge*. Pressure has once again begun to build in Mr. Blank's body. Unlike the earlier episode, which was situated in the general area of his stomach, this one appears in a spot several inches lower, in the southernmost region of Mr. Blank's belly. From long experience with such matters, the old man understands that he has to pee. He considers traveling over to the bathroom in the chair, but knowing that the chair will not fit through the bathroom doorway, and further knowing that he cannot execute the pee while sitting in the chair, that a moment will inevitably come when he will have to stand up (if only to sit down again on the toilet seat if he is attacked by another rush of dizziness), he decides to make the journey on foot. He therefore rises from the chair, pleased to note as he does so that his equilibrium is steady, with no signs of the vertigo that plagued him earlier. What Mr. Blank has forgotten, however, is that he is no longer wearing the white tennis shoes, not to speak of no longer wearing the black slippers, and that there is nothing on his feet anymore but the white nylon socks. In that the material of those socks is exceedingly thin, and in that the wooden floor is exceedingly smooth, Mr. Blank discovers after the first step that it is possible to slide his way forward—not with the rasping shuffle of the slippers, but as if he were moving along on ice skates.

A new form of pleasure has become available to him, and after two or three experimental glides between the desk and the bed, he concludes that it is no less enjoyable than rocking back and forth and spinning around in the chair—perhaps even more so. The pressure in his bladder is mounting, but Mr. Blank delays his trip to the bathroom in order to prolong his turn on the imaginary ice by a few moments, and as he skates around the room, now lifting one foot into the air, now the other, or else floating along with both feet on the floor, he again returns to the distant past, not as far back as the era of Whitey the rocking horse or the mornings when he would sit in his mother's lap as she dressed him on the bed, but a long while ago just the same: Mr. Blank in his high middle boyhood, roughly ten years old, perhaps eleven, but on no account as advanced as twelve. It's a cold Saturday afternoon in January or February. The pond in the little town where he grew up has frozen over, and there is the young Mr. Blank, who was then referred to as Master Blank, skating hand in hand with his first love, a girl with green eyes and reddish brown hair, long reddish brown hair tousled by the wind, her cheeks red from the cold, her name now forgotten, but beginning with the letter *S*, Mr. Blank says to himself, he is certain of that, perhaps Susie, he thinks, or Samantha or Sally or Serena, but no, none of those, and yet no matter, for in that it was the first time he ever held a girl's hand, what he remembers most keenly now is the sensation of having entered a new world, a world in which holding a girl's hand was a good to be desired above all others, and such was his ardor for this young creature whose name began with the letter *S* that once they stopped skating and sat down on a tree stump at the edge of the pond, Master Blank was bold enough to lean forward and kiss her on the lips. For reasons that both baffled and wounded him at the time, Miss S. burst out laughing, turned away her head, and rebuked him with a sentence that has stayed with him ever since—even now, in his present abject circumstances, when all is not right in his head and so many other things have vanished: Don't be silly. For the object of his affections understood nothing of such matters, being but ten or eleven years old and not yet ripened to the point where amorous advances from a member of the opposite sex would have any meaning for her. And so, rather than respond to Master Blank's kiss with a kiss of her own, she laughed.

The rebuff lingered for days afterward, causing such pain in his soul that one morning, noticing her son's grim demeanor, his mother asked him what was wrong. Mr. Blank was still young enough to feel no compunctions about confiding in his mother, and therefore he told her the full story. To which she replied: Don't worry; there are other pebbles on the shore. It was the first time Mr. Blank had heard the expression, and he found it curious that girls should be compared to pebbles, whom they in no way resembled, he felt, at least not in his experience. Nevertheless, he grasped the metaphor, but in spite of understanding what his mother was trying to tell him, he disagreed with her, since passion is and always will be blind to all but one thing, and as far as Mr. Blank was concerned, there was only one pebble on the shore that counted, and if he couldn't have that one, he wasn't interested in any of the others. Time changed all that, of course, and as the years went on he came to see the wisdom of his mother's remark. Now, as he continues to glide around the room in his white nylon socks, he wonders how many pebbles there have been since then. Mr. Blank can't be sure, for his memory is nothing if not defective, but he knows there are dozens, perhaps even scores of them—more pebbles in his past than he can possibly count, right up to and including Anna, the long-lost girl of so many years ago, rediscovered this very day on the infinite shore of love.

These musings fly through Mr. Blank's head in a matter of seconds, perhaps twelve, perhaps twenty, and all the while, as the past wells up within him, he struggles to maintain his concentration so as not to lose his balance as he skates around the room. Short as those seconds may be, however, a moment comes when the bygone days overtake the present, and instead of thinking and moving at the same time, Mr. Blank forgets that he is moving and focuses exclusively on his thoughts, and not long after that, perhaps less than a second, two seconds at most, his feet slip out from under him and he falls to the floor.

Luckily, he does not land on his head, but in all other respects the tumble qualifies as a nasty spill. Pitching backward into the void as his stockinged feet struggle to gain a purchase on the slippery wooden planks, he thrusts his hands out behind him in the vain hope of softening the impact, but he nevertheless hits the floor smack on his tailbone, which sends forth a cascade of volcanic fire through his legs and torso, and given that he has also fallen on his hands, his wrists and elbows are suddenly ablaze as well. Mr. Blank writhes around on the floor, too stunned even to feel sorry for himself, and as he wrestles to absorb the pain that has engulfed him, he forgets to contract the muscles in and around his penis, which he has been doing for the last little while as he skated into his past. For Mr. Blank's bladder is full to bursting, and without making a conscious effort to hold it in, as it were, he is on the verge of producing a shameful and embarrassing accident. But the pain is too much for him. It has pushed all other thoughts out of his mind, and once he begins to relax the aforementioned muscles, he feels his urethra give way to the inevitable, and a moment later he is pissing in his pants. No better than an infant, he says to himself as the warm urine flows out of him and runs down his leg. Then he adds: Mewling and puking in his nurse's arms. And then, once the deluge has ceased, he shouts at the top of his lungs: Idiot! Idiot old man! What the hell is wrong with you?

Now Mr. Blank is in the bathroom, stripping off his pants, underwear, and socks, all of which have been drenched and yellowed by his involuntary loss of control. Still rattled by the blunder, his bones still aching from the crash to the floor, he flings each article of clothing angrily into the tub, then takes the white washcloth Anna used for the sponge bath earlier and wipes down his legs and crotch with warm water. As he does so, his penis begins to swell from its present flaccid state, rising from the perpendicular to a forty-five-degree angle. In spite of the multiple indignities Mr. Blank has been subjected to in the past minutes, he can't help feeling consoled by this development, as if it somehow proved that his honor was still intact. After a few more tugs, his old companion is sticking out from his body at a full ninety-degree thrust, and in this way, preceded by his second erection of the morning, Mr. Blank exits the bathroom, walks over to the bed, and climbs into the pajama bottoms that Anna stowed under the pillow. Mr. Bigshot has already begun to shrink by the time the old man pushes his feet into his leather slippers, but what else can be expected in the absence of further friction or mental stimulation of some kind? Mr. Blank feels more comfortable in the pajama bottoms and slippers than he did in the white trousers and tennis shoes, but at the same time he can't help feeling guilty about these sartorial changes, for the fact is that he is no longer dressed all in white, which means that he has broken his promise to Anna—as per the demand of Peter Stillman, Junior—and this pains him deeply, even more deeply than the physical pain that is still reverberating through his body. As he shuffles over to the desk to resume his reading of the typescript, he resolves to make a clean breast of it the next time he sees her, hoping she will find it in her heart to forgive him.

Several moments later, he is once again sitting in the chair, his tailbone throbbing as he wriggles his backside around until he settles into a more or less acceptable position. Then he begins to read:

I first heard about the trouble in the Alien Territories six months ago. It was a late afternoon in midsummer, and I was sitting alone in my office, working on the last pages of my semiannual report. We were well into the season of white cotton suits by then, but the air that day had been especially hot, bearing down with such stifling heaviness that even the thinnest clothing felt excessive. At ten o'clock, I had instructed the men in my department to remove their coats and ties, but as that seemed to have little effect, I dismissed them at noon. Since the staff had done nothing all morning but fan their faces and wipe sweat from their foreheads, it seemed pointless to hold them hostage any longer.

I remember dining at the Bruder Hof, a small restaurant around the corner from the Foreign Ministry building. Afterward, I took a stroll down Santa Victoria Boulevard, going as far as the river to see if I couldn't coax a breeze to blow against my face. I saw the children launching their toy boats into the water, the women walking by in groups of three and four with their yellow parasols and bashful smiles, the young men loafing on the grass. I have always loved the capital in summer. There is a stillness that envelops us at that time of year, a trancelike quality that seems to blur the difference between animate and inanimate things, and with the crowds along the avenues so much thinner and quieter, the frenzy of the other seasons becomes almost unimaginable. Perhaps it is because the Protector and his family are gone from the city then, and with the palace standing empty and blue shutters covering the familiar windows, the reality of the Confederation begins to feel less substantial. One is aware of the great distances, of the endless territories and people, of the chaos and clamor of lives being lived—but they are all at a remove, somehow, as if the Confederation had become something internal, a dream that each person carried within himself.

After I returned to the office, I worked steadily until four o'clock. I had just put down my pen to mull over the concluding paragraphs when I was interrupted by the arrival of the Minister's secretary—a young man named Jensen or Johnson, I can't recall which. He handed me a note and then looked off discreetly in the other direction while I read it, waiting for an answer to carry back to the Minister. The message was very brief. *Would it be possible for you to stop by my house this evening? Excuse the last-minute invitation, but there is a matter of great importance I need to discuss with you. Joubert.*

I wrote out a reply on department stationery, thanking the Minister for his invitation and telling him that he could expect me at eight. The redheaded secretary went off with the letter, and for the next few minutes I remained at my desk, puzzling over what had just happened. Joubert had been installed as Minister three months earlier, and in that time I had seen him only once—at a formal banquet held by the Bureau to celebrate his appointment. Under ordinary circumstances, a man in my position would have little direct contact with the Minister, and I found it odd to have been invited to his house, especially on such short notice. From all I had heard about him so far, he was neither an impulsive nor flamboyant administrator, and he did not flaunt his power in an arbitrary or unreasonable way. I doubted that I had been summoned to this private meeting because he was planning to criticize my work, but at the same time, judging from the urgency of his message, it was clear that this was to be more than just a social visit.

For a person who had attained such an exalted rank, Joubert did not cut an impressive figure. Just short of his sixtieth birthday, he was a squat and diminutive man with bad eyesight and a bulbous nose who continually adjusted and readjusted his pince-nez throughout our conversation. A servant led me down the central corridor to a small library on the ground floor of the Minister's residence, and when Joubert rose to welcome me, dressed in an out-of-fashion brown frock coat and a ruffled white cravat, I had the feeling that I was shaking hands with an assistant law clerk rather than one of the most important men in the Confederation. Once we began to speak, however, that illusion was quickly dispelled. He had a clear and attentive mind, and each one of his remarks was delivered with authority and conviction. After he had apologized for calling me to his house at such an inopportune moment, he gestured to the gilded leather chair on the opposite side of his desk, and I sat down.

—I take it you've heard of Ernesto Land, he said, wasting no more time on empty formalities.

—He was one of my closest friends, I replied. We fought together in the Southeast Border Wars and then worked as colleagues in the same intelligence division. After the Consolidation Treaty of the Fourth of March, he introduced me to the woman I eventually married—my late wife, Beatrice. A man of exceptional courage and ability. His death during the cholera epidemic was a great loss to me.

—That's the official story. A death certificate is on file at the Municipal Hall of Records, but Land's name has cropped up again recently on several occasions. If these reports are true, it would appear he's still alive.

—That's excellent news, sir. It makes me very glad.

—For the past several months, rumors have been drifting back to us from the garrison at Ultima. Nothing has been confirmed, but according to these stories, Land crossed over the border into the Alien Territories sometime after the cholera epidemic ended. It's a three-week journey from the capital to Ultima. That would mean Land departed just after the outbreak of the scourge. Not dead, then—simply missing.

—The Alien Territories are off-limits. Everyone knows that. The No-Entrance Decrees have been in force for ten years now.

—Nevertheless, Land is there. If the intelligence reports are correct, he was traveling with an army of more than a hundred men.

—I don't understand.

—We think he's stirring up discontent among the Primitives, preparing to lead them in an insurrection against the western provinces.

—That's impossible.

—Nothing is impossible, Graf. You of all people should know that.

—No one believes in the principles of the Confederation more fervently than he does. Ernesto Land is a patriot.

—Men sometimes change their views.

—You must be mistaken. An uprising is impossible. Military action would require unity among the Primitives, and that has never happened and never will. They're as various and divided as we are. Their social customs, their languages, and their religious beliefs have kept them at odds for centuries. The Tackamen in the east bury their dead, just as we do. The Gangi in the west put their dead on elevated platforms and leave the corpses to rot in the sun. The Crow People in the south burn their dead. The Vahntoo in the north cook the bodies and eat them. We call it an offense against God, but to them it's a sacred ritual. Each nation is divided into tribes, which are further subdivided into small clans, and not only have all the nations fought against one another at various times in the past, but tribes within those nations have waged war against one another as well. I simply can't see them banding together, sir. If they were capable of unified action, they never would have been defeated in the first place.

—I understand that you know the Territories quite well.

—I spent more than a year among the Primitives during my early days with the Bureau. That was before the No-Entrance Decrees, of course. I moved from one clan to another, studying the workings of each society, investigating everything from dietary laws to mating rituals. It was a memorable experience. My work since then has always engaged me, but I consider that to have been the most challenging assignment of my career.

—Everything used to be theirs. Then the ships arrived, bringing settlers from Iberia and Gaul, from Albion, Germania, and the Tartar kingdoms, and little by little the Primitives were pushed off their lands. We slaughtered them and enslaved them and then we herded them together in the parched and barren territories beyond the western provinces. You must have encountered much bitterness and resentment during your travels.

—Less than you would think. After four hundred years of conflict, most of the nations were glad to be at peace.

—That was more than ten years ago. Perhaps they've rethought their position by now. If I were in their place, I'd be sorely tempted to reconquer the western provinces. The ground is fertile there. The forests are full of game. It would give them a better, easier life.

—You're forgetting that all the Primitive nations endorsed the No-Entrance Decrees. Now that the fighting has stopped, they would prefer to live in their own separate world, with no interference from the Confederation.

—I hope you're right, Graf, but it's my duty to protect the welfare of the Confederation. Whether they prove groundless or not, the reports about Land must be investigated. You know him, you've spent time in the Territories, and of all the members of the Bureau, I can think of no one better qualified to handle the job. I'm not ordering you to go, but I would be deeply grateful if you accepted. The future of the Confederation could depend on it.

—I feel honored by your confidence in me, sir. But what if I'm not allowed to cross the border?

—You'll be carrying a personal letter from me to Colonel De Vega, the officer in charge of the garrison. He won't be pleased about it, but he'll have no choice. An order from the central government must be obeyed.

—But if what you say is true, and Land is in the Alien Territories with a hundred men, it raises a perplexing question, doesn't it?

—A question?

—How did he manage to get there? From what I'm told, there are troops stationed along the entire frontier. I can imagine one man slipping past them, but not a hundred men. If Land got through, then he must have done it with Colonel De Vega's knowledge.

—Possibly. Possibly not. That's one of the mysteries you'll be entrusted to solve.

—When do you want me to leave?

—As soon as you can. A carriage from the Ministry will be at your disposal. We'll furnish you with supplies and make all the necessary arrangements. The only things you'll need to carry with you are the letter and the clothes on your back.

—Tomorrow morning, then. I've just finished writing my semi-annual report, and my desk is clear.

—Come to the Ministry at nine o'clock for the letter. I'll be waiting for you in my office.

—Very good, sir. Tomorrow morning at nine.

The moment he comes to the end of the conversation between Graf and Joubert, the telephone starts to ring, and once again Mr. Blank is forced to interrupt his reading of the typescript. Cursing under his breath as he extricates himself from the chair, he hobbles slowly across the room toward the bedside table, moving with difficulty because of his recent injuries, and so plodding is his progress that he doesn't pick up the receiver until the seventh ring, whereas he was nimble enough to answer the previous call from Flood on the fourth.

What do you want? Mr. Blank says harshly, as he sits down on the bed, suddenly feeling a flutter of the old dizziness whirling around inside him.

I want to know if you've finished the story, a man's voice calmly answers.

Story? What story is that?

The one you've been reading. The story about the Confederation.

I didn't know it was a story. It sounds more like a report, like something that really happened.

It's make-believe, Mr. Blank. A work of fiction.

Ah. That explains why I've never heard of that place. I know my mind isn't working too well today, but I thought Graf's manuscript must have been found by someone years after he wrote it and then copied out by a typist.

An honest mistake.

A stupid mistake.

Don't worry about it. The only thing I need to know is whether you've finished it or not.

Almost. Just a few more pages to go. If you hadn't interrupted me with this goddamned call, I'd probably be at the end by now.

Good. I'll come round in fifteen or twenty minutes, and we can begin the consultation.

Consultation? What are you talking about?

I'm your doctor, Mr. Blank. I come to see you every day.

I don't remember having a doctor.

Of course not. That's because the treatment is beginning to take effect.

Does my doctor have a name?

Farr. Samuel Farr.

Farr . . . Hmm . . . Yes, Samuel Farr . . . You wouldn't happen to know a woman named Anna, would you?

We'll talk about that later. For now, the only thing you have to do is finish the story.

All right, I'll finish the story. But when you come to my room, how will I know it's you? What if it's someone else pretending to be you?

There's a picture of me on your desk. The twelfth one in from the top of the pile. Take a good look at it, and when I show up, you won't have any trouble recognizing me.

Now Mr. Blank is sitting in the chair again, hunched over the desk. Rather than look for Samuel Farr's picture in the pile of photographs as he was instructed to do, he reaches for the pad and ballpoint pen and adds another name to his list:

> James P. Flood
> Anna
> David Zimmer
> Peter Stillman, Jr.
> Peter Stillman, Sr.
> Fanshawe
> Man with house
> Samuel Farr

Pushing aside the pad and pen, he immediately picks up the typescript of the story, forgetting all about his intention to look for Samuel Farr's photograph, in the same way that he has long since forgotten about looking for the closet that is supposedly in the room. The last pages of the text read as follows:

The long journey to Ultima gave me ample time to reflect upon the nature of my mission. A series of coachmen took over the reins at two-hundred-mile intervals, and with nothing for me to do but sit in the carriage and stare out at the landscape, I felt a growing sense of dread as I neared my destination. Ernesto Land had been my comrade and intimate friend, and I had the greatest trouble accepting Joubert's verdict that he had turned traitor to a cause he had defended all his life. He had remained in the military after the Consolidations of Year 31, continuing his work as an intelligence officer under the aegis of the Ministry of War, and whenever he had dined with us at our house or I had met with him for an afternoon meal at one of the taverns near the Ministry Esplanade, he had talked with enthusiasm about the inevitable victory of the Confederation, confident that all we had dreamed of and fought for since our earliest youth would finally come to pass. Now, according to Joubert's agents in Ultima, not only had Land escaped death during the cholera epidemic, he had in fact falsified his death in order to disappear into the wilderness with a small army of anti-Confederationists to foment rebellion among the Primitives. Judging from all I knew about him, this seemed an absurd and preposterous accusation.

Land had grown up in the northwestern farming region of Tierra Vieja Province, the same part of the world where my wife, Beatrice, was born. They had been playmates as small children, and for many years it was taken for granted by their two families that they would eventually marry. Beatrice once confessed to me that Ernesto had been her first love, and when he later turned his back on her and was betrothed to Hortense Chatterton, the daughter of a wealthy shipping family from Mont Sublime, she felt as if her life had ended. But Beatrice was a strong girl, too proud to share her suffering with anyone, and in a demonstration of remarkable courage and dignity, she accompanied her parents and two brothers to the lavish wedding festival at the Chatterton estate. That was where we were introduced. I lost my heart to her that first evening, but it was only after a prolonged courtship of eighteen months that she finally accepted my proposal of marriage. I knew that in her eyes I was no match for Land. I was neither as handsome nor as brilliant as he was, and it took some time before she understood that my steadiness of character and fierce devotion to her were no less important qualities on which to build a lifelong union. Much as I admired Land, I was also aware of his flaws. There had always been something wild and obstreperous about him, a headstrong assurance in his superiority to others, and despite his charm and persuasiveness, that inborn power to draw attention to himself wherever he happened to be, one also sensed an incurable vanity lurking just below the surface. His marriage to Hortense Chatterton proved to be an unhappy one. He was unfaithful to her almost from the start, and when she died in childbirth four years later, he recovered quickly from his loss. He went through all the rituals of mourning and public sorrow, but at bottom I felt he was more relieved than brokenhearted. We saw quite a bit of him after that, much more than had been the case in the early years of our marriage. To his credit, Land became deeply attached to our little daughter, Marta, always bringing presents when he visited the house and showering her with such affection that she came to regard him as a heroic figure, the greatest man who walked the earth. He behaved with utmost decorum whenever he was among us, and yet who could fault me if I sometimes questioned whether the fires that had once burned in my wife's soul for him had been fully extinguished? Nothing untoward ever happened—no words or glances between them that could have aroused my jealousy—but in the aftermath of the cholera epidemic that had supposedly killed them both, what was I to make of the fact that Land was now reported to be alive and that in spite of my assiduous efforts to learn something about Beatrice's fate, I hadn't uncovered a single witness who had seen her in the capital during the scourge? If not for my disastrous run-in with Giles McNaughton, which had been set off by ugly innuendos concerning my wife, it seemed doubtful that I would have tormented myself with such dark suspicions on my way to Ultima. But what if Beatrice and Marta had run off with Land while I was traveling through the Independent Communities of Tierra Blanca Province? It seemed impossible, but as Joubert had said to me the night before my departure, nothing was impossible, and of all the people in the world, I was the one who should know that best.

The wheels of the carriage turned, and by the time I'd reached the outskirts of Wallingham, the midway point of the journey, I understood that I was approaching a twofold horror. If Land had betrayed the Confederation, my instructions from the minister were to put him under arrest and transport him back to the capital in chains. That thought was gruesome enough, but if my friend had betrayed me by stealing my wife and daughter, then I was planning to kill him. That much was certain, no matter what the consequences were. May God damn me for thinking it, but for Ernesto's sake and my own, I prayed that Beatrice was already dead.

Mr. Blank tosses the typescript onto the desk, snorting with dissatisfaction and contempt, furious that he has been compelled to read a story that has no ending, an unfinished work that has barely even begun, a mere bloody fragment. What garbage, he says out loud, and then, swiveling the chair around by a hundred and eighty degrees, he wheels himself over to the bathroom door. He is thirsty. With no beverages on hand, the only solution is to pour himself a glass of water from the bathroom sink. He stands up from the chair, opens the door, and shuffles forward to do just that, all the while regretting having wasted so much time on that misbegotten excuse of a story. He drinks one glass of water, then another, leaning his left hand on the sink to steady his balance as he gazes forlornly at the soiled clothes in the tub. Now that he happens to be in the bathroom, Mr. Blank wonders if he shouldn't take another shot at peeing, just to play it safe. Worried that he might fall again if he stays on his feet too long, he lets his pajama bottoms drop to his ankles and sits down on the toilet. Just like a woman, he says to himself, suddenly amused by the thought of how different his life would have been if he hadn't been born a man. After his recent accident, his bladder has little to say for itself, but eventually he manages to dribble forth a few measly squirts. He pulls up the pajama bottoms as he climbs to his feet, flushes, rinses his hands at the sink, dries those same hands with a towel, then turns around and opens the door—whereupon he sees a man standing in the room. Another lost opportunity, Mr. Blank says to himself, realizing that the noise of the flushing toilet must have drowned out the sound of the stranger's entrance, thus leaving the question of whether the door is locked from the outside or not unanswered.

Mr. Blank sits down in the chair and does an abrupt half-turn in order to take a look at the new arrival, a tall man in his mid-thirties dressed in blue jeans and a red button-down shirt open at the collar. Dark hair, dark eyes, and a gaunt face that looks as if it hasn't cracked a smile in years. No sooner does Mr. Blank make this observation, however, than the man smiles at him and says: Hello, Mr. Blank. How are you feeling today?

Do I know you? Mr. Blank asks.

Didn't you look at the picture? the man replies.

What picture?

The photograph on your desk. The twelfth one in from the top of the pile. Remember?

Oh, that. Yes. I think so. I was supposed to look at it, wasn't I? And?

I forgot. I was too busy reading that dumb story.

No problem, the man says, turning around and walking toward the desk, where he picks up the photographs and searches through the pile until he comes to the picture in question. Then, putting the other photographs back on the desk, he walks over to Mr. Blank and hands him the portrait. You see, Mr. Blank? the man says. There I am.

You must be the doctor, then, Mr. Blank says. Samuel . . . Samuel something.

Farr.

That's right. Samuel Farr. I remember now. You have something to do with Anna, don't you?

I did. But that was a long time ago.

Holding the picture firmly in his two hands, Mr. Blank lifts it up until it is directly in front of his face, then studies it for a good twenty seconds. Farr, looking very much as he does now, is sitting in a garden somewhere dressed in a white doctor's coat with a cigarette burning between the second and third fingers of his left hand.

I don't get it, Mr. Blank says, suddenly besieged by a new attack of anguish that burns like a hot coal in his chest and tightens his stomach into the shape of a fist.

What's wrong? Farr asks. It's a good likeness, don't you think?

A perfect likeness. You might be a year or two older now, but the man in the picture is definitely you.

Is that a problem?

It's just that you're so young, Mr. Blank says in a tremulous voice, doing all he can to fight back the tears that are forming in his eyes. Anna is young in her picture, too. But she told me it was taken more than thirty years ago. She's not a girl anymore. Her hair is gray, her husband is dead, and time is turning her into an old woman. But not you, Farr. You were with her. You were in that terrible country I sent her to, but that was more than thirty years ago, and you haven't changed.

Farr hesitates, clearly uncertain about how to answer Mr. Blank. He sits down on the edge of the bed, spreads his palms out on his knees, and looks down at the floor, inadvertently settling into the same position the old man was discovered in at the beginning of this report. A long moment of silence follows. At last he says, speaking in a low voice: I'm not allowed to talk about it.

Mr. Blank looks at him in horror. You're telling me you're dead, he cries out. That's it, isn't it? You didn't make it. Anna lived, but you didn't.

Farr lifts his head and smiles. Do I look dead, Mr. Blank? he asks. We all go through our rough moments, of course, but I'm just as alive as you are, believe me.

Well, who's to say if I'm alive or not? Mr. Blank says, staring grimly at Farr. Maybe I'm dead, too. The way things have been going for me this morning, I wouldn't be a bit surprised. Talk about *the treatment*. It's probably just another word for death.

You don't remember now, Farr says, standing up from the bed and taking the photograph out of Mr. Blank's hands, but the whole thing was your idea. We're just doing what you asked us to do.

Bullshit. I want to see a lawyer. He'll get me out of here. I have my rights, you know.

That can be arranged, Farr answers, carrying the photograph back to the desk, where he reinserts it into the pile. If you like, I'll have someone stop in to see you this afternoon.

Good, Mr. Blank mumbles, somewhat thrown by Farr's so-licitous and accommodating manner. That's more like it.

Glancing at his watch, Farr returns from the desk and once again sits down on the bed facing Mr. Blank, who is still in his chair beside the bathroom door. It's getting late, the young man says. We have to begin our talk.

Talk? What kind of talk?

The consultation.

I understand the word, but I have no idea what you mean by it.

We're supposed to discuss the story.

What's the point? It's only the beginning of a story, and where I come from, stories are supposed to have a beginning, a middle, and an end.

I couldn't agree with you more.

Who wrote that piece of drivel, by the way? The bastard should be taken outside and shot.

A man named John Trause. Ever hear of him?

Trause . . . Hmmm . . . Perhaps. He wrote novels, didn't he? It's all a bit fuzzy now, but I think I might have read some of them.

You have. Rest assured that you have.

So why not give me one of those to read—instead of some half-assed, unfinished story without a title?

Trause did finish it. The manuscript comes to a hundred and ten pages, and he wrote it in the early fifties, when he was just starting out as a novelist. You might not think much of it, but it's not bad work for a kid of twenty-three or twenty-four.

I don't understand. Why not let me see the rest of it?

Because it's part of the treatment, Mr. Blank. We didn't put all those papers on the desk just to amuse you. They're here for a purpose.

Such as?

To test your reflexes, for one thing.

My reflexes? What do they have to do with it?

Mental reflexes. Emotional reflexes.

And?

What I want you to do is tell me the rest of the story. Starting at the point where you stopped reading, tell me what you think should happen now, right up to the last paragraph, the last word. You have the beginning. Now I want you to give me the middle and the end.

What is this, some kind of parlor game?

If you like. I prefer to think of it as an exercise in imaginative reasoning.

A pretty phrase, doctor. *Imaginative reasoning.* Since when does the imagination have anything to do with reason?

Since now, Mr. Blank. From the moment you begin to tell me the rest of the story.

All right. It's not as if I have anything better to do, is there?

That's the spirit.

Mr. Blank closes his eyes in order to concentrate on the task at hand, but blocking out the room and his immediate surroundings has the disturbing effect of summoning forth the procession of figment beings who marched through his head at earlier points in the narrative. Mr. Blank shudders at the ghastly vision, and an instant later he opens his eyes again to make it disappear.

What's wrong? Farr asks, with a look of concern on his face.

The damned specters, Mr. Blank says. They're back again.

Specters?

My victims. All the people I've made suffer over the years. They're coming after me now to take their revenge.

Just keep your eyes open, Mr. Blank, and they won't be there anymore. We have to get on with the story.

All right, all right, Mr. Blank says, letting out a long, self-pitying sigh. Give me a minute.

Why don't you tell me some of your thoughts about the Confederation. That might help get you started.

The Confederation . . . The Con-fed-e-ra-tion . . . It's all very simple, isn't it? Just another name for America. Not the United States as we know it, but a country that has evolved in another way, that has another history. But all the trees, all the mountains, and all the prairies of that country stand exactly where they do in ours. The rivers and oceans are identical. Men walk on two legs, see with two eyes, and touch with two hands. They think double thoughts and speak out of both sides of their mouths at once.

Good. Now what happens to Graf when he gets to Ultima?

He goes to see the Colonel with Joubert's letter, but De Vega acts as if he's just been handed a note from a child, since he's in on the plot with Land. Graf reminds him that an order from an official of the central government must be obeyed, but the Colonel says that he works for the Ministry of War, and they've put him under strict orders to abide by the No-Entrance Decrees. Graf mentions the rumors about Land and the hundred soldiers who have entered the Alien Territories, but De Vega pretends to know nothing about it. Graf then says he has no alternative but to write to the Ministry of War and ask for an exemption to bypass the No-Entrance Decrees. Fine, De Vega says, but it takes six weeks for a letter to travel back and forth from the capital, and what are you going to do in the meantime? Take in the sights of Ultima, Graf says, and wait for the response to come— knowing full well that the Colonel will never allow his letter to get through, that it will be intercepted the moment he tries to send it.

Why is De Vega in on the plot? From all I can gather, he appears to be a loyal officer.

He is loyal. And so is Ernesto Land with his hundred troops in the Alien Territories.

I don't follow.

The Confederation is a fragile, newly formed state composed of previously independent colonies and principalities, and in order to hold this tenuous union together, what better way to unite the people than to invent a common enemy and start a war? In this case, they've chosen the Primitives. Land is a double agent who's been sent into the Territories to stir up rebellion among the tribes there. Not so different from what we did to the Indians after the Civil War. Get the natives riled up and then slaughter them.

But how does Graf know that De Vega is in on it, too?

Because he didn't ask enough questions. He should have at least pretended to be curious. And then there's the fact that he and Land both work for the Ministry of War. Joubert and his crowd at the Bureau of Internal Affairs know nothing about the plot, of course, but that's perfectly normal. Government agencies keep secrets from one another all the time.

And then?

Joubert has given Graf the names of three men, spies who work for the Bureau in Ultima. None of them is aware of the others' existence, but collectively they've been the source of Joubert's information about Land. After his conversation with the Colonel, Graf goes out to look for them. But one by one he discovers that all three, as the saying goes, have been dispatched to other parts. Let's find some names for them. It's always more interesting when a character has a name. Captain . . . hmmm . . . Lieutenant Major Jacques Dupin was transferred to a post in the high central mountains two months earlier. Dr. Carlos . . . Woburn . . . left town in June to volunteer his services after an outbreak of smallpox in the north. And Declan Bray, Ultima's most prosperous barber, died from food poisoning in early August. Whether by accident or design it's impossible to know, but there's poor Graf, completely cut off from the Bureau now, without a single ally or confidant, all alone in that bleak, godforsaken corner of the earth.

Very nice. The names are a good touch, Mr. Blank.

My brain is turning at a hundred miles an hour. Haven't felt so full of beans all day.

Old habits die hard, I suppose.

What's that supposed to mean?

Nothing. Just that you're in good form, beginning to hit your stride. What happens next?

Graf hangs around Ultima for more than a month, trying to

figure out a way to cross the border into the Territories. He can't go on foot, after all. He needs a horse, a rifle, provisions, probably a donkey as well. In the meantime, with nothing else to occupy his days, he finds himself getting drawn into Ultima society—such as it is, considering that it's nothing more than a pukey little garrison town in the middle of nowhere. Of all people, it's the hypocrite De Vega who makes a great show of befriending him. He invites Graf to dinner parties—long, tedious affairs attended by military officers, town officials, members of the merchant class, along with their wives, their lady friends, and so on—takes him to the best brothels, and even goes out hunting with him a couple of times. And then there's the Colonel's mistress . . . Carlotta . . . Carlotta Hauptmann . . . a debauched sensualist, the proverbial horny widow, whose principal entertainments in life are fucking and playing cards. The Colonel is married, of course, married with two small children, and since he can visit Carlotta only once or twice a week, she's available for romps with other men. It isn't long before Graf enters into a liaison with her. One night, as they're lying in bed together, he questions her about Land, and Carlotta confirms the rumors. Yes, she says, Land and his men crossed into the Territories a little more than a year ago. Why does she tell him this? Her motives aren't quite clear. Perhaps she's smitten with Graf and wants to be helpful, or perhaps the Colonel has put her up to it for hidden reasons of his own. This part has to be handled delicately. The reader can never be certain if Carlotta is luring Graf into a trap or if she simply talks too much for her own good. Don't forget that this is Ultima, the dreariest outpost of the Confederation, and sex, gambling, and gossip are about the only fun to be had.

How does Graf make it across the border?

I'm not sure. Probably a bribe of some sort. It doesn't really matter. The important thing is that he gets across one night, and the second part of the story begins. We're in the desert now. Emptiness all around, a ferocious blue sky overhead, pounding light, and then, when the sun goes down, a chill to freeze the marrow in your bones. Graf rides west for several days, mounted on a chestnut horse who goes by the name of Whitey, so called because of a splash of white between the animal's eyes, and since Graf knows the terrain well from his visit twelve years before, he heads in the direction of the Gangi, the tribe with whom he got along best during his earlier travels and whom he found to be the most peaceful of all the Primitive nations. Late one morning, he finally approaches a Gangi encampment, a small village of fifteen or twenty hogans, which would suggest a population of somewhere between seventy and a hundred people. When he's approximately thirty yards from the edge of the settlement, he calls out a greeting in the local Gangi dialect to signal his arrival to the inhabitants—but no one responds. Growing alarmed now, Graf quickens the horse's pace and trots into the heart of the village, where not a single sign of human life can be seen. He dismounts, walks over to one of the hogans, and pushes aside the buffalo skin that serves as the door to the little house. The moment he enters, he's greeted by the overpowering stench of death, the sickening smell of decomposing bodies, and there, in the dim light of the hogan, he sees a dozen slaughtered

Gangi—men, women, and children—all of them shot down in cold blood. He staggers out into the air, covering his nose with a handkerchief, and then one by one inspects the other hogans in the village. They're all dead, every last soul is dead, and among them Graf recognizes a number of people he befriended twelve years before. The girls who have since grown into young women, the boys who have since grown into young men, the parents who have since become grandparents, and not a single one is breathing anymore, not a single one will grow a day older for the rest of time.

Who was responsible? Was it Land and his men?

Patience, doctor. A thing like this can't be rushed. We're talking about brutality and death, the murder of the innocent, and Graf is still reeling from the shock of his discovery. He's in no shape to absorb what's happened, but even if he were, why would he think Land had anything to do with it? He's working on the assumption that his old friend is trying to start a rebellion, to form an army of Primitives that will invade the western provinces of the Confederation. An army of dead men can't fight very well, can it? The last thing Graf would conclude is that Land has killed his own future soldiers.

I'm sorry. I won't interrupt anymore.

Interrupt all you like. We're involved in a complicated story here, and not everything is quite what it seems to be. Take Land's troops, for example. They have no idea what their real mission is, no idea that Land is a double agent working for the Ministry of War. They're a bunch of well-educated dreamers, political radicals opposed to the Confederation, and when Land enlisted them to follow him into the Alien Territories, they took him at his word and assumed they were going to help the Primitives annex the western provinces.

Does Graf ever find Land?

He has to. Otherwise, there wouldn't be any story to tell. But that doesn't happen until later, until several weeks or months down the road. About two days after Graf leaves the massacred Gangi village, he comes across one of Land's men, a delirious soldier staggering through the desert with no food, no water, no horse. Graf tries to help him, but it's already too late, and the kid hangs on for just a few more hours. Before he gives up the ghost, he raves on to Graf in a stream of incoherent babble about how everyone is dead, how they never had a chance, how the whole thing was a fraud from the start. Graf has trouble following him. Who does he mean by *everyone*? Land and his troops? The Gangi? Other tribes among the Primitives? The boy doesn't answer, and before the sun goes down that evening, he's dead. Graf buries the body and moves on, and a day or two after that, he comes to another Gangi settlement filled with corpses. He no longer knows what to think. What if Land is responsible, after all? What if the rumor of an insurrection is no more than a blind to cover up a far more sinister undertaking: a quiet slaughter of the Primitives that would enable the government to open their territory to white settlement, to expand the reach of the Confederation all the way to the shores of the western ocean? And yet, how can such a thing be accomplished with such a paucity of troops? One hundred men to wipe out tens of thousands? It doesn't seem possible, and yet if Land has nothing to do with it, then the only other explanation is that the Gangi were killed by another tribe, that the Primitives are at war among themselves.

Mr. Blank is about to continue, but before he can get another word out of his mouth, he and the doctor are interrupted by a knocking at the door. Engrossed as he is in elaborating the story, content as he is to be spinning out his version of far-flung, imaginary events, Mr. Blank instantly understands that this is the moment he's been waiting for: the mystery of the door is about to be solved at last. Once the knock is heard, Farr turns his head in the direction of the sound. Come in, he says, and just like that the door opens, and in walks a woman pushing a stainless steel cart, perhaps the same one Anna used earlier, perhaps one that is identical to it. For once, Mr. Blank has been paying attention, and to the best of his knowledge he heard no sound of a lock being opened—nothing that resembled the sound of a bolt or a latch or a key—which would suggest that the door was unlocked to begin with, unlocked all along. Or so Mr. Blank surmises, beginning to rejoice at the thought of his liberty to come and go as he wants, but a moment later he understands that things are possibly not quite as simple as that. It could be that Dr. Farr forgot to lock the door when he entered. Or, even more likely, that he didn't bother to lock it, knowing he would have no trouble overpowering Mr. Blank if his prisoner tried to escape. Yes, the old man says to himself, that's probably the answer. And he, who is nothing if not pessimistic about his prospects for the future, once again resigns himself to living in a state of constant uncertainty.

Hello, Sam, the woman says. Sorry to barge in on you like this, but it's time for Mr. Blank's lunch.

Hi, Sophie, Farr says, simultaneously looking down at his watch and standing up from the bed. I hadn't realized it was so late.

What's happening? Mr. Blank asks, pounding the arm of his chair and speaking in a petulant tone of voice. I want to go on telling the story.

We've run out of time, Farr says. The consultation is over for today.

But I haven't finished! the old man shouts. I haven't come to the end!

I know, Farr replies, but we're working on a tight schedule around here, and it can't be helped. We'll go on with the story tomorrow.

Tomorrow? Mr. Blank roars, both incredulous and confused. What are you talking about? Tomorrow I won't remember a word I said today. You know that. Even I know that, and I don't know a blasted thing.

Farr walks over to Mr. Blank and pats him on the shoulder, a classic gesture of appeasement for one skilled in the subtle art of bedside manner. All right, he says, I'll see what I can do. I have to get permission first, but if you want me to come back this evening, I can probably work it out. Okay?

Okay, Mr. Blank mumbles, feeling somewhat mollified by the gentleness and concern in Farr's voice.

Well, I'm off then, the doctor announces. See you later.

Without another word, he waves good-bye to Mr. Blank and the woman called Sophie, walks to the door, opens it, steps across the threshold, and shuts the door behind him. Mr. Blank hears the click of the latch, but nothing more. No clatter of a bolt, no turning of a key, and he wonders now if the door isn't simply one of those contraptions that locks automatically the instant you close it.

All the while, the woman called Sophie has been busy wheeling the stainless steel cart alongside the bed and transferring the various dishes of Mr. Blank's lunch from the bottom shelf of the cart to the upper surface. Mr. Blank notes that there are four dishes in all and that each plate is hidden by a round metal cover with a hole in the center. Seeing those covers, he is suddenly reminded of room-service meals in hotels, which in turn provokes him to speculate on how many nights he has spent in hotels over the course of his life. Too many to count, he hears a voice within him say, a voice that is not his own, at least not a voice he recognizes as his own, and yet because it speaks with such authority and conviction, he acknowledges that it must be telling the truth. If that is the case, he thinks, then he has done a good deal of traveling in his time, moving around from place to place in cars, trains, and airplanes, and yes, he further says to himself, airplanes have taken him all over the world, to many countries on several continents, and no doubt those trips had something to do with the missions he sent all those people on, the poor people who suffered so much because of him, and that is surely why he is confined to this room now, no longer permitted to travel anywhere, stuck inside these four walls because he is being punished for the grave harm he has inflicted on others.

This fleeting reverie is cut off in mid-flow by the sound of the woman's voice. Are you ready for your lunch? she asks, and as he lifts his head to take a look at her, Mr. Blank realizes that he can no longer remember her name. She is somewhere in her late forties or early fifties, and although he finds her face both delicate and attractive, her body is too full and chunky to allow her to be classified as an ideal woman. For the record, it should be noted that her clothes are identical to the ones worn by Anna earlier in the day.

Where's my Anna? Mr. Blank asks. I thought she was the one who takes care of me.

She does, the woman says. But she had some last-minute errands to do, and she asked me to fill in for her.

That's terrible, Mr. Blank says, in a mournful tone of voice. Nothing against you, of course, whoever you might be, but I've been waiting for hours to see her again. That woman is everything to me. I can't live without her.

I know that, the woman says. We all know that. But—and here she gives him a friendly little smile—what can I do about it? I'm afraid you're stuck with me.

Alas, Mr. Blank sighs. I'm sure you mean well, but I'm not going to pretend I'm not disappointed.

You don't have to pretend. You have the right to feel what you feel, Mr. Blank. It's not your fault.

As long as we're stuck with each other, as you put it, I suppose you should tell me who you are.

Sophie.

Ah. That's right. Sophie . . . A very pretty name. And it begins with the letter *S*, doesn't it?

It would seem so.

Think back, Sophie. Are you the little girl I kissed at the pond when I was ten years old? We had just finished ice skating, and then we sat down on a tree stump, and I kissed you. Unfortunately, you didn't kiss me back. You laughed.

It couldn't have been me. When you were ten, I hadn't even been born.

Am I that old?

Not old, exactly. But a lot older than I am.

All right. If you're not that Sophie, which Sophie are you?

Instead of answering him, the Sophie who was not the girl Mr. Blank kissed when he was ten walks over to the desk, retrieves one of the photographs from the pile, and holds it up in the air. That's me, she says. Me as I was about twenty-five years ago.

Come closer, Mr. Blank says. You're too far away.

Several seconds later, Mr. Blank is holding the picture in his hands. It turns out to be the photograph he lingered over so attentively earlier in the day—the one of the young woman who has just opened the door of what appears to be a New York apartment.

You were much thinner then, he says.

Middle age, Mr. Blank. It tends to do funny things to a girl's figure.

Tell me, Mr. Blank says, tapping the photo with his index finger. What's going on here? Who's the person standing in the hallway, and why do you look like that? Apprehensive, somehow, but at the same time pleased. If not, you wouldn't be smiling.

Sophie crouches down beside Mr. Blank, who is still sitting in the chair, and studies the photo in silence for several moments.

It's my second husband, she says, and I think it's the second time he came to see me. The first time, I was holding my baby in my arms when I opened the door, I remember that distinctly— so this must be the second time.

Why so apprehensive?

Because I wasn't sure how he felt about me.

And the smile?

I'm smiling because I was happy to see him.

Your second husband, you say. And what about the first? Who was he?

A man named Fanshawe.

Fanshawe . . . Fanshawe . . . , Mr. Blank mutters to himself. I think we're finally getting somewhere.

With Sophie still crouching beside him, with the black-and-white photograph of her younger self still on his lap, Mr. Blank abruptly begins to waddle forward in the chair, moving as quickly as he can in the direction of the desk. Once he arrives, he tosses the picture of Sophie on top of Anna's portrait, reaches for the small pad, and opens it to the first page. Running his finger down the list of names, he stops when he comes to *Fanshawe* and then swivels around in the chair to face Sophie, who has climbed to her feet by now and is slowly walking toward him.

Aha, Mr. Blank says, tapping the pad with his finger. I knew it. Fanshawe is implicated in all this, isn't he?

I don't know what you mean, Sophie says, stopping at the foot of the bed and then sitting down in more or less the same spot occupied earlier by James P. Flood. Of course he's implicated. We're all implicated in this, Mr. Blank. I thought you understood that.

Confused by her response, the old man nevertheless struggles to stick to his train of thought. Have you ever heard of someone called Flood? James P. Flood. English fellow. Ex-policeman. Talks with a Cockney accent.

Wouldn't you rather eat your lunch now? Sophie asks. The food is getting cold.

In a minute, Mr. Blank snaps back at her, peeved that she has changed the subject. Just give me a minute. Before we talk about eating, I want you to tell me everything you know about Flood.

I don't know anything. I heard he was around here this morning, but I've never met him.

But your husband . . . your first husband, I mean . . . this Fanshawe . . . He wrote books, didn't he? In one of them, one of them called . . . damn it . . . I can't remember the title. *Never . . . Never-something* . . .

Neverland.

That's it. *Neverland.* He used Flood as one of the characters in that book, and in chapter . . . chapter thirty I think it was, or maybe it was chapter seven, Flood has a dream.

I don't remember, Mr. Blank.

Are you saying that you didn't read your husband's novel?

No, I read it. But it was such a long time ago, and I haven't looked at it since. You probably won't understand, but for my own peace of mind I've made a conscious decision not to think about Fanshawe and his work.

What ended the marriage? Did he die? Were you divorced?

I married him when I was very young. We lived together for a few years, I got pregnant, and then he vanished.

Did something happen, or did he leave you on purpose?

On purpose.

The man must have been insane. Walking out on a beautiful young thing like you.

Fanshawe was an extremely troubled person. So many good qualities, so many fine things in him, but at bottom he wanted to destroy himself, and in the end he managed to do it. He turned against me, he turned against his work, and then he walked out of his life and disappeared.

His work. You mean he stopped writing?

Yes. He gave up everything. He had great talent, Mr. Blank, but he came to despise that part of himself, and one day he just stopped, he just quit.

It was my fault, wasn't it?

I wouldn't go that far. You played a part in it, of course, but you were only doing what you had to do.

You must hate me.

No, I don't hate you. I went through a tough period for a while, but everything worked out pretty well after that. I got married again, remember, and it's been a good marriage, a long and good marriage. And then there are my two boys, Ben and Paul.

They're all grown up now. Ben is a doctor, and Paul's studying to become an anthropologist. Not too bad, if I do say so myself. I hope you get to meet them one day. I think you'll be very proud.

Now Sophie and Mr. Blank are sitting beside each other on the bed, facing the stainless steel cart with the various dishes of Mr. Blank's lunch lying on the surface, each plate hidden by a round metal cover with a hole in the center. Mr. Blank has worked up an appetite and is eager to begin, but before he is allowed to touch a morsel of food, Sophie tells him, he must first take his afternoon pills. In spite of the understanding that has developed between them over the past several minutes, and in spite of the pleasure Mr. Blank feels at being so close to So-phie's warm and ample body, he balks at this demand and re-fuses to swallow the medication. Whereas the pills he ingested that morning were green, purple, and white, the ones now sitting on the surface of the stainless steel cart are pink, red, and orange. Sophie explains that they are indeed different pills, designed to produce different effects from the ones he took earlier, and that the treatment will fail unless he takes these in conjunction with the others. Mr. Blank follows the argument, but that in no way convinces him to change his mind, and as Sophie picks up the first pill between her thumb and middle finger and tries to give it to him, Mr. Blank stubbornly shakes his head.

Please, Sophie implores him. I know you're hungry, but one way or another these pills are going into your system before you take a bite of food.

Fuck the food, Mr. Blank says, with bitterness in his voice.

Sophie sighs with exasperation. Look, old-timer, she says, I only want to help you. I'm one of the few people around here who's on your side, but if you won't cooperate, I can think of at least a dozen men who'd be happy to come in here and force these pills down your throat.

All right, Mr. Blank says, beginning to relent somewhat. But only on one condition.

Condition? What are you talking about?

I'll swallow the pills. But first you have to take off your clothes and let me run my hands over your body.

Sophie finds the proposition so ludicrous, she bursts out in a fit of laughter—little realizing that this is exactly how the other Sophie responded under similar circumstances all those many years ago at the frozen pond of Mr. Blank's boyhood. And then, to add insult to injury, she delivers the fatal words: *Don't be silly.*

Ah, says Mr. Blank, tipping backward as if someone has just smacked him across the face. Ah, he groans. Say anything you want, woman. But not that. Please. Not that. Say anything but that.

Within seconds, Mr. Blank's eyes have filled with tears, and before he knows what is happening, the tears are rolling down his cheeks and the old man is crying in earnest.

I'm sorry, Sophie says. I didn't mean to hurt your feelings.

What's wrong with wanting to look at you? Mr. Blank asks, choking through his sobs. You have such beautiful breasts. I just want to see them and touch them. I want to put my hands on your skin, to run my fingers through your pubic hair. What's so terrible about that? I'm not going to hurt you. I just want a little tenderness, that's all. After everything that's been done to me in this place, is that too much to ask?

Well, Sophie says thoughtfully, doubtless feeling some compassion for Mr. Blank's plight, maybe we can come up with a compromise.

Such as? Mr. Blank asks, as he wipes away the tears with the back of his hand.

Such as . . . Such as, you take the pills, and each time you swallow one, I'll let you touch my breasts.

Bare breasts?

No. I'd rather keep my blouse on.

That's not good enough.

All right. I'll take off the blouse. But the bra stays where it is. Understood?

It's not quite paradise, but I suppose I'll have to accept it.

And in that way the matter is resolved. Sophie sheds the blouse, and as she does so Mr. Blank is heartened to see that the bra she is wearing is of the flimsy, lacy variety and not some drab piece of equipment worn by elderly matrons and others who have thrown in the towel on physical love. The upper halves of Sophie's round and abundant breasts are uncovered, and even lower down, the material of the bra is so thin as to allow him a clear view of her nipples jutting against the fabric. Not quite paradise, Mr. Blank says to himself as he downs the first pill with a sip of water, but rather satisfying all the same. And then his hands are upon them—his left hand on the right breast, his right hand on the left breast—and as he savors the bulk and softness of Sophie's somewhat pendulous but noble mammaries, he is further gladdened to observe that she is smiling. Not from pleasure, perhaps, but at least from amusement, thereby demonstrating that she bears him no ill will and is taking the adventure in stride.

You're a dirty old man, Mr. Blank, she says.

I know, he answers. But I was a dirty young man, too.

They work their way through the process twice more—the downing of a pill followed by another delicious encounter with the breasts—and then Sophie puts on her blouse again, and the moment for lunch has arrived.

Unfortunately, the repeated fondling of a desirable woman's flesh has wrought a predictable change in the flesh of the fondler himself. Mr. Blank's old friend is acting up again, and because our hero is no longer wearing the cotton trousers and underpants and is quite naked under the pajama bottoms, there is no barrier to prevent Mr. Bigshot from bounding out through the slit and poking his head into the light of day. This happens at the precise moment Sophie leans forward to begin removing the metal covers from the plates, and as she bends down to store the covers on the lower shelf of the cart, her eyes are just inches from the offending culprit.

Look at you, Sophie says, addressing her words to Mr. Blank's erect penis. Your master squeezes my tits a few times, and now you're all ready for action. Forget it, pal. The fun is over.

I'm sorry, Mr. Blank says, for once truly embarrassed by his behavior. It just kind of popped out on its own. I wasn't expecting it.

No apologies necessary, Sophie replies. Just stick that thing back in your pants, and we'll get down to business.

Business in this case is Mr. Blank's lunch, which consists of a small bowl of now tepid vegetable soup, a club sandwich on white toast, a tomato salad, and a cup of red Jell-O. We will not give an exhaustive account of the consumption of this meal, but one event nevertheless bears mentioning. As was the case after Mr. Blank took his pills in the morning, his hands begin to tremble uncontrollably the instant he tries to eat his food. These might be different pills, designed for different purposes and swathed in different colors, but in the matter of the trembling hands their effect is identical. Mr. Blank begins the meal by attacking the soup. As one might imagine, the inaugural journey of the spoon as it departs from the bowl toward Mr. Blank's mouth is a difficult one, and not a single drop makes it to the intended destination. Through no fault of his own, everything in the spoon comes raining down on Mr. Blank's white shirt.

Good God, he says. I've done it again.

Before the meal can continue, or, more exactly, before the meal can begin, Mr. Blank is obliged to remove the shirt, which is the last article of white clothing he has on, and replace it with the pajama top, thus reverting to the same attire he was discovered in at the beginning of this report. It is a sad moment for Mr. Blank, for now there is not a single trace left of Anna's gentle and meticulous efforts to dress him and prepare him for the day. Even worse, he has now entirely reneged on his promise to wear white.

As Anna did before her, Sophie now takes it upon herself to feed Mr. Blank. Although she is no less kind and patient with him than Anna was, Mr. Blank does not love Sophie in the way he loves Anna, and therefore he looks over her left shoulder at a spot on the far wall as she brings the various spoons and forks to his mouth, pretending it is Anna who is sitting beside him and not Sophie.

Do you know Anna well? he asks.

I met her only a few days ago, Sophie replies, but we've already had three or four long talks. We're very different in all sorts of ways, but we see eye to eye on the stuff that really counts.

Like what?

You, for one thing, Mr. Blank.

Is that why she asked you to fill in for her this afternoon?

I think so.

I've had a pretty awful day so far, but finding her again has done me a lot of good. I don't know what I'd do without her.

She feels the same way about you.

Anna . . . But Anna what? I've spent hours trying to remember her last name. I think it begins with a *B*, but I can't get any further than that.

Blume. Her name is Anna Blume.

Of course! shouts Mr. Blank, striking his forehead with the palm of his left hand. What the hell is wrong with me? I've known that name all my life. Anna Blume. Anna Blume. Anna Blume . . .

Now Sophie is gone. The stainless steel cart is gone, the soup-splattered white shirt is gone, the wet and dirty clothes from the tub are gone, and once again, having taken a proper, uneventful pee in the bathroom with Sophie's help, Mr. Blank is alone, sitting on the edge of the narrow bed, palms spread out on his knees, head down, staring at the floor. He ponders the details of Sophie's recent visit, chastising himself for not having asked her any questions about the things that concern him most. Where he is, for example. Whether he is allowed to walk in the park without supervision. Where the closet is, if indeed there is a closet, and why he hasn't been able to find it. Not to mention the eternal enigma of the door—and whether it is locked from the outside or not. Why did he hesitate to bare his soul to her, he wonders, she who is nothing if not a sympathetic person who holds no grudge against him? Is it simply a question of fear, he asks himself, or does it have something to do with the treatment, the noxious, debilitating treatment that has slowly robbed him of the power to stand up for himself and fight his own battles?

Not knowing what to think, Mr. Blank shrugs, slaps his hands on his knees, and rises from the bed. Several seconds later, he is sitting at the desk, the ballpoint pen in his right hand, the little pad in front of him, opened to the first page. He searches the list for Anna's name, discovers it on the second line directly below James P. Flood, and prints out the letters B-l-u-m-e, thus changing the entry from *Anna* to *Anna Blume*. Then, because all the lines on the first page have been filled, he turns to the second page and adds two more entries to the list:

John Trause
Sophie

As he closes the pad, Mr. Blank is dumbfounded to realize that Trause's name returned to him with no effort at all. After so many struggles, so many failures to remember names and faces and events, he considers this to be a triumph of the first magnitude. He rocks back and forth in the chair to celebrate his accomplishment, wondering if the afternoon pills aren't responsible in some way for counteracting his memory loss of the previous hours, or if it isn't just a lucky fluke, one of those unexpected things that happen to us for no apparent reason. Whatever the cause, he decides to go on thinking about the story now, in anticipation of a visit from the doctor that evening, since Farr told him he would do everything possible to allow him to go on telling the story to the end—not tomorrow, when Mr. Blank will no doubt have forgotten the bulk of what he has recounted so far, but today. As the old man goes on tipping back and forth in the chair, however, his eyes fall upon the strip of white tape affixed to the surface of the desk. He has looked at that piece of tape no less than fifty or a hundred times during the course of the day, and each time he did so the white strip was clearly marked with the word DESK. Now, to his astonishment, Mr. Blank sees that it is marked with the word LAMP. His initial response is to think that his eyes have fooled him in some way, so he stops rocking back and forth in order to take a closer look. He leans forward, lowers his head until his nose is nearly touching the tape, and carefully studies the word. To his immense chagrin, he discovers that it still reads LAMP.

With a growing sense of alarm, Mr. Blank clambers out of the chair and begins shuffling around the room, stopping at each strip of white tape attached to an object in order to find out if any other words have been altered. After a thorough investigation, he is horrified to discover that not a single label occupies its former spot. The wall now reads CHAIR. The lamp now reads BATHROOM. The chair now reads DESK. Several possible explanations flare up in Mr. Blank's mind at once. He has suffered a stroke or brain injury of some kind; he has lost the ability to read; someone has played a nasty trick on him. But if he is the victim of a prank, he asks himself, who can be responsible for it? Several people have visited his room in the past few hours: Anna, Flood, Farr, and Sophie. He finds it inconceivable that either one of the women would have done such a thing to him. It's true, however, that his mind was elsewhere when Flood came in, and it's also true that he was in the bathroom flushing the toilet when Farr entered, but he can't imagine how either one of those men could have pulled off such an elaborate switching operation in the short period of time they were not in his field of vision—several seconds at most, scarcely any time at all. Mr. Blank knows that he is not in top form, that his mind is not working as well as it ought to, but he also knows that he is no worse now than he was when the day began, which would dispense with the stroke theory, and if he has lost the ability to read, how could he have made the two recent additions to his list of names? He sits down on the edge of the narrow bed and wonders if he didn't doze off for a few minutes after Sophie left the room. He doesn't remember having fallen asleep, but in the end that is the only explanation that makes sense. A fifth person entered the room, a person who was not Anna or Flood or Farr or Sophie, and switched the labels during Mr. Blank's brief, now forgotten plunge into oblivion.

An enemy is stalking the premises, Mr. Blank says to himself, perhaps several or many of them working in league with one another, and their only intention is to frighten him, to disorient him, to make him think he is losing his mind, as if they were trying to persuade him that the shadow-beings lodged in his head had transformed themselves into living phantoms, bodiless souls conscripted to invade his little room and cause as much havoc as possible. But Mr. Blank is a man of order, and he is offended by the childish mischief-making of his captors. From long experience, he has come to appreciate the importance of precision and clarity in all things, and during the years when he was sending out his charges on their various missions around the world, he always took great pains to write up his reports on their activities in a language that would not betray the truth of what they saw and thought and felt at each step along the way. It will not do, then, to call a chair a desk or a desk a lamp. To indulge in such infantile whimsy is to throw the world into chaos, to make life intolerable for all but the mad. Mr. Blank has not reached the point where he cannot identify objects that do not have their names affixed to them, but there is no question that he is in decline, and he understands that a day might come, perhaps soon, perhaps even tomorrow, when his brain will erode still further and it will become necessary for him to have the name of the thing on the thing in order for him

to recognize it. He therefore decides to reverse the damage created by his unseen enemy and return each one of the scrambled
labels to its proper spot.

The job takes longer to complete than he thinks it will, for
Mr. Blank soon learns that the strips of tape on which the words
have been written are endowed with almost supernatural powers of adhesion, and to peel one of them off the surface to which
it is attached requires unstinting concentration and effort.
Mr. Blank begins by using his left thumbnail to pry the first strip
loose (the word WALL, which has landed on the oak board at the
foot of the bed), but no sooner does he manage to slide his nail
under the lower right-hand corner of the tape than the tip of the
nail snaps. He tries again with the nail of his middle finger,
which is somewhat shorter and therefore less frangible, and
diligently hacks away at the stubborn right-hand corner until
enough tape has detached itself from the bed for Mr. Blank to
put a small section between his thumb and middle finger and,
tugging gently so as not to cause a tear, pull the whole strip from
the oak board. A satisfying moment, yes, but one that has required a good two minutes of laborious preparation. Considering that there are twelve strips of tape to be removed in all, and
considering that Mr. Blank breaks three more fingernails in the
process (thus diminishing the number of usable fingers to six),
the reader will understand why it takes him more than half an
hour to finish the job.

These strenuous activities have worn out Mr. Blank, and instead of pausing to look around the room and admire his work
(which, however small and insignificant it might appear to be, is

for him nothing short of a symbolic undertaking to restore harmony to a broken universe), he shuffles off into the bathroom to
rinse the sweat from his face. The old dizziness has returned,
and he clutches the sink with his left hand as he splashes water
onto himself with his right. By the time he turns off the spigot
and begins to reach for a towel, he is suddenly feeling worse,
worse than he has felt at any moment of the day so far. The
trouble seems to be located somewhere in his stomach, but before
he can pronounce the word *stomach* to himself, it is traveling up
his windpipe, accompanied by an unpleasant tingling in his jaws.
He instinctively clutches the sink with both hands and lowers
his head, bracing himself against the attack of nausea that has
inexplicably overcome him. He fights against it for a second or
two, praying that he can ward off the coming explosion, but it
is a hopeless cause, and an instant later he is vomiting into the
sink. They've poisoned me! Mr. Blank shouts, once the onslaught
is over. The monsters have poisoned me!

When the action resumes, Mr. Blank is stretched out on the bed,
looking up at the white, freshly painted ceiling. Now that the
murderous toxins have been flushed from his system, he feels
drained of energy, half-dead from the savage bout of puking,
retching, and weeping that took place in the bathroom just minutes ago. And yet, if such a thing is possible, he also feels better,
more tranquil in the core of his debilitated self, more prepared
to face the trials that no doubt lie ahead.

As Mr. Blank continues to study the ceiling, its whiteness

gradually conjures up an image to him, and instead of looking at a ceiling he fancies that he is staring at a sheet of blank paper. Why this should be so he cannot say, but perhaps it has something to do with the dimensions of the ceiling, which is rectilinear and not square, meaning that the room is rectilinear and not square as well, and although the ceiling is much larger than a sheet of paper, its proportions are roughly similar to those of the standard eight-and-a-half-by-eleven-inch page. As Mr. Blank pursues this thought, something stirs inside him, some distant memory he cannot fix in his mind, that keeps breaking apart the closer he gets to it, but through the murk that is blocking him from seeing the thing clearly in his head, he can dimly make out the contours of a man, a man who is undoubtedly himself, sitting at a desk and rolling a sheet of paper into an old manual typewriter. It's probably one of the reports, he says out loud, speaking in a soft voice, and then Mr. Blank wonders how many times he must have repeated that gesture, how many times over the years, understanding now that it was no less than thousands of times, thousands upon thousands of times, more sheets of paper than a man could possibly count in a day or a week or a month.

Thinking about the typewriter recalls the typescript he read earlier in the day, and now that he has more or less recovered from the exasperating job of peeling off the strips of white tape and returning them to their correct spots in the room, and now that the battle that flared up so violently in his stomach has been quelled, Mr. Blank remembers that he was planning to go on with the story, to map out the tale to its conclusion in order to

TRAVELS IN THE SCRIPTORIUM 115

prepare himself for the supplementary visit from the doctor that evening. Still stretched out on the bed with his eyes open, he considers for a moment whether to carry on in silence, that is, to tell the story to himself in his mind, or else to continue improvising the events out loud, even if there is no one in the room to follow what he is saying. Because he is feeling particularly alone just now, fairly crushed by the weight of his enforced solitude, he decides to pretend that the doctor is in the room with him and to proceed as before, that is, to tell the story with his voice rather than merely think it in his head.

Let's get on with it, shall we? he says. The Confederation. Sigmund Graf. The Alien Territories. Ernesto Land. What year is it in this imaginary place? About eighteen-thirty, I'd guess. No trains, no telegraph. You travel by horse, and you can wait as long as three weeks for a letter to arrive. Much like America, but not identical. No black slaves, for one thing, at least none mentioned in the text. But more ethnic variety than here for that moment in history. German names, French names, English names, Spanish names. All right, where were we? Graf is in the Alien Territories, looking for Land, who might or might not be a double agent, who might or might not have absconded with Graf's wife and daughter. Let's back up a little bit. I think I went too fast before, jumped to too many hasty conclusions. According to Joubert, Land is a traitor to the Confederation who's formed his own private army to help lead the Primitives in an invasion of the western provinces. I detest that word, by the way. Primitives. It's too flat, too blunt, has no flair. Let's try to think of something more colorful. Hmmm . . . I don't know . . .

Maybe something like . . . the Spirit People. No. No good. The
Dolmen. The Olmen. The Tolmen. Awful. What's wrong with
me? The Djiin. That's it. The Djiin. Sounds a little like Injun,
but with other connotations mixed in as well. All right, the
Djiin. Joubert thinks Land is in the Alien Territories to lead
the Djiin in an attack on the western provinces. But Graf thinks
it's more complicated than that. Why? For one thing, he believes
Land is loyal to the Confederation. For another, how could Land
have crossed the border accompanied by a hundred men without Colonel De Vega's knowledge? De Vega claims to know
nothing about it, but Carlotta has told Graf that Land entered
the Territories more than a year ago, and unless she's lying, De
Vega is in on the plot. Or else—and this is something I didn't
think of before—Land bribed De Vega with a large sum of
money, and the Colonel isn't involved at all. But that has nothing to do with Graf, who never suspects the possibility of a bribe.
According to his reasoning, Land, De Vega, and the entire military are planning to hatch a phony war with the Djiin in order
to hold the Confederation together. Maybe they intend to wipe
out the Djiin in the process, maybe not. For the moment, there
are only two possibilities: Joubert's position and Graf's position.
If this story is going to add up to anything, though, there has to
be a third explanation, something no one ever would have expected. Otherwise, it's just too damned predictable.

All right, Mr. Blank continues, after a short pause to focus
his thoughts. Graf has come to two Gangi villages, and the inhabitants of both have been massacred. He's buried the raving
white soldier, and now he doesn't know what to think. For the

time being, as he slowly wends his way toward Land, let's separate the two main questions he's confronted with. The professional question and the private question. What is Land doing in the Territories, and where are his wife and daughter? To be perfectly honest, this domestic issue bores me. It can be resolved in any one of several ways, but each solution is an embarrassment: too trite, too hackneyed, not worth thinking about. One: Beatrice and Marta have run away with Land. If Graf finds them together, he's vowed to kill Land. Either he'll succeed or he won't, but at that point the story devolves into a simple melodrama of a cuckold trying to defend his honor. Two: Beatrice and Marta have run away with Land, but Beatrice has died—either from the effects of the cholera epidemic or from the hardships of living in the Territories. Assume that Marta, now sixteen, has grown into a woman and is traveling with Land as his lover. What does Graf do then? Does he still try to kill Land, murdering his old friend while his only daughter begs him to spare the life of the man she loves? Oh Daddy, please, Daddy, don't do it! Or does Graf let bygones be bygones and forget the whole thing? One way or the other, it won't wash. Three: Beatrice and Marta have run away with Land, but both of them have died. Land won't mention their names to Graf, and that element of the story turns into a defunct red herring. Trause was apparently quite young when he wrote this piece, and it doesn't surprise me that he never published it. He worked himself into a corner with the two women. I don't know what solution he came up with, but I'd bet good money that it was the second one—which is just as bad as the first and the third. As far as I'm concerned, I'd just

separate the different nations from one another, looking for Land and his men, yes, encountering the raving soldier, yes, but once he finds what he's looking for, it's altogether the opposite of what he was expecting. On a barren plain in the north-central region of the Territories, a stretch of country similar to the salt flats in Utah, he chances upon a mound of a hundred and fifteen corpses, some of them mutilated, some of them intact, all of them rotting and decomposing in the sun. Not Gangi bodies, not the bodies of any members of the Djiin nations, but white men, white men in soldiers' uniforms, at least those who weren't stripped naked and hacked to pieces, and as Graf stumbles around this putrid, nauseating mass of the slaughtered dead, he discovers that one of the victims is his old friend Ernesto Land—lying on his back with a bullet hole in his forehead and a swarm of flies and maggots crawling over his half-eaten face. We won't dwell on Graf's response to this horror: the puking and weeping, the howling, the rending of his garments. What matters is this. Because his encounter with the raving soldier took place only two weeks earlier, Graf knows the massacre must be fairly recent. But most of all, what matters is this: he has no doubt that Land and his men were murdered by the Djiin.

Mr. Blank pauses to emit another laugh, more restrained than the last one, perhaps, but nevertheless a laugh that manages to express both joy and bitterness at the same time, for even if Mr. Blank is happy to have reshaped the story according to his own design, he knows that it is a gruesome story for all that, and a part of him recoils in terror from what he has yet to tell.

But Graf is wrong, he says. Graf knows nothing about the

sinister scheme he's been drawn into. He's the fall guy, as they
say in the movies, the patsy who's been set up by the government
to put the machinery in motion. They're all in on it—Joubert,
the Ministry of War, De Vega, the whole lot of them. Yes, Land
was sent into the Territories as a double agent, with instructions
to stir up the Djiin into invading the western provinces, which
would unleash the war the government so desperately wants.
But Land fails in his mission. A year goes by, and when nothing
happens after all that time, the men in power conclude that
Land has betrayed them, that for one reason or another his conscience has gotten the better of him and he's made peace with
the Djiin. So they cook up a new plan and send a second army
into the Territories. Not from Ultima, but from another garrison
several hundred miles to the north, and this contingent is much
larger than the first, at least ten times larger, and with a thousand troops against a hundred, Land and his ragtag bunch of
idealists don't have a chance. Yes, you heard me correctly. The
Confederation sends in a second army to wipe out the first army.
All in secret, of course, and if a man such as Graf should be
sent out to look for Land, he would naturally conclude that the
Djiin are responsible for that pile of stinking, mutilated corpses.
At this point, Graf becomes the key figure in the operation.
Without knowing it, he's the person who's going to get the war
started. How? By being allowed to write his story in that crummy
little cell in Ultima. De Vega works him over in the beginning,
beats him constantly for a whole week, but that's only to put the
fear of God in him and convince him that he's about to be executed. And when a man thinks he's about to die, he's going to

spill his guts on paper the moment he's allowed to write. So Graf does what they want him to do. He tells about his mission to track down Land, and when he comes to the massacre he discovered in the salt flats, he omits nothing, describes the whole abomination down to the last gory detail. That's the crucial point: a vivid, eyewitness account of what happened, with all the blame put on the Djiin. When Graf finishes his story, De Vega takes possession of the manuscript and releases him from prison. Graf is stunned. He was expecting to be shot, and here he is being paid a large bonus for his work and given a free ride back to the capital in a first-class carriage. By the time he makes it home, the manuscript has been skillfully edited and released to every newspaper in the country. CONFEDERATION SOLDIERS MASSACRED BY DJIIN: A Firsthand Report by Sigmund Graf, Deputy Assistant Director of the Bureau of Internal Affairs.

Graf returns to find the entire population of the capital up in arms, clamoring for an invasion of the Alien Territories. He understands now how cruelly he's been tricked. War on this scale could potentially destroy the Confederation, and it turns out that he, and he alone, was the match that ignited this deadly fire. He goes to Joubert and demands an explanation. Now that things have worked out so well, Joubert is all too happy to give it to him. Then he offers Graf a promotion with a large increase in salary, but Graf counters with an offer of his own: I resign, he says, and then he marches out of the room, slamming the door behind him. That evening, in the darkness of his empty house, he picks up a loaded revolver and fires a bullet through his skull. And that's it. End of story. *Finità, la commedia.*

Mr. Blank has been talking steadily for nearly twenty minutes, and he is tired now, and not only from the exertions of his vocal cords, for his throat was irritated to begin with (brought on by the upchuck binge in the bathroom just minutes before), and he delivers the final sentences of his tale with a noticeable rasp in his voice. He closes his eyes, forgetting that such an action is likely to bring back the procession of figment beings blundering through the wilderness, the mob of the damned, the faceless ones who will eventually surround him and tear his body apart, but this time luck spares Mr. Blank from the demons, and when he closes his eyes he is once again in the past, sitting in a wooden chair of some kind, an Adirondack chair he believes it is called, on a lawn somewhere in the country, some remote and rustic spot he cannot identify, with green grass all around him and bluish mountains in the distance, and the weather is warm, warm in the way summer is warm, with a cloudless sky above and the sun pouring down on his skin, and there is Mr. Blank, many years ago now it would seem, back in the days of his early manhood, sitting in the Adirondack chair and holding a small child in his arms, a one-year-old girl child dressed in a white T-shirt and a white diaper, and Mr. Blank is looking into the eyes of the little girl and talking to her, what words he cannot say, for this excursion into the past is unfolding in silence, and as Mr. Blank talks to the little girl, she is looking back at him with an intent and serious expression in her eyes, and he wonders now, lying on the bed with his eyes now closed, if this small person isn't Anna Blume at the beginning of her life, his beloved Anna Blume, and if it isn't Anna, whether the child might not be his daughter, but what daughter, he asks himself, what daughter and what is her name, and if he is the father of a child, where is the mother and what is her name, he asks himself, and then he makes a mental note to inquire about these matters the next time a person enters the room, to find out if he has a home somewhere with a wife and children, or once had a wife, or once had a home, or if this room is not the place where he has always lived, but Mr. Blank is about to forget this mental note and therefore will forget to ask these questions, for he is extremely tired now, and the image of himself in the Adirondack chair with the young child in his arms has just vanished, and Mr. Blank has fallen asleep.

Because of the camera, which has gone on taking one picture per second throughout this report, we know for certain that Mr. Blank's nap lasts for exactly twenty-seven minutes and twelve seconds. He might have gone on sleeping much longer than that, but a man has now entered the room, and he is tapping Mr. Blank on the shoulder in an effort to wake him. When the old man opens his eyes, he feels entirely refreshed by his brief sojourn in the Land of Nod, and he sits up immediately, alert and ready for the encounter, with no trace of grogginess clouding his mind.

The visitor appears to be in his late fifties or early sixties, and like Farr before him, he is dressed in a pair of blue jeans, but whereas Farr was wearing a red shirt, this man's shirt is black, and while Farr came into the room empty-handed, the man in the black shirt is carrying a thick bundle of files and folders in his arms. His face is deeply familiar to Mr. Blank, but as with so many of the faces he has seen today, whether in photographs or in the flesh, he is at a loss to attach a name to it.

Are you Fogg? he asks. Marco Fogg?

The visitor smiles and shakes his head. No, he says, I'm afraid not. Why would you think I'm Fogg?

I don't know, but when I woke up just now I suddenly remembered that Fogg stopped by around this time yesterday. A minor miracle, actually, now that I think about it. Remembering, I mean. But Fogg came in. I'm certain of that. For afternoon tea. We played cards for a while. We talked. And he told me a number of funny jokes.

Jokes? the visitor asks, walking over to the desk, swiveling the chair by a hundred and eighty degrees, and sitting down with the pile of dossiers on his lap. As he does so, Mr. Blank stands up, shuffles forward for several feet, and then sits down on the bottom edge of the mattress, settling into roughly the same spot that Flood occupied earlier in the day.

Yes, jokes, Mr. Blank continues. I can't remember them all, but there was one that struck me as especially good.

You wouldn't mind telling it to me, would you? the visitor asks. I'm always on the lookout for good jokes.

I can try, Mr. Blank answers, and then he pauses for a few moments to collect his thoughts. Let's see, he says. Hmmm. Let me see. I think it begins like this. A man walks into a bar in Chicago at five o'clock in the afternoon and orders three scotches.

Not one after the other, but all three at once. The bartender is a little puzzled by this unusual request, but he doesn't say anything and gives the man what he wants—three scotches, lined up on the bar in a row. The man drinks them down one by one, pays the bill, and leaves. The next day, he comes back at five o'clock and orders the same thing. Three scotches all at once. And the day after that, and every day after that for two weeks. Finally, curiosity gets the better of the barman. I don't mean to be nosy, he says, but you've been in here every day for the past two weeks ordering your three scotches, and I'd just like to know why. Most people take them one at a time. Ah, the man says, the answer is very simple. I have two brothers. One of them lives in New York, one lives in San Francisco, and the three of us are very close. As a way of honoring our friendship, we all go into a bar at five in the afternoon and order three scotches, silently toasting one another's health, pretending that we're all together in the same place. The barman nods, finally understanding the reason for this strange ritual, and thinks no more about it. The business goes on for another four months. The man comes in every day at five o'clock, and the bartender serves him the three drinks. Then something happens. The man shows up at his regular hour one afternoon, but this time he orders only two scotches. The bartender is worried, and after a while he plucks up his courage and says: I don't mean to be nosy, but every day for the past four and a half months you've come in here and ordered three scotches. Now you order two. I know it's none of my business, but I just hope nothing's gone wrong with your family. Nothing's wrong, the man says, as bright and chipper as ever. What is it, then? the bartender asks. The answer is very simple, the man says. I've stopped drinking.

The visitor erupts in a prolonged fit of laughter, and while Mr. Blank does not join in, since he already knew the punch line, he nevertheless smiles at the man in the black shirt, pleased with himself for having pulled off the joke so well. When the hilarity at last dies down, the visitor looks at Mr. Blank and says: Do you know who I am?

I'm not sure, the old man replies. Not Fogg, in any case. But there's no question that I've met you before—many times, I think.

I'm your lawyer.

My lawyer. That's good . . . very good. I was hoping I'd see you today. We have a lot to talk about.

Yes, says the man in the black shirt, patting the bundle of files and folders on his lap. A great deal to talk about. But before we get down to that, I want you to take a good look at me and try to remember my name.

Mr. Blank looks carefully at the man's thin, angular face, peers into his large gray eyes, studies his jaw and forehead and mouth, but in the end he can do no more than let out a sigh and shake his head in defeat.

I'm Quinn, Mr. Blank, the man says. Daniel Quinn. Your first operative.

Mr. Blank groans. He is mortified with shame, embarrassed to such a point that a part of him, the innermost part of him, wants to crawl into a hole and die. Please forgive me, he says. My dear Quinn—my brother, my comrade, my loyal friend. It's these rotten pills I've been swallowing. They've screwed up my head, and I can't tell if I'm coming or going anymore.

You sent me on more missions than anyone else, Quinn says. Do you remember the Stillman case?

A little, Mr. Blank replies. Peter Stillman. Junior and Senior, if I'm not mistaken. One of them wore white clothes. I forget which now, but I think it was the son.

Exactly right. The son. And then there was that strange business with Fanshawe.

Sophie's first husband. The madman who disappeared.

Right again. But we mustn't forget the passport either. A small point, I suppose, but it was tough work just the same.

What passport?

My passport. The one that Anna Blume found when you sent her on her mission.

Anna? Do you know Anna?

Of course. Everyone knows Anna. She's something of a legend around here.

She deserves to be. There's no woman like her in the world.

And then, last but not least, there was my aunt, Molly Fitzsimmons, the woman who married Walt Rawley. I helped him write his memoirs.

Walt who?

Rawley. Once known as Walt the Wonder Boy.

Ah, yes. That was a long time ago, wasn't it?

Correct. A very long time ago.

And then?

That's it. You retired me after that.

Why would I do such a thing? What was I thinking?

I'd put in all those years, and the time came for me to go. Operatives don't last forever. It's the nature of the business.

When was that?

Nineteen ninety-three.

And what year is it now?

Two thousand and five.

Twelve years. What have you been doing with yourself since . . . since I retired you?

Traveling, mostly. By now, I've visited nearly every country in the world.

And now you're back, working as my lawyer. I'm glad it's you, Quinn. I always felt I could trust you.

You can, Mr. Blank. That's why I was given the job. Because we go so far back together.

You have to get me out of here. I don't think I can take it anymore.

That won't be easy. So many charges have been filed against you, I'm drowning in paperwork. You have to be patient. I wish I could give you an answer, but I have no idea how long it will take to sort things out.

Charges? What kind of charges?

The whole gamut, I'm afraid. From criminal indifference to sexual molestation. From conspiracy to commit fraud to negligent homicide. From defamation of character to first-degree murder. Shall I go on?

But I'm innocent. I've never done any of those things.

That's a debatable point. It all depends on how you look at it.

And what happens if we lose?

The nature of the punishment is still open to question. One group is advocating clemency, an across-the-board pardon on every count. But others are out for blood. And not just one or two of them. There's a whole gang, and they're becoming more and more vociferous.

Blood. I don't understand. You mean blood as in *death*?

Instead of answering, Quinn reaches into the pocket of his black shirt and pulls out a piece of paper, which he then unfolds in order to share what is written on it with Mr. Blank.

There was a meeting just two hours ago, Quinn says. I don't want to scare you, but someone got up and actually proposed this as a possible solution. I quote: *He shall be drawn through the streets to the place of his execution, there to be hanged and cut down alive, and his body shall be opened, his heart and bowels plucked out, and his privy members cut off and thrown into the fire before his eyes. Then his head shall be stricken off from his body, and his body shall be divided into four quarters, to be disposed of at our discretion.*

Lovely, Mr. Blank sighs. And what gentle soul came up with that plan?

It doesn't matter, Quinn says. I just want you to get a sense of what we're dealing with. I'll fight for you to the bitter end, but we have to be realistic. The way it looks now, we're probably going to have to work out some compromises.

It was Flood, wasn't it? Mr. Blank asks. That odious little man who came in here and insulted me this morning.

No, as a matter of fact it wasn't Flood, but that doesn't mean he isn't a dangerous person. You were very wise to refuse his invitation to go to the park. Later on, we discovered that he'd concealed a knife in his jacket. Once he got you out of the room, he was planning to kill you.

Ah. I figured as much. That lousy, good-for-nothing piece of shit.

I know it's hard being cooped up in this room, but I would suggest you stay here, Mr. Blank. If someone else invites you out for a walk in the park, invent some excuse and say no.

So there really is a park?

Yes, there really is a park.

And the birds. Are they in my head, or can I really hear them?

What kind of birds?

Crows or seagulls, I can't tell which.

Seagulls.

Then we must be near the ocean.

You picked the spot yourself. In spite of everything that's been going on here, you've gathered us all in a beautiful place. I'm thankful to you for that.

Then why don't you let me see it? I can't even open the goddamned window.

It's for your own protection. You wanted to be on the top floor, but we can't take any chances, can we?

I'm not going to commit suicide, if that's what you mean.

I know that. But not everyone shares my opinion.

Another one of your compromises, huh?

By way of response, Quinn shrugs his shoulders, glances down, and looks at his watch.

Time is running short, he says. I've brought along the files of one case, and I think we should get to it now. Unless you're feeling too tired, of course. If you prefer, I could always come back tomorrow.

No, no, Mr. Blank answers, waving his arm in disgust. Let's get it over with now.

Quinn opens the top folder and removes four eight-by-ten black-and-white photographs. Wheeling himself forward in the chair, he hands them to Mr. Blank and says: Benjamin Sachs. Does the name ring any bells?

I think so, the old man replies, but I'm not sure.

It's a bad one. One of the worst, as a matter of fact, but if we can mount a compelling defense against this charge, we might be able to set a precedent for the others. Do you follow me, Mr. Blank?

Mr. Blank nods in silence, already beginning to look through the pictures. The first one shows a tall, gangly man of about forty, perched on the railing of a fire escape in what appears to be Brooklyn, New York, looking out into the night in front of him—but then Mr. Blank moves on to the second photo, and suddenly that same man has lost his grip on the railing and is falling through the darkness, a silhouette of splayed limbs caught in midair, plunging toward the ground below. That is disturbing enough, but once Mr. Blank comes to the third picture, a shudder of recognition passes through him. The tall man is on a dirt road somewhere out in the country, and he is swinging a metal softball bat at a bearded man who is standing in front of him. The image is frozen at the precise instant the bat makes contact with the bearded man's head, and from the look on his face it is clear that the blow will kill him, that within a matter of seconds he will fall to the ground with his skull crushed as blood pours from the wound and gathers in a puddle around his corpse.

Mr. Blank clutches his face, tearing at the skin with his fingers. He is finding it difficult to breathe now, for he already knows the subject of the fourth picture, even if he can't remember how or why he knows it, and because he can anticipate the explosion of the homemade bomb that will tear the tall man apart and cast his mangled body to the four winds, he does not have the strength to look at it. Instead, he lets the four photographs slip out of his hands and fall to the floor, and then, bringing those same hands up to his face, he covers his eyes and begins to weep.

Now Quinn is gone, and once again Mr. Blank is alone in the room, sitting at the desk with the ballpoint pen in his right hand. The onrush of tears stopped more than twenty minutes ago, and as he opens the pad and turns to the second page, he says to himself: I was only doing my job. If things turned out badly, the report still had to be written, and I can't be blamed for telling the truth, can I? Then, applying himself to the task at hand, he adds three more names to his list:

John Trause
Sophie
Daniel Quinn
Marco Fogg
Benjamin Sachs

Mr. Blank puts down the pen, closes the pad, and pushes both articles aside. He realizes now that he was hoping for a visit from Fogg, the man with all the funny stories, but even though there is no clock in the room and no watch on his wrist, meaning that he has no idea of the time, not even an approximate one, he senses that the hour for tea and light conversation has passed. Perhaps, before long, Anna will be coming back to serve him dinner, and if by chance it isn't Anna who comes, but another woman or man sent in as a substitute, then he means to protest, to misbehave, to rant and shout, to cause such a ruckus that it will blow the very roof clear into the sky.

For want of anything better to do just now, Mr. Blank decides to go on with his reading. Directly below Trause's story about Sigmund Graf and the Confederation there is a longer manuscript of some one hundred and forty pages, which, unlike the previous work, comes with a cover page that announces the title of the piece and the author's name:

Travels in the Scriptorium

by

N. R. Fanshawe

Aha, Mr. Blank says out loud. That's more like it. Maybe we're finally getting somewhere, after all.

Then he turns to the first page and begins to read:

The old man sits on the edge of the narrow bed, palms spread out on his knees, head down, staring at the floor. He has no idea that a camera is planted in the ceiling directly above him. The shutter clicks silently once every second, producing eighty-six thousand four hundred still photos with each revolution of the earth. Even if he knew he was being watched, it wouldn't make any difference. His mind is elsewhere, stranded among the figments in his head as he searches for an answer to the question that haunts him.

Who is he? What is he doing here? When did he arrive and how long will he remain? With any luck, time will tell us all. For the moment, our only task is to study the pictures as attentively as we can and refrain from drawing any premature conclusions.

There are a number of objects in the room, and on each one a strip of white tape has been affixed to the surface, bearing a single word written out in block letters. On the bedside table, for example, the word is TABLE. On the lamp, the word is LAMP. Even on the wall, which is not strictly speaking an object, there is a strip of tape that reads WALL. The old man looks up for a moment, sees the wall, sees the strip of tape attached to the wall, and pronounces the word *wall* in a soft voice. What cannot be known at this point is whether he is reading the word on the strip of tape or simply referring to the wall itself. It could be that he has forgotten how to read but still recognizes things for what they are and can call them by their names, or, conversely, that he has lost the ability to recognize things for what they are but still knows how to read.

He is dressed in blue-and-yellow striped cotton pajamas, and his feet are encased in a pair of black leather slippers. It is unclear to him exactly where he is. In the room, yes, but in what building is the room located? In a house? In a hospital? In a prison? He can't remember how long he has been here or the nature of the circumstances that precipitated his removal to this place. Perhaps he has always been here; perhaps this is where he has lived since the day he was born. What he knows is that his heart is filled with an implacable sense of guilt. At the same time, he can't escape the feeling that he is the victim of a terrible injustice.

There is one window in the room, but the shade is drawn, and as far as he can remember he has not yet looked out of it. Likewise with the door and its white porcelain knob. Is he locked in, or is he free to come and go as he wishes? He has yet to investigate this matter—for, as stated in the first paragraph above, his mind is elsewhere, adrift in the past as he wanders among the phantom beings that clutter his head, struggling to answer the question that haunts him.

The pictures do not lie, but neither do they tell the whole story. They are merely a record of time passing, the outward evidence. The old man's age, for example, is difficult to determine from the slightly out-of-focus black-and-white images. The only fact that can be set down with any certainty is that he is not young, but the word *old* is a flexible term and can be used to describe a person anywhere between sixty and a hundred.

We will therefore drop the epithet *old man* and henceforth refer to the person in the room as Mr. Blank. For the time being, no first name will be necessary.

Mr. Blank stands up from the bed at last, pauses briefly to steady his balance, and then shuffles over to the desk at the other end of the room. He feels tired, as if he has just woken from a fitful, too short night of sleep, and as the soles of his slippers scrape along the bare wood floor, he is reminded of the sound of sandpaper. Far off in the distance, beyond the room, beyond the building in which the room is located, he hears the faint cry of a bird— perhaps a crow, perhaps a seagull, he can't tell which . . .

By now, Mr. Blank has read all he can stomach, and he is not the least bit amused. In an outburst of pent-up anger and frustration, he tosses the manuscript over his shoulder with a violent flick of the wrist, not even bothering to turn around to see where it lands. As it flutters through the air and then thuds to the floor behind him, he pounds his fist on the desk and says in a loud voice: When is this nonsense going to end?

It will never end. For Mr. Blank is one of us now, and struggle though he might to understand his predicament, he will always be lost. I believe I speak for all his charges when I say he is getting what he deserves—no more, no less. Not as a form of punishment, but as an act of supreme justice and compassion. Without him, we are nothing, but the paradox is that we, the figments of another mind, will outlive the mind that made us, for once we are thrown into the world, we continue to exist forever, and our stories go on being told, even after we are dead.

Mr. Blank might have acted cruelly toward some of his charges over the years, but not one of us thinks he hasn't done everything in his power to serve us well. That is why I plan to keep him where he is. The room is his world now, and the longer the treatment goes on, the more he will come to accept the generosity of what has been done for him. Mr. Blank is old and enfeebled, but as long as he remains in the room with the shuttered window and the locked door, he can never die, never disappear, never be anything but the words I am writing on this page.

In a short while, a woman will enter the room and feed him his dinner. I haven't yet decided who that woman will be, but if all goes well between now and then, I will send in Anna. That will make Mr. Blank happy, and when all is said and done, he has probably suffered enough for one day. Anna will feed Mr. Blank his dinner, then wash him and put him to bed. Mr. Blank will lie awake in the dark for some time, listening to the cries of birds in the far distance, but then his eyes will at last grow heavy, and his lids will close. He will fall asleep, and when he wakes up in the morning, the treatment will begin again. But for now it is still the day it has always been since the first word of this report, and now is the moment when Anna kisses Mr. Blank on the cheek and tucks him in, and now is the moment when she stands up from the bed and begins walking toward the door. Sleep well, Mr. Blank.

Lights out.

MAN IN
THE DARK

———

For David Grossman
and his wife Michal
his son Jonathan
his daughter Ruthi
and in memory of Uri

I am alone in the dark, turning the world around in my head as I struggle through another bout of insomnia, another white night in the great American wilderness. Upstairs, my daughter and granddaughter are asleep in their bedrooms, each one alone as well, the forty-seven-year-old Miriam, my only child, who has slept alone for the past five years, and the twenty-three-year-old Katya, Miriam's only child, who used to sleep with a young man named Titus Small, but Titus is dead now, and Katya sleeps alone with her broken heart.

Bright light, then darkness. Sun pouring down from all corners of the sky, followed by the black of night, the silent stars, the wind stirring in the branches. Such is the routine. I have been living in this house for more than a year now, ever since they released me from the hospital. Miriam insisted that I come here, and at first it was just the two of us, along with a day nurse who looked after me when Miriam was off at work. Then, three months later, the roof fell in on Katya, and she dropped out of film school in New York and came home to live with her mother in Vermont.

His parents named him after Rembrandt's son, the little boy of the paintings, the golden-haired child in the red hat, the day-dreaming pupil puzzling over his lessons, the little boy who turned into a young man ravaged by illness and who died in his twenties, just as Katya's Titus did. It's a doomed name, a name that should be banned from circulation forever. I think about Titus's death often, the horrifying story of that death, the images of that death, the pulverizing consequences of that death on my grieving granddaughter, but I don't want to go there now, I can't go there now, I have to push it as far away from me as possible. The night is still young, and as I lie here in bed looking up into the darkness, a darkness so black that the ceiling is invisible, I begin to remember the story I started last night. That's what I do when sleep refuses to come. I lie in bed and tell myself stories. They might not add up to much, but as long as I'm inside them, they prevent me from thinking about the things I would prefer to forget. Concentration can be a problem, however, and more often than not my mind eventually drifts away from the story I'm trying to tell to the things I don't want to think about. There's nothing to be done. I fail again and again, fail more often than I succeed, but that doesn't mean I don't give it my best effort.

I put him in a hole. That felt like a good start, a promising way to get things going. Put a sleeping man in a hole, and then see what happens when he wakes up and tries to crawl out. I'm talking about a deep hole in the ground, nine or ten feet deep, dug in such a way as to form a perfect circle, with sheer inner walls of dense, tightly packed earth, so hard that the surfaces have the texture of baked clay, perhaps even glass. In other words, the man in the hole will be unable to extricate himself from the hole once he opens his eyes. Unless he is equipped with a set of mountaineering tools—a hammer and metal spikes, for example, or a rope to lasso a neighboring tree—but this man has no tools, and once he regains consciousness, he will quickly understand the nature of his predicament.

And so it happens. The man comes to his senses and discovers that he is lying on his back, gazing up at a cloudless evening sky. His name is Owen Brick, and he has no idea how he has landed in this spot, no memory of having fallen into this cylindrical hole, which he estimates to be approximately twelve feet in diameter. He sits up. To his surprise, he is dressed in a soldier's uniform made of rough, dun-colored wool. A cap is on his head, and a pair of sturdy, well-worn black leather boots are on his feet, laced above the ankles with a firm double knot. There are two military stripes on each sleeve of the jacket, indicating that the uniform belongs to someone with the rank of corporal. That person might be Owen Brick, but the man in the hole, whose name is Owen Brick, cannot recall having served in an army or fought in a war at any time in his life.

For want of any other explanation, he assumes he has received a knock on the head and has temporarily lost his memory. When he puts his fingertips against his scalp and begins to search for bumps and gashes, however, he finds no traces of swelling, no cuts, no bruises, nothing to suggest that such an injury has occurred. What is it, then? Has he suffered some debilitating trauma that has blacked out large portions of his brain? Perhaps. But unless the memory of that trauma suddenly returns to him, he will have no way of knowing. After that, he begins to explore the possibility that he is asleep in his bed at home, trapped inside some supernaturally lucid dream, a dream so lifelike and intense that the boundary between dreaming and consciousness has all but melted away. If that is true, then he simply has to open his eyes, hop out of bed, and walk into the kitchen to prepare the morning coffee. But how can you open your eyes when they're already open? He blinks a few times, childishly wondering if that won't break the spell—but there is no spell to be broken, and the magic bed fails to materialize.

A flock of starlings passes overhead, entering his field of vision for five or six seconds, and then vanishes into the twilight. Brick stands up to inspect his surroundings, and as he does so he becomes aware of an object bulging in the left front pocket of his trousers. It turns out to be a wallet, his wallet, and in addition to seventy-six dollars in American money, it contains a driver's license issued by the state of New York to one Owen Brick, born June 12, 1977. This confirms what Brick already knows: that he is a man approaching thirty who lives in Jackson Heights, Queens. He also knows that he is married to a woman named Flora and that for the past seven years he has worked as a professional magician, performing mostly at children's birthday parties around the city under the stage name of the Great Zavello. These facts only deepen the mystery. If he is so certain of who he is, then how did he wind up at the bottom of this hole, dressed in a corporal's uniform no less, without papers or dog tags or a military ID card to prove his status as a soldier?

It doesn't take long for him to understand that escape is out of the question. The circular wall is too high, and when he kicks it with his boot in order to dent the surface and create some kind of foothold that would help him climb up, the only result is a sore big toe. Night is falling rapidly, and there is a chill in the air, a damp vernal chill worming itself into his body, and while Brick has begun to feel afraid, for the moment he is still more baffled than afraid. Nevertheless, he can't stop himself from calling out for help. Until now, all has been quiet around him, suggesting that he is in some remote, unpopulated stretch of countryside, with no sounds other than an occasional bird cry and the rustling of the wind. As if on command, however, as if by some skewed logic of cause and effect, the moment he shouts the word *HELP*, artillery fire erupts in the distance, and the darkening sky lights up with streaking comets of destruction. Brick hears machine guns, exploding grenades, and under it all, no doubt miles away, a dull chorus of howling human voices. This is war, he realizes, and he is a soldier in that war, but with no weapon at his disposal, no way to defend himself against attack, and for the first time since waking up in the hole, he is well and truly afraid.

The shooting goes on for more than an hour, then gradually dissipates into silence. Not long after that, Brick hears the faint

sound of sirens, which he takes to mean that fire engines are
rushing to buildings damaged during the assault. Then the sirens stop as well, and quiet descends on him once again. Cold
and frightened as he is, Brick is also exhausted, and after pacing around the confines of his cylindrical jail until the stars
appear in the sky, he stretches out on the ground and manages
to fall asleep at last.

Early the next morning, he is woken by a voice calling to him
from the top of the hole. Brick looks up and sees the face of a man
jutting over the rim, and since the face is all he can see, he assumes the man is lying flat on his stomach.

Corporal, the man says. Corporal Brick, it's time to get moving.

Brick stands up, and now that his eyes are only three or four
feet from the stranger's face, he can see that the man is a swar-
thy, square-jawed fellow with a two-day stubble of beard and
that he is wearing a military cap identical to the one on his own
head. Before Brick can protest that much as he'd like to get
moving, he's in no position to do anything of the sort, the man's
face disappears.

Don't worry, he hears him say. We'll have you out of there in
no time.

Some moments later, there follows the sound of a hammer or
iron mallet pounding on a metal object, and because the sound
becomes increasingly muted with each successive blow, Brick
wonders if the man isn't driving a stake into the ground. And if
it's a stake, then perhaps a length of rope will soon be attached
to it, and with that rope Brick will be able to climb out of the

hole. The clanging stops, another thirty or forty seconds go by, and then, just as he predicted, a rope drops down at his feet.

Brick is a magician, not a bodybuilder, and even if climbing a yard or so of rope is not an inordinately strenuous task for a healthy man of thirty, he nevertheless has a good deal of trouble hoisting himself to the top. The wall is of no use to him, since the soles of his boots keep sliding off the smooth surface, and when he tries to clamp his boots onto the rope itself, he fails to gain a secure purchase, which means that he has to rely on the strength of his arms alone, and given that his are not muscular or powerful arms, and given that the rope is made of coarse material and therefore chafes his palms, this simple operation is turned into something of a battle. When he finally nears the rim and the other man takes hold of his right hand and pulls him onto level ground, Brick is both out of breath and disgusted with himself. After such a dismal performance, he is expecting to be mocked for his ineptitude, but by some miracle the man refrains from making any disparaging comments.

As Brick struggles slowly to his feet, he notes that his rescuer's uniform is the same as his, with the single exception that there are three stripes on the sleeves of his jacket, not two. The air is dense with fog, and he has difficulty making out where he is. Some isolated spot in the country, as he suspected, but the city or town that was under attack last night is nowhere to be seen. The only things he can distinguish with any clarity are the metal stake with the rope tied around it and a mud-splattered jeep parked about ten feet from the edge of the hole.

Corporal, the man says, shaking Brick's hand with a firm, enthusiastic grip. I'm Serge Tobak, your sergeant. Better known as Sarge Serge.

Brick looks down at the man, who is a good six inches shorter than he is, and repeats the name in a low voice: Sarge Serge.

I know, Tobak says. Very funny. But the name stuck, and there's nothing I can do about it. If you can't lick 'em, join 'em, right?

What am I doing here? Brick asks, trying to suppress the anguish in his voice.

Get a grip on yourself, boy. You're fighting a war. What did you think this was? A trip to Fun World?

What war? Does that mean we're in Iraq?

Iraq? Who cares about Iraq?

America's fighting a war in Iraq. Everyone knows that.

Fuck Iraq. This is America, and America is fighting America.

What are you talking about?

Civil war, Brick. Don't you know anything? This is the fourth year. But now that you've turned up, it's going to end soon. You're the guy who's going to make it happen.

How do you know my name?

You're in my platoon, dumbbell.

And what about the hole? What was I doing down there?

Normal procedure. All new recruits come to us like that.

But I didn't sign up. I didn't enlist.

Of course not. No one does. But that's the way it is. One minute you're living your life, and the next minute you're in the war.

Brick is so confounded by Tobak's statements, he doesn't know what to say.

It's like this, the sergeant rattles on. You're the chump they've picked for the big job. Don't ask me why, but the general staff thinks you're the best man for the assignment. Maybe because no one knows you, or maybe because you have this . . . this what? . . . this bland look about you, and no one would suspect you're an assassin.

Assassin?

That's it, assassin. But I like to use the word *liberator*. Or *maker of the peace*. Whatever you want to call it, without you the war will never end.

Brick would like to run away on the spot, but because he's unarmed, he can't think of anything else to do but play along. And who am I supposed to kill? he asks.

It's not *who* so much as *what*, the sergeant replies enigmatically. We're not even sure of his name. It could be Blake. It could be Black. It could be Bloch. But we have an address, and if he hasn't slipped away by now, you shouldn't have any trouble. We'll set you up with a contact in the city, you'll go undercover, and in a few days it should all be over.

And why does this man deserve to die?

Because he owns the war. He invented it, and everything that happens or is about to happen is in his head. Eliminate that head, and the war stops. It's that simple.

Simple? You make him sound like God.

Not God, Corporal, just a man. He sits in a room all day writing it down, and whatever he writes comes true. The intelligence reports say he's racked with guilt, but he can't stop himself. If the bastard had the guts to blow his brains out, we wouldn't be having this conversation.

You're saying it's a story, that a man is writing a story, and we're all part of it.

Something like that.

And after he's killed, then what? The war ends, but what about us?

Everything goes back to normal.

Or maybe we just disappear.

Maybe. But that's the risk we have to take. Do or die, son. More than thirteen million dead already. If things go on like this much longer, half the population will be gone before you know it.

Brick has no intention of killing anyone, and the longer he listens to Tobak, the more certain he becomes that the man is a raving lunatic. For the time being, however, he has no choice but to pretend to understand, to act as if he's eager to carry out the assignment.

Sarge Serge walks over to the jeep, fetches a bulging plastic bag from the back, and hands it to Brick. Your new duds, he says, and right there in the open he instructs the magician to strip off his army uniform and put on the civilian clothes contained in the bag: a pair of black jeans, a blue oxford shirt, a red V-neck sweater, a belt, a brown leather jacket, and black leather shoes. Then he hands him a green nylon backpack filled with more clothes, shaving equipment, a toothbrush and toothpaste, a hairbrush, a .38-caliber revolver, and a box of bullets. Finally, Brick is given an envelope with twenty fifty-dollar bills in it and a slip of paper with the name and address of his contact.

Lou Frisk, the sergeant says. A good man. Go to him as soon as you get to the city, and he'll tell you everything you need to know.

What city are we talking about? Brick asks. I have no idea where I am.

Wellington, Tobak says, swiveling to his right and pointing into the heavy morning fog. Twelve miles due north. Just stay on this road, and you'll be there by the middle of the afternoon.

I'm supposed to walk?

Sorry. I'd give you a lift, but I have to go in the other direction. My men are waiting for me.

And what about breakfast? Twelve miles on an empty stomach . . .

Sorry about that, too. I was supposed to bring you an egg sandwich and a thermos of coffee, but I forgot.

Before leaving to join his men, Sarge Serge pulls the rope up from the hole, yanks the metal stake out of the ground, and tosses them into the back of the jeep. Then he climbs in behind the steering wheel and starts the engine. Giving Brick a farewell salute, he says: Hang in there, soldier. You don't look like much of a killer to me, but what do I know? I'm never right about anything.

Without another word, Tobak presses his foot on the accelerator, and just like that he is gone, disappearing into the fog within a matter of seconds. Brick doesn't budge. He is both cold and hungry, both destabilized and frightened, and for more than a minute he just stands there in the middle of the road, wondering what to do next. Eventually, he starts to shiver in the frosty air. That decides it for him. He has to get his limbs moving, to warm himself up, and so, without the faintest notion of what lies ahead of him, he turns around, thrusts his hands into his pockets, and begins walking toward the city.

A door has just opened upstairs, and I can hear the sound of footsteps traveling down the hall. Miriam or Katya, I can't tell which. The bathroom door opens and shuts; faintly, very faintly, I detect the familiar music of pee hitting water, but whoever has done the peeing is thoughtful enough not to flush the toilet and risk waking the household, even if two-thirds of its members are already awake. Then the bathroom door opens, and once again the quiet tread down the hall and the closing of a bedroom door. If I had to choose, I would say it was Katya. Poor, suffering Katya, as resistant to sleep as her immobilized grandfather. I would love to be able to walk up the stairs, go into her room, and talk to her for a while. Tell some of my bad jokes, maybe, or else just run my hand over her head until her eyes closed and she fell asleep. But I can't climb the stairs in a wheelchair, can I? And if I used my crutch, I would probably fall in the dark. Damn this idiot leg. The only solution is to sprout a pair of wings, giant wings of the softest white down. Then I'd be up there in a flash.

For the past couple of months, Katya and I have spent our days watching movies together. Side by side on the living room sofa, staring at the television set, knocking off two, three, even four films in a row, then breaking for dinner with Miriam, and once dinner has been eaten, returning to the sofa for another film or two before going to bed. I should be working on my manuscript, the memoir I promised to write for Miriam after I retired three years ago, the story of my life, the family history, a chronicle of a vanished world, but the truth is I'd rather be on the sofa with Katya, holding her hand, letting her rest her head on my shoulder, feeling my mind grow numb from the endless parade of images dancing across the screen. For over a year I went at it every day, building up a hefty pile of pages, about half the story I'd guess, perhaps a little more, but now I seem to have lost the stomach for it. Maybe it started when Sonia died, I don't know, the end of married life, the loneliness of it all, the fucking loneliness after I lost her, and then I cracked up that rented car, destroying my leg, nearly killing myself in the process, maybe that added to it as well: the indifference, the feeling that after seventy-two years on this earth, who gives a damn if I write about myself or not? It was never anything that interested me, not even when I was young, and I certainly never had any ambition to write a book. I liked to read them, that was all, to read books and then write about them afterward, but I was always a sprinter, never a long-distance man, a greyhound working on deadline for forty years, an expert at cranking out the seven-hundred-word piece, the fifteen-hundred-word piece, the twice-weekly column, the occasional magazine assignment, how many thousands of them did I vomit forth? Decades of ephemera, mounds of burned-up and recycled newsprint, and unlike most of my colleagues, I never had the slightest inclination to collect the good ones, assuming there were any, and republish them in books that no sane person would bother to read. Let my half-finished manuscript go on gathering dust for now. Miriam is hard at it, coming to the end of her biography of Rose Hawthorne, squeezing in her hours at night, on the weekends, on the days when she doesn't have to drive to Hampton to teach her courses, and for the time being maybe one writer in the house is enough.

Where was I? Owen Brick . . . Owen Brick walking down the road to the city. The cold air, the confusion, a second civil war in America. A prelude to something, but before I figure out what to do with my befuddled magician, I need a few moments to reflect on Katya and the films, since I still can't decide if this is a good thing or a bad thing. When she started ordering the DVDs through the Internet, I took it as a sign of progress, a small step in the right direction. If nothing else, it showed me that she was willing to let herself be distracted, to think about something other than her dead Titus. She's a film student, after all, training to become an editor, and when the DVDs started pouring into the house, I wondered if she wasn't thinking about going back to school or, if not school, then furthering her education on her own. After a while, though, I began to see this obsessive movie watching as a form of self-medication, a homeopathic drug to anesthetize herself against the need to think about her future. Escaping into a film is not like escaping into a book. Books force you to give something back to them, to exercise your intelligence and imagination, whereas you can watch a film—and even enjoy it—in a state of mindless passivity. That said, I don't mean to suggest that Katya has turned herself into a stone. She smiles and sometimes even emits a small laugh during the funny scenes in comedies, and her tear ducts have frequently been active during the touching scenes in dramas. It has more to do with her posture, I think, the way she slumps back on the sofa with her feet stretched out on the coffee table, unmoving for hours on end, refusing to stir herself even to pick up the phone, showing little or no signs of life except when I'm touching or holding her. It's probably my fault. I've encouraged her to lead this flattened-out existence, and maybe I should put a stop to it— although I doubt she'd listen to me if I tried.

On the other hand, some days are better than others. Each time we finish a movie, we talk about it for a little while before Katya puts on the next one. I usually want to discuss the story and the quality of the acting, but her remarks tend to focus on the technical aspects of the film: the camera setups, the editing, the lighting, the sound, and so on. Just tonight, however, after we watched three consecutive foreign films—*Grand Illusion, The Bicycle Thief,* and *The World of Apu*—Katya delivered some sharp and incisive comments, sketching out a theory of filmmaking that impressed me with its originality and acumen.

Inanimate objects, she said.

What about them? I asked.

Inanimate objects as a means of expressing human emotions. That's the language of film. Only good directors understand how to do it, but Renoir, De Sica, and Ray are three of the best, aren't they?

No doubt.

Think about the opening scenes of *The Bicycle Thief.* The
hero is given a job, but he won't be able to take it unless he gets
his bicycle out of hock. He goes home feeling sorry for himself.
And there's his wife outside their building, lugging two heavy
buckets of water. All their poverty, all the struggles of this
woman and her family are contained in those buckets. The husband is so wrapped up in his own troubles, he doesn't bother to
help her until they're halfway to the door. And even then, he
only takes one of the buckets, leaving her to carry the other.
Everything we need to know about their marriage is given to us
in those few seconds. Then they climb the stairs to their apartment, and the wife comes up with the idea to pawn their bed
linens so they can redeem the bicycle. Remember how violently
she kicks the bucket in the kitchen, remember how violently
she opens the bureau drawer. Inanimate objects, human emotions. Then we're at the pawnshop, which isn't a shop, really, but
a huge place, a kind of warehouse for unwanted goods. The wife
sells the sheets, and after that we see one of the workers carry
their little bundle to the shelves where pawned items are stored.
At first, the shelves don't seem very high, but then the camera
pulls back, and as the man starts climbing up, we see that they
go on and on and on, all the way to the ceiling, and every shelf
and cubby is crammed full of bundles identical to the one the
man is now putting away, and all of a sudden it looks as if every
family in Rome has sold their bed linens, that the entire city is
in the same miserable state as the hero and his wife. In one shot,
Grandpa. In one shot we're given a picture of a whole society
living at the edge of disaster.

Not bad, Katya. The wheels are turning . . .

It just hit me tonight. But I think I'm on to something, since I saw examples in all three films. Remember the dishes in *Grand Illusion*?

The dishes?

Right near the end. Gabin tells the German woman that he loves her, that he'll come back for her and her daughter when the war is over, but the troops are closing in now, and he and Dalio have to try to cross the border into Switzerland before it's too late. The four of them have a last meal together, and then the moment comes to say good-bye. It's all very moving, of course. Gabin and the woman standing in the doorway, the possibility that they'll never see each other again, the woman's tears as the men vanish into the night. Renoir then cuts to Gabin and Dalio running through the woods, and I'd bet money that every other director in the world would have stayed with them until the end of the film. But not Renoir. He has the genius—and when I say *genius,* I mean the understanding, the depth of heart, the compassion—to go back to the woman and her little daughter, this young widow who has already lost her husband to the madness of war, and what does she have to do? She has to go back into the house and confront the dining room table and the dirty dishes from the meal they've just eaten. The men are gone now, and because they're gone, those dishes have been transformed into a sign of their absence, the lonely suffering of women when men go off to war, and one by one, without saying a word, she picks up the dishes and clears the table. How long does the scene last? Ten seconds? Fifteen seconds? No time at all, but it takes your breath away, doesn't it? It just knocks the stuffing out of you.

You're a brave girl, I said, suddenly thinking about Titus.

Stop it, Grandpa. I don't want to talk about him. Some other time, maybe, but not now. Okay?

Okay. Let's stick to the movies. There's still one to go. The Indian film. I think it's the one I liked best.

That's because it's about a writer, Katya said, cracking a brief, ironic smile.

Maybe. But that doesn't mean it isn't good.

I wouldn't have chosen it unless it was good. No junk. That's the rule, remember? All sorts of movies, from the wacky to the sublime, but no junk.

Agreed. But where's the inanimate object in *Apu*?

Think.

I don't want to think. It's your theory, so you tell me.

The curtains and the hairpin. A transition from one life into another, the turning point of the story. Apu has gone to the country to attend his friend's cousin's wedding. A traditional arranged marriage, and when the bridegroom shows up, he turns out to be an idiot, a blithering numskull. The wedding is called off, and the friend's cousin's parents begin to panic, afraid their daughter will be cursed for life if she doesn't get married that afternoon. Apu is asleep somewhere under the trees, not a care in the world, happy to be out of the city for a few days. The girl's family approaches him. They explain that he's the only available unmarried man, that he's the only one who can solve the problem for them. Apu is appalled. He thinks they're nuts, a bunch of superstitious country bumpkins, and refuses to go along. But then he mulls it over for a while and decides to do it. As a good deed, as an altruistic gesture, but he has no intention of taking the girl back to Calcutta with him. After the wedding ceremony, when they're finally alone together for the first time, Apu learns that this meek young woman is a lot tougher than he thought she was. I'm poor, he says, I want to be a writer, I have nothing to offer you. I know, she says, but that makes no difference, she's determined to go with him. Exasperated, flummoxed, but also moved by her resolve, Apu reluctantly gives in. Cut to the city. A carriage pulls up in front of the ramshackle building where Apu lives, and he and his bride step out. All the neighbors come to gawk at the beautiful girl as Apu leads her up the stairs to his squalid little garret. A moment later, he's called away by someone and leaves. The camera stays on the girl, alone in this strange room, this strange city, married to a man she hardly knows. Eventually, she walks to the window, which has a cruddy piece of burlap hanging over it instead of a real curtain. There's a hole in the burlap, and she looks through the hole into the backyard, where a baby in diapers is toddling along through the dust and debris. The camera angle reverses, and we see her eye through the hole. Tears are falling from that eye, and who can blame her for feeling overwrought, scared, lost? Apu reenters the room and asks her what's wrong. Nothing, she says, shaking her head, nothing at all. Then we fade to black, and the big question is: what next? What's in store for this unlikely couple who wound up marrying each other by pure accident? With a few deft and decisive strokes, everything is revealed to

us in less than a minute. Object number one: the window. We
fade in, it's early morning, and the first thing we see is the window the girl was looking through in the previous scene. But the
ratty burlap is gone, replaced by a pair of clean checkered curtains. The camera pulls back a little, and there's object number
two: potted flowers on the windowsill. These are encouraging
signs, but we can't be sure what they mean yet. Domesticity, hom-
eyness, a woman's touch, but this is what wives are supposed to
do, and just because Apu's wife has carried out her duties well
doesn't prove that she cares for him. The camera continues pulling back, and we see the two of them asleep in bed. The alarm
clock rings, and the wife climbs out of bed as Apu groans and
buries his head in the pillow. Object number three: her sari.
After she gets out of bed and starts walking off, she suddenly
can't move—because her clothes are tied to Apu's. Very odd.
Who could have done this—and why? The expression on her
face is both peeved and amused, and we instantly know that
Apu was responsible. She returns to the bed, thwacks him gently on the butt, and then unties the knot. What does this moment say to me? That they're having good sex, that a sense of
playfulness has developed between them, that they're really
married. But what about love? They seem to be contented, but
how strong are their feelings for each other? That's when object
number four appears: the hairpin. The wife leaves the frame to
prepare breakfast, and the camera closes in on Apu. He finally
manages to open his eyes, and as he yawns and stretches and
rolls around in bed, he sees something in the crevice between
the two pillows. He reaches in and pulls out one of his wife's

hairpins. That's the crowning moment. He holds up the hairpin and studies it, and when you look at Apu's eyes, the tenderness and adoration in those eyes, you know beyond a doubt that he's madly in love with her, that she's the woman of his life. And Ray makes it happen without using a single word of dialogue.

Same with the dishes, I said. Same with the bundle of sheets. No words.

No words needed, Katya replied. Not when you know what you're doing.

There's another thing about those three scenes. I wasn't aware of it while we were watching the films, but listening to you describe them now, it jumped right out at me.

What?

They're all about women. How women are the ones who carry the world. They take care of the real business while their hapless men stumble around making a hash of things. Or else just lie around doing nothing. That's what happens after the hairpin. Apu looks across the room at his wife, who's crouching down over a pot making breakfast, and he doesn't make a move to help her. In the same way the Italian guy doesn't notice how hard it is for his wife to carry those water buckets.

At last, Katya said, giving me a small poke in the ribs. A man who gets it.

Let's not exaggerate. I'm just adding a footnote to your theory. Your very astute theory, I might add.

And what kind of husband were you, Grandpa?

Just as distracted and lazy as the jokers in those films. Your grandmother did everything.

That's not true.

Yes, it is. When you were with us, I was always on my best behavior. You should have seen us when we were alone.

I pause for a moment to shift my position in bed, to adjust the pillow, to take a sip of water from the glass on the bedside table. I don't want to start thinking about Sonia. It's still too early, and if I let myself go now, I'll wind up brooding about her for hours. Stick to the story. That's the only solution. Stick to the story, and then see what happens if I make it to the end.

Owen Brick. Owen Brick on his way to the city of Wellington, in which state he doesn't know, in which part of the country he doesn't know, but because of the dampness and chill in the air, he suspects that he's in the north, perhaps New England, perhaps New York State, perhaps somewhere in the Upper Midwest, and then, remembering Sarge Serge's talk about a civil war, he wonders what the fighting is about and who is fighting whom. Is it North against South again? East against West? Red against Blue? White against Black? Whatever caused the war, he tells himself, and whatever issues or ideas happen to be at stake, none of it makes any sense. How can this be America if Tobak knows nothing about Iraq? Utterly at a loss, Brick reverts to his earlier speculation that he is trapped in a dream, that in spite of the physical evidence around him, he is lying next to Flora in his bed at home.

Visibility is poor, but through the fog Brick can dimly apprehend that he is flanked by woods on both sides, that there are no houses or buildings anywhere in sight, no telephone poles, no traffic signs, no indication of human presence except the road itself, a badly paved stretch of tar and asphalt with numerous cracks and potholes, no doubt unrepaired for years. He walks on for a mile, then another mile, and still no cars drive past, no people emerge from the emptiness. Finally, after twenty minutes or so, he hears something approaching him, a clanking, whooshing sound that he is at pains to identify. Out of the fog, a man on a bicycle comes pedaling toward him. Brick raises his hand to catch the man's attention, calls out *Hello, Please, Sir,* but the cyclist ignores him and scoots on past. After a while, more people on bicycles start showing up, some riding in one direction, some in the other, but for all the notice they pay to Brick as he urges them to stop, he might as well be invisible.

Five or six miles farther down the road, signs of life begin to appear—or rather signs of former life: burned-out houses, collapsed food markets, a dead dog, several exploded cars. An old woman dressed in tattered clothes and pushing a shopping cart filled with her possessions suddenly looms up in front of him.

Excuse me, Brick says. Could you tell me if this is the road to Wellington?

The woman stops and looks at Brick with uncomprehending eyes. He notes a small tuft of whiskers sprouting from her chin, her wrinkled mouth, her gnarled, arthritic hands. Wellington? she says. Who asked you?

No one asked me, Brick says. I'm asking you.

Me? What do I have to do with it? I don't even know you.

And I don't know you. All I'm asking is if this is the road to Wellington.

The woman scrutinizes Brick for a moment and says, It'll cost you five bucks.

Five bucks for a yes or no? You must be crazy.

Everyone's crazy around here. Are you trying to tell me you're not?

I'm not trying to tell you anything. I just want to know where I am.

You're standing on a road, nitwit.

Yes, fine, I'm standing on a road, but what I want to know is if this road leads to Wellington.

Ten bucks.

Ten bucks?

Twenty bucks.

Forget it, Brick says, by now at the limit of his patience. I'll figure it out for myself.

Figure out what? the woman asks.

Instead of answering her, Brick starts walking again, and as he strides off through the fog, he hears the woman burst out laughing behind him, as if someone has just told her a good joke . . .

The streets of Wellington. It's past noon by the time he enters the city, exhausted and hungry, his feet aching from the rigors of the long trek. The sun has burned off the early morning fog, and as he wanders around in the fine, sixty-degree weather, Brick is heartened to discover that the place is still

more or less intact, not some bombed-out war zone heaped with
rubble and the bodies of dead civilians. He sees a number of
destroyed buildings, some cratered streets, a few demolished
barricades, but otherwise Wellington appears to be a function-
ing city, with pedestrians walking to and fro, people going in
and out of shops, and no imminent threat hanging in the air.
The only thing that distinguishes it from your normal American
metropolis is the fact that there are no cars, trucks, or buses.
Nearly everyone is moving around on foot, and those who aren't
walking are mounted on bicycles. It's impossible for Brick to
know yet if this is a result of a gasoline shortage or municipal
policy, but he has to admit that the quiet has a pleasant effect,
that he prefers it to the clamor and chaos of the streets in New
York. Beyond that, however, Wellington has little to recommend
it. It's a shabby, down-at-the-heels kind of place, with ugly, poorly
constructed buildings, nary a tree in sight, and mounds of un-
collected garbage littering the sidewalks. A glum burg, perhaps,
but not the out-and-out hellhole Brick was expecting.

His first order of business is to fill his stomach, but restaurants seem to be scarce in Wellington, and he prowls around for
some time before spotting a small diner on a side street off one
of the main avenues. It's almost three o'clock, long past lunch
hour, and the place is empty when he walks in. To his left is a
counter with six vacant stools in front of it; to his right, running
along the opposite wall, are four narrow booths, also vacant. Brick
decides to sit at the counter. A few seconds after he settles onto
one of the stools, a young woman emerges from the kitchen and

slaps down a menu in front of him. She's in her mid- to late twenties, a thin, pale blonde with a weary look in her eyes and the hint of a smile on her lips.

What's good today? Brick asks, not bothering to open the menu.

More like, what do we *have* today, the waitress replies.

Oh? Well, what are the choices?

Tuna salad, chicken salad, and eggs. The tuna's from yesterday, the chicken's from two days ago, and the eggs came in this morning. We'll cook them any way you like. Fried, scrambled, poached. Hard, medium, soft. Whatever, however.

Any bacon or sausage? Any toast or potatoes?

The waitress rolls her eyes in mock disbelief. Dream on, honey, she says. Eggs are eggs. Not eggs with something else. Just eggs.

All right, Brick says, feeling disappointed but nevertheless trying to keep up a good front, let's go for the eggs.

How do you want them?

Let's see. . . . How do I want them? Scrambled.

How many?

Three. No, make that four.

Four? That'll cost you twenty bucks, you know. The waitress narrows her eyes, and she looks at Brick as if seeing him for the first time. Shaking her head, she adds: What are you doing in a dump like this with twenty dollars in your pocket?

Because I want eggs, Brick answers. Four scrambled eggs, served to me by . . .

Molly, the waitress says, giving him a smile. Molly Wald.

. . . by Molly Wald. Any objections to that?

None that I can think of.

So Brick orders his four scrambled eggs, struggling to maintain a light, bantering tone with the skinny, not unfriendly Molly Wald, but underneath it all he's calculating that with prices like these—eggs going at five dollars a pop in a no-account greasy spoon—the money Tobak gave him that morning isn't going to last very long. As Molly turns around and calls out the order into the kitchen behind her, Brick wonders if he should start questioning her about the war or play it closer to the vest and keep his mouth shut. Still undecided, he asks for a cup of coffee.

Sorry, no can do, Molly says, we're all out. Hot tea. I can give you some hot tea if you like.

Okay, Brick says. A pot of tea. After a moment's hesitation, he plucks up his courage and asks: Just out of curiosity, how much is it?

Five bucks.

Five bucks? It seems that everything in here costs five bucks.

Clearly thrown by his comment, Molly leans forward, plants her arms on the counter, and shakes her head. You're kind of dumb, aren't you?

Probably, Brick says.

We stopped using singles and coins six months ago. Where have you been, pal? Are you a foreigner or something?

I don't know. I'm from New York. Does that make me a foreigner or not?

New York City?

Queens.

Molly lets out a sharp little laugh, which seems to convey both contempt and pity for her know-nothing customer. That's rich, she says, really rich. A guy from New York who can't tell his ass from his elbow.

I . . . uh . . . , Brick stammers, I've been sick. Out of commission. You know, in a hospital, and I haven't kept up with what's been going on.

Well, for your information, Mr. Stupid, Molly says, we're in a war, and New York started it.

Oh?

Yes, *oh*. Secession. Maybe you've heard of it. When a state declares independence from the rest of the country. There are sixteen of us now, and God knows when it will end. I'm not saying it's a bad thing, but enough is enough. It wears you out, and pretty soon you're just sick of the whole business.

There was a lot of gunfire last night, Brick says, finally daring to ask a direct question. Who won?

The Federals attacked, but our troops fought them off. I doubt they'll try that again anytime soon.

Which means that things are going to be fairly quiet in Wellington.

At least for now, yeah. Or so they say. But who knows?

A voice from the kitchen announces: *Four scrambled,* and a moment later a white plate appears on the shelf behind Molly. She pivots, takes hold of Brick's meal, and sets it down in front of him. Then she begins preparing the tea.

The eggs prove to be dry and overcooked, and not even some healthy doses of salt and pepper can draw much flavor from them. Half-starved after his twelve-mile walk, Brick shovels one forkful of food into his mouth after another, chewing diligently on the rubbery eggs and washing them down with frequent sips of tea—which isn't hot as advertised, but tepid. No matter, he says to himself. With so many unanswered questions to be dealt with, the quality of the food is the least of his worries. Pausing for a moment about midway through his combat with the eggs, Brick looks over at Molly, who is still standing behind the counter, watching him eat with her arms folded across her chest, shifting the weight of her body now onto her left leg, now onto her right, her green eyes flickering with what appears to be a kind of suppressed mirth.

What's so funny? he asks.

Nothing, she says, shrugging her shoulders. It's just that you're eating so fast, you remind me of a dog we used to have when I was a kid.

Sorry, Brick says. I'm hungry.

So I gathered.

You also might have gathered that I'm new around here, he says. I don't know a soul in Wellington, and I need a place to stay. I was wondering if you had any ideas.

For how long?

I don't know. Maybe a night, maybe a week, maybe forever. It's too soon to tell.

You're pretty vague about it, aren't you?

It can't be helped. I'm in a situation, you see, an odd situation, and I'm kind of stumbling around in the dark. The fact is, I don't even know what day it is.

Thursday, April nineteenth.

April nineteenth. Good. That's just what I would have said. But what year?

Are you kidding?

No, unfortunately not. What year is it?

Two thousand and seven.

Strange.

Why strange?

Because it's the right year, but everything else is wrong. Listen to me, Molly . . .

I'm listening, friend. I'm all ears.

Good. Now, if I said the words *September eleventh* to you, would they have any special meaning?

Not particularly.

And *the World Trade Center*?

The twin towers? Those tall buildings in New York?

Exactly.

What about them?

They're still standing?

Of course they are. What's wrong with you?

Nothing, Brick says, muttering to himself in a barely audible voice. Then, looking down at his half-eaten eggs, he whispers: One nightmare replaces another.

What? I didn't hear you.

Lifting his head and looking Molly straight in the eyes, Brick asks her a final question: And there's no war in Iraq, is there?

If you already know the answer, why ask me?

I just had to be sure. Forgive me.

Look, mister—

Owen. Owen Brick.

All right, Owen. I don't know what your problem is, and I don't know what happened to you in that hospital, but if I were you, I'd finish those eggs before they get cold. I'm going back into the kitchen to make a call. One of my cousins is the night manager of a little hotel around the corner. There could be a vacancy.

Why are you being so nice? You don't even know me.

I'm not being nice. My cousin and I have a deal. Whenever I bring him a new customer, he gives me a ten percent cut on the first night. It's strictly business, spaceman. If he has a room for you, you don't owe me a thing.

It turns out that he does. By the time Brick has swallowed the last of his food (with the aid of yet another gulp of the now-cold tea), Molly has come back from the kitchen to give him the good news. There are three rooms available, she says, two of them for three hundred a night and the third for two hundred. Not knowing how much he can afford, she's taken it upon herself to book him the room for two hundred, a clear indication, Brick thankfully notes, that despite her tough talk about *strictly business*, Molly has reduced her finder's fee by ten dollars as a favor to him. Not such a bad girl, he thinks, no matter how hard she works at hiding it. Brick is feeling so lonely, so discombobulated by the events of the past twenty hours, he wishes she would abandon her post behind the counter and accompany him to the hotel, but he knows she can't, and he's too timid to ask her to make an exception for him. Instead, Molly sketches a

diagram on a paper napkin, indicating the route he should follow to reach the Exeter Hotel, which is only one block away.
Then he settles the tab, insisting that she accept a ten-dollar
tip, and shakes her hand good-bye.

I hope I see you again, he says, suddenly and moronically on
the verge of tears.

I'm always around, she replies. From eight to six, Monday
through Friday. If you ever want another lousy meal, you know
where to come.

The Exeter Hotel is a six-story limestone building in the
middle of a block of discount shoe stores and dimly lit bars. It
might have been an attractive place sixty or seventy years ago,
but one look at the lobby, with its sagging, moth-eaten velvet
chairs and dead potted palms, and Brick understands that two
hundred dollars doesn't buy you much in Wellington. He's a bit
stunned when the clerk behind the front desk insists that he
pay for the night in advance, but since he's unfamiliar with
local customs, he doesn't bother to protest. The clerk, who could
pass for Serge Tobak's twin brother, counts out the four fifty-
dollar bills, sweeps them into a drawer below the cracked marble
counter, and hands Brick the key to room 406. No signature or
proof of identity required. When Brick asks where he can find
the elevator, the clerk informs him that it's broken.

Somewhat winded after climbing the four flights of stairs,
Brick unlocks the door and enters his room. He observes that the
bed has been made, that the white walls look and smell as if
they've been freshly painted, that everything is relatively clean,
but once he begins to look around in earnest, he is gripped by a

pulverizing sense of dread. The room is so bleak and unwelcoming, he imagines that dozens of desperate people have checked into this place over the years with no other purpose than to commit suicide. Where has this impression come from? Is it his own state of mind, he wonders, or can it be borne out by the facts? The sparseness of the furniture, for example: just one bed and one battered wardrobe stranded in an overly large space. No chair, no phone. The absence of any pictures on the walls. The blank, cheerless bathroom, with a single miniature bar of soap lying in its wrapper on the white sink, a single white hand towel hanging on the rack, the rusted enamel in the white tub. Pacing around in an ever-spiraling funk, Brick decides to turn on the old black-and-white television next to the window. Maybe that will calm him down, he thinks, or, if luck is with him, maybe a newscast will be on and he can learn something about the war. A hollow, echoing ping emerges from the box as he pushes the button. A promising sign, he says to himself, but then, after a long wait as the machine slowly warms up, no image appears on the screen. Nothing but snow, and the strident hiss of static. He changes the channel. More snow, more static. He goes around the dial, but each stop produces the same result. Rather than simply turn off the television, Brick yanks the cord out of the wall. Then he sits down on the ancient bed, which groans under the weight of his body.

Before he has a chance to slump into a miasma of useless self-pity, someone knocks on the door. No doubt an employee of the hotel, Brick thinks, but secretly he's hoping it's Molly Wald, that somehow or other she's managed to dash out of the diner for a couple of minutes to check on him and make sure he's all right. Not very probable, of course, and no sooner does he unlock the door than his fleeting hope is crushed. His visitor isn't Molly, but neither is it an employee of the hotel. Instead, he finds himself standing in front of a tall, attractive woman with dark hair and blue eyes dressed in black jeans and a brown leather jacket—clothes similar to the ones Sarge Serge gave him that morning. As Brick studies her face, he is convinced they have met before, but his mind refuses to conjure up a memory of where or when.

Hi there, Owen, the woman says, flashing him a bright, brittle smile, and as he looks at her mouth, he notices that she's wearing an intense shade of red lipstick.

I know you, don't I? Brick answers. At least I think I do. Or maybe you just remind me of someone.

Virginia Blaine, the woman announces cheerfully, triumph ringing in her voice. Don't you remember? You had a crush on me in the tenth grade.

Good God, Brick mutters, more lost than ever now. Virginia Blaine. We sat next to each other in Miss Blunt's geometry class.

Aren't you going to let me in?

Of course, of course, he says, stepping out of the doorway and watching her stride across the threshold.

Once she has cast her eyes around the grim, barren room, Virginia turns to him and says: What a horrible place. Why on earth did you check in here?

It's a long story, Brick replies, not wanting to go into it.

This won't do, Owen. We'll have to find you something better.

Maybe tomorrow. I've already paid up for tonight, and I doubt they'd give me my money back now.

There isn't even a chair to sit in.

I realize that. You can sit on the bed if you want to.

Thanks, Virginia says, glancing over at the worn-out green bedspread, I think I'll stand.

What are you doing here? Brick asks, abruptly changing the subject.

I saw you walk into the hotel, and I came up to—

No, no, I don't mean that, he says, cutting her off in midsentence. I'm talking about *here,* in Wellington, a city I've never even heard of. In this country, which is supposed to be America but isn't America, at least not the America I know.

I can't tell you. Not yet, anyway.

I go to bed with my wife in New York. We make love, we fall asleep, and when I wake up I'm lying in a hole in the middle of goddamned nowhere, dressed in a fucking army uniform. What the hell is going on?

Calm down, Owen. I know it's a bit disorienting at first, but you'll get used to it, I promise.

I don't want to get used to it. I want to go back to my life.

You will. And a lot sooner than you think.

Well, at least that's something, Brick says, not sure whether he should believe her or not. But if I'm able to go back, what about you?

I don't want to go back. I've been here a long time now, and I like it better than where I used to be.

A long time. . . . So when you stopped coming to school, it wasn't because you and your parents had moved away.

No.

I missed you a lot. For about three months, I'd been screwing up my courage to ask you out on a date, and then, just when I was ready to do it, you were gone.

It couldn't be helped. I didn't have any choice.

What keeps you here? Are you married? Do you have any kids?

No kids, but I used to be married. My husband was killed at the beginning of the war.

I'm sorry.

I'm sorry, too. And I'm also a little sorry to hear that you're married. I haven't forgotten you, Owen. I know it was a long time ago, but I wanted to go out on that date just as much as you did.

Now you tell me.

It's the truth. I mean, whose idea do you think it was to bring you here?

You're joking. Come on, Virginia, why would you do something that awful to me?

I wanted to see you again. And I also thought you'd be the perfect man for the job.

What job?

Don't be coy, Owen. You know what I'm talking about.

Tobak. The clown who calls himself Sarge Serge.

And Lou Frisk. You were supposed to go to him straightaway, remember?

I was tired. I'd been walking all day on an empty stomach,

and I needed to eat something and take a nap. I was about to climb into bed when you knocked on the door.

Bad luck. We're working on a tight schedule, and we have to go to Frisk now.

I can't. I'm just too exhausted. Let me sleep for a couple of hours, and then I'll go with you.

I really shouldn't . . .

Please, Virginia. For old times' sake.

All right, she says, looking down at her wristwatch. I'll give you an hour. It's four-thirty now. Expect a knock on your door at five-thirty sharp.

Thank you.

But no funny business, Owen. Okay?

Of course not.

After giving him a warm, affectionate smile, Virginia opens her arms and hugs Brick good-bye. It's so good to see you again, she whispers into his ear. Brick remains mute, his arms at his sides, a hundred thoughts darting through his head. Finally, Virginia lets go of him, pats him on the cheek, and makes her way to the door, which she opens with a quick, downward thrust on the handle. Before letting herself out, she turns and says: Five-thirty.

Five-thirty, Brick echoes, and then the door bangs shut, and Virginia Blaine is gone.

Brick already has a plan—and a set of principles. Under no circumstances does he want to meet Frisk or carry out the job they've assigned him. He is not going to murder anyone, he will not do anyone's bidding, he will keep himself out of sight for as long as necessary. Since Virginia knows where he is, he will have to leave the hotel at once and never return. Where to go next is the most immediate problem, and he can think of only three possible solutions. Return to the diner and ask Molly Wald for help. If she isn't willing to give it, then what? Roam the streets and look for another hotel, or else wait for nightfall and then slip out of Wellington.

He gives himself ten minutes, more than enough time for Virginia to get down the four flights of stairs and leave the Exeter. She could be waiting in the lobby, of course, or keeping watch on the hotel entrance from across the street, but if she isn't in the lobby, he will make his exit through a back door, assuming there is a back door and he can find it. And what if she happens to be in the lobby, after all? He will make a run for it, pure and simple. Brick might not be the fastest man in the world, but during his conversation with Virginia he noticed that she was wearing high-heeled boots, and surely a man in flat shoes can outrun a woman in high-heeled boots any day of the week.

As for the hug and the affectionate smile, as for professing to want to see him again and her regret at not having gone out with him in high school, Brick is nothing if not skeptical. Virginia Blaine, the heartthrob of his fifteen-year-old self, was the prettiest girl in the class, and every boy swooned with lust and silent longing whenever she walked by. He wasn't telling the truth when he said he was about to ask her out on a date. There was no question that he wanted to ask, but at that point in his life, he never would have dared.

Leather jacket zipped, backpack slung over his right shoulder, down Brick goes, taking the rear stairwell, the fire exit, which mercifully allows him to bypass the lobby altogether and leads to a metal door that opens onto a street parallel to the front entrance of the hotel. No sign of Virginia anywhere, and so heartened is our frazzled hero by his successful escape, he feels a momentary surge of optimism, sensing that he can finally add the word *hope* to the lexicon of his miseries. He walks along quickly, sliding past knots of pedestrians, dodging a boy on a pogo stick, slackening his pace briefly at the approach of four soldiers carrying rifles, listening to the ever-present clank of bicycles rolling down the street. A turn, another turn, and then one more, and there he is, standing in front of the Pulaski Diner, the restaurant where Molly works.

Brick goes in, and once again the place is empty. Now that he understands the circumstances, this hardly comes as a surprise to him, since why would anyone bother to go to a restaurant that has no food? Not a customer to be seen, therefore, but more distressing is the absence of Molly as well. Wondering if she hasn't gone home early, Brick calls out her name, and when she fails to appear, he calls it out again. After several anxious seconds, he is relieved to see her walk into the room, but once she recognizes him, the boredom in her face instantly turns to worry, perhaps even anger.

Is everything okay? she asks, her voice sounding tight and defensive.

Yes and no, Brick says.

What does that mean? Did they give you any trouble at the hotel?

No trouble. They were expecting me. I paid for one night in advance and went upstairs.

What about the room? Any problem with that?

Let me tell you, Molly, Brick says, unable to suppress the smile that is spreading across his lips, I've traveled all over the world, and when it comes to first-class accommodations, I mean top-of-the-line comfort and elegance, nothing comes close to room four-oh-six at the Exeter Hotel in Wellington.

Molly smiles broadly at his facetious remark, and all at once she looks like a different person. Yeah, I know, she says. It's a classy place, isn't it?

Seeing that smile, Brick suddenly understands the cause of her alarm. Her initial assumption was that he marched back here to complain, to accuse her of having swindled him, but now that she knows otherwise, she has let down her guard, relaxed into a more amiable attitude.

It has nothing to do with the hotel, he says. It's about that situation I mentioned to you before. A bunch of people are after me. They want me to do something I don't want to do, and now they know I'm staying at the Exeter. Which means I can't stay there anymore. That's why I came back. To ask for your help.

Why me?

Because you're the only person I know.

You don't know me, Molly says, shifting the weight of her body from her right leg to her left. I served you some eggs, I found a room for you, we talked for about five minutes. I hardly call that knowing me.

You're right. I don't know you. But I couldn't think of any-where else to go.

Why should I stick my neck out for you? You're probably in some kind of trouble. Police trouble or army trouble. Or maybe you escaped from that hospital. The loony bin would be my guess. Give me one good reason why I should help you.

I can't. Not a single one, Brick says, dismayed at how badly he misjudged this girl, how foolish he was to think he could count on her. The only thing I can offer you is money, he adds, re-membering the envelope of fifties in the backpack. If you know of a place where I could hide out for a while, I'll be glad to pay you.

Ah, well, that's different, isn't it? says the transparent, not-so-cunning Molly. How much money are we talking about?

I don't know. You tell me.

I suppose I could put you up in my apartment for a night or two. The sofa's long enough to hold that body of yours, I think. But no hanky-panky. My boyfriend lives with me, and he has a bad temper, if you know what I mean, so don't get any dumb ideas.

I'm married. I don't go in for stuff like that.

That's a good one. There isn't a married man in this world who'd pass up some extra nooky if it came his way.

Maybe I don't live in this world.

Yeah, maybe you don't at that. That would explain a lot of things, wouldn't it?

So, how much are you going to charge? Brick asks, eager to complete the transaction.

Two hundred bucks.

Two hundred? That's pretty steep, don't you think?

You don't know crap, mister. Around here, that's rock bottom, as low as it gets. Take it or leave it.

All right, Brick says, bowing his head and letting out a long, mournful sigh. I'll take it.

Suddenly, an urgent need to empty my bladder. I shouldn't have drunk that last glass of wine, but the temptation was too strong, and the fact is I like going to bed a little tipsy. The apple juice bottle is sitting on the floor next to the bed, but as I reach out and grope for it in the dark, I can't seem to find it. The bottle was Miriam's idea—to spare me the pain and difficulty of having to get out of bed and hobble off to the bathroom in the middle of the night. An excellent idea, but the whole point is to have the bottle close at hand, and on this particular night my waving, extended fingers make no contact with the glass. The only solution is to turn on the bedside lamp, but once that happens, any chance I have of falling asleep will be gone for good. The bulb is just fifteen watts, but in the ink-black dark of this room, switching it on will be like exposing myself to a searing blast of fire. I'll go blind for a few seconds, and then, as my pupils gradually expand, I'll be wide awake, and even after I turn off the lamp, my brain will go on churning until dawn. I know this from long experience, a lifetime of battling against myself in the trenches of night. Oh well, nothing to be done, not one bloody thing. I switch on. I go blind. I blink slowly as my eyes adjust, and then I catch sight of the bottle, standing on the floor a mere two inches from its usual spot. I lean over, extend my body a little farther, and take hold of the damn thing. Then, throwing back the covers, I inch myself into a sitting position—carefully, carefully, so as not to rouse the ire of my shattered leg—twist off the top of the bottle, stick my pecker into the hole, and let the pee come pouring out. It never fails to satisfy, that moment when the gush begins, and then watching the bubbling yellow liquid cascade into the bottle as the glass grows warm in my hand. How many times does a person urinate over the course of seventy-two years? I could do the calculations, but why bother now that the job is nearly done? As I remove my penis from the hole, I look down at my old comrade and wonder if I'll ever have sex again, if I'll ever run across another woman who will want to go to bed with me and spend a night in my arms. I push down the thought, tell myself to desist, for therein lies the way to madness. Why did you have to die, Sonia? Why couldn't I have gone first?

I recap the bottle, return it to its proper place on the floor, and pull the blankets over me. What now? To turn off the light or not to turn off the light? I want to go back to my story and discover what happens to Owen Brick, but the latest installments of Miriam's book are lying on the lower shelf of the bedside table, and I promised to read them and give her my comments. After all the movie watching with Katya, I've fallen behind, and it irks me to think I've let her down. Just for a while, then, another chapter or two—for Miriam's sake.

Rose Hawthorne, the youngest of Nathaniel Hawthorne's

three children, born in 1851, just thirteen when her father died, redheaded Rose, known to the family as Rosebud, a woman who lived two lives, the first one sad, tormented, failed, the second one remarkable. I've often asked myself why Miriam chose to take on this project, but I think I'm beginning to understand now. Her last book was a life of John Donne, the crown prince of poets, the genius of geniuses, and then she embarks on an investigation of a woman who floundered through the world for forty-five years, a truculent and difficult person, a confessed "stranger to herself," trying her hand first at music, then at painting, and after getting nowhere with either of those pursuits, turning to poetry and short stories, some of which she managed to publish (no doubt on the strength of her father's name), but the work was heavy and awkward, mediocre at best—excluding one line from a poem quoted in Miriam's manuscript, which I like enormously: *As the weird world rolls on.*

Add to the public portrait the private facts of her elopement at twenty with young writer George Lathrop, a man of talent who never fulfilled his promise, the bitter conflicts of that marriage, the separation, the reconciliation, the death of their only child at the age of four, the final separation, Rose's protracted squabbles with her brother and sister, and one begins to think: why bother, why spend your time exploring the soul of such an insignificant, unhappy person? But then, in midlife, Rose underwent a transformation. She became a Catholic, took holy vows, and founded an order of nuns called the Servants of Relief for Incurable Cancer, devoting her last thirty years to caring for the terminally ill poor, a passionate defender of every person's right to die with dignity. *The weird world rolls on.* In other words, as with Donne, Rose Hawthorne's life was a story of conversion, and that must have been the attraction, the thing that sparked Miriam's interest in her. Why that should interest her is another question, but I believe it comes directly from her mother: a fundamental conviction that people have the power to change. That was Sonia's influence, not mine, and Miriam is probably a better person for it, but brilliant as my daughter is, there's also something naïve and fragile about her, and I wish to God she would learn that the rotten acts human beings commit against one another are not just aberrations—they're an essential part of who we are. She would suffer less that way. The world wouldn't collapse every time something bad happened to her, and she wouldn't be crying herself to sleep every other night.

I'm not going to pretend that divorce isn't a cruel business. Unspeakable suffering, crippling despair, demonic rage, and the constant cloud of sorrow in the head, which gradually turns into a kind of mourning, as if one were grieving a death. But Richard walked out on Miriam five years ago, and you'd think by now that she would have adjusted to her new circumstances, put herself back in circulation, attempted to reconfigure her life. But all her energy has gone into her teaching and writing, and whenever I bring up the subject of other men, she bristles. Luckily, Katya was already eighteen and off at college when the breakup happened, and she was old enough and strong enough to absorb the shock without going to pieces. Miriam had a much harder time of it when Sonia and I split up. She was just fifteen, a far more vulnerable age, and even though Sonia and I got back together nine years later, the damage had already been done. It's hard enough for grown-ups to live through a divorce, but it's worse for the kids. They're entirely powerless, and they bear the brunt of the pain.

Miriam and Richard made the same mistake that Sonia and I did: they married too young. In our case, we were both twenty-two—not such an uncommon occurrence back in 1957. But when Miriam and Richard walked down the aisle a quarter of a century later, she was the same age her mother had been. Richard was a little older, twenty-four or twenty-five, I think, but the world had changed by then, and they were little more than babies, two crackerjack baby students doing postgraduate work at Yale, and within a couple of years they had a baby of their own. Didn't Miriam understand that Richard might eventually grow restless? Didn't she realize that a forty-year-old professor standing in front of a room of female undergraduates could become entranced by those young bodies? It's the oldest story in the world, but the hardworking, loyal, high-strung Miriam wasn't paying attention. Not even with her own mother's story burned deeply in her mind—that awful moment when her wretch of a father, after eighteen years of marriage, ran off with a woman of twenty-six. I was forty then. Beware of men in their forties.

Why am I doing this? Why do I persist in traveling down these old, tired paths; why this compulsion to pick at old wounds and make myself bleed again? It would be impossible to exaggerate the contempt I sometimes feel for myself. I was supposed to be looking at Miriam's manuscript, but here I am staring at a crack in the wall and dredging up remnants from the past, broken things that can never be repaired. Give me my story. That's all I want now—my little story to keep the ghosts away. Before switching off the lamp, I turn at random to another page in the manuscript and fall upon this: the final two paragraphs of Rose's memoir of her father, written in 1896, describing the last time she ever saw him.

It seemed to me a terrible thing that one so peculiarly strong, sentient, luminous as my father should grow feebler and fainter, and finally ghostly still and white. Yet when his step was tottering and his frame that of a wraith, he was as dignified as in the days of greater pride, holding himself, in military self-command, even more erect than before. He did not omit to come in his very best black coat to the dinner-table, where the extremely prosaic fare had no effect on the distinction of the meal. He hated failure, dependence, and disorder, broken rules and weariness of discipline, as he hated cowardice. I cannot express how brave he seemed to me. The last time I saw him, he was leaving the house to take the journey for his health which led suddenly to the next world. My mother was to go to the station with him—she who, at the moment when it was said that he died, staggered and groaned, though so far from him, telling us that something seemed to be sapping all her strength; I could hardly bear to let my eyes rest upon her shrunken, suffering form on this day of farewell. My father certainly knew, what she vaguely felt, that he would never return.

Like a snow image of an unbending but old, old man, he stood for a moment gazing at me. My mother sobbed as she walked beside him to the carriage. We have missed him in the sunshine, in the storm, in the twilight, ever since.

I switch off, and once again I'm in the dark, engulfed by the endless, soothing dark. Somewhere in the distance, I hear the sounds of a truck driving down an empty country road. I listen to the air rushing in and out of my nostrils. According to the clock on the bedside table, which I checked before turning off the lamp, the time is twenty past twelve. Hours and hours until daybreak, the bulk of the night still in front of me. . . . Hawthorne didn't care. If the South wanted to secede from the country, he said, let them go and good riddance. The weird world, the battered world, the weird world rolling on as wars flame all around us: the chopped-off arms in Africa, the chopped-off heads in Iraq, and in my own head this other war, an imaginary war on home ground, America cracking apart, the noble experiment finally dead. My thoughts drift back to Wellington, and suddenly I can see Owen Brick again, sitting in one of the booths at the Pulaski Diner, watching Molly Wald wipe down the tables and counter as six o'clock approaches. Then they're outdoors, walking together in silence as she leads him toward her place, the sidewalks clogged with exhausted-looking men and women shuffling home from work, soldiers with rifles standing guard at the main intersections, a pinkish sky gloaming overhead. Brick has lost all confidence in Molly. Realizing that she can't be trusted, that no one can be trusted, he ducked into the men's room at the diner about twenty minutes before they left and transferred the envelope of fifty-dollar bills from the backpack to the right front pocket of his jeans. A smaller chance of being robbed that way, he felt, and when he goes to bed that night, he has every intention of keeping his pants on. In the men's room, he finally took the trouble to examine the money and was encouraged to see the face of Ulysses S. Grant engraved on the front of each bill. That proved to him that this America, this other America, which hasn't lived through September 11 or the war in Iraq, nevertheless has strong historical links to the America he knows. The question is: at what point did the two stories begin to diverge?

Molly, Brick says, breaking the silence ten minutes into their walk, do you mind if I ask you something?

It depends on what it is, she answers.

Have you ever heard of the Second World War?

The waitress lets out a short, ill-tempered grunt. What do you think I am? she says. A retard? Of course I've heard of it.

And what about Vietnam?

My grandfather was one of the first soldiers they shipped out.

If I said *the New York Yankees*, what would you say?

Come on, everybody knows that.

What would you say? Brick repeats.

With an exasperated sigh, Molly turns to him and announces in a sardonic voice: The New York Yankees? They're those girls who dance at Radio City Music Hall.

Very good. And the Rockettes are a baseball team, right?

Exactly.

Okay. One last question, and then I'll stop.

You're a real pain in the ass, you know that?

Sorry. I know you think I'm stupid, but it isn't my fault.

No, I guess not. You just happened to be born that way.

Who's the president?

President? What are you talking about? We don't have a president.

No? Then who's in charge of the government?

The prime minister, birdbrain. Jesus Christ, what planet do you come from?

I see. The independent states have a prime minister. But what about the Federals? Do they still have a president?

Of course.

What's his name?

Bush.

George W.?

That's right. George W. Bush.

Sticking to his word, Brick refrains from asking any more questions, and once again the two of them walk through the streets in silence. A couple of minutes later, Molly points to a four-story wood-frame building on a low-rent residential block lined with similar four-story wooden buildings, all of them in need of a paint job. 628 Cumberland Avenue. Here we are, she says, extracting a key from her purse and unlocking the front door, and then Brick follows her up two flights of wobbly stairs to the apartment she occupies with her unnamed boyfriend. It's a small but tidy flat, consisting of one bedroom, a living room, a kitchen, and a bathroom with a shower but no tub. Looking around the place, Brick is struck by the fact that there's no television or radio either. When he remarks on this to Molly, she tells him that all the transmission towers in the state were blown up in the first weeks of the war, and the government doesn't have enough money to rebuild them.

Maybe after the war is over, Brick says.

Yeah, maybe, Molly answers, sitting down on the living room sofa and lighting up a cigarette. But the thing is, nobody seems to care anymore. It was hard at first—*my God, no TV!*—but then you kind of get used to it, and after another year or two, you begin to like it. The stillness, I mean. No more voices shouting at you twenty-four hours a day. It's an old-fashioned sort of life now, I guess, the way things must have been a hundred years ago. You want news, you read the paper. You want to see a movie, you go to the theater. No more couch potatoes. I know a lot of people have died, and I know things are really tough out there, but maybe it's all been worth it. *Maybe.* Just maybe. If the war doesn't end soon, everything will turn to shit.

Brick is at a loss to explain it, but he realizes that Molly is no longer talking to him as if he were a dunce. How to account for this unexpected shift in tone? The fact that her job is done for the day and she's sitting comfortably in her apartment puffing on a cigarette? The fact that she's begun to feel sorry for him? Or, conversely, the fact that he's made her two hundred dollars richer and she's decided to stop poking fun at him? In any case, Brick thinks, a girl of many moods, perhaps not as crass as she seems to be, but not so terribly bright either. There are a hundred more questions he would like to ask her, but he decides not to push his luck.

Stubbing out her cigarette, Molly stands up and tells Brick that she's meeting her boyfriend for dinner across town in less than an hour. She walks over to a closet between the bedroom and the kitchen, pulls out two sheets, two blankets, and a pillow, then carries them into the living room and plops them down on the sofa.

There you are, she says. Bedding for your bed, which isn't a real bed. I hope it's not too lumpy.

I'm so tired, Brick answers, I could sleep on a pile of rocks.

If you get hungry, there's some stuff to eat in the kitchen. A can of soup, a loaf of bread, some sliced turkey. You can make yourself a sandwich.

How much?

What do you mean?

How much will it cost me?

Cut it out. I'm not going to charge you for a little food. You've already paid me enough.

And what about breakfast tomorrow morning?

Fine by me. We don't have a lot, though. Just coffee and toast.

Without waiting for Brick to answer, Molly rushes off to the bedroom to change her clothes. The door slams shut, and Brick begins making the bed that isn't a bed. When he's finished, he walks around the room looking for newspapers and magazines, hoping to find something that will tell him about the war, something that will give him a clue about where he is, some scrap of information that will help him understand a little more about the bewildering country he's landed in. But there are no magazines or newspapers in the living room—only a small bookcase crammed with paperback mysteries and thrillers, which he has no desire to read.

He returns to the sofa, sits down, leans his head against the upholstered backrest, and promptly dozes off.

When he opens his eyes thirty minutes later, the bedroom door is ajar, and Molly is gone.

He searches the bedroom for newspapers and magazines—with no success.

Then he walks into the kitchen to heat up a can of vegetable soup and fix himself a turkey sandwich. He notes that the brands are familiar to him: Progresso, Boar's Head, Arnold's. Washing the dishes after eating this *prosaic fare,* he looks at the white telephone attached to the wall and wonders what would happen if he tried to call Flora.

He takes the receiver off the hook, dials the number of his apartment in Jackson Heights, and quickly learns the answer. The number is out of service.

He dries the dishes and puts them back in the cupboard. Then, after turning off the kitchen light, he walks into the living room and thinks about Flora, his dark-haired Argentinian bedmate, his little spitfire, his wife of the past three years. What she must be going through, he says to himself.

He turns off the lights in the living room. He undoes the laces of his shoes. He crawls under the covers. He falls asleep.

Some hours later, he is woken by the sound of a key entering the lock of the apartment door. Keeping his eyes shut, Brick listens to the scraping of footsteps, the low-pitched rumble of a male voice, the sharper, more metallic voice of his female companion, no doubt Molly, yes, indeed Molly, who addresses the man as Duke, and then a light goes on, which registers as a

crimson glare undulating on the surface of his eyelids. They
both sound a bit drunk, and as the light goes off and they clomp
into the bedroom—where another light immediately goes on—
Brick gathers that they're quarreling about something. Before
the door shuts, he catches the words *don't like it, two hundred,*
risky, harmless, and understands that he is the subject of the
argument and that Duke is none too happy about his presence
in the house.

Managing to fall asleep again after the ruckus in the bedroom dies down (sounds of copulation: a grunting Duke, a yelp-
ing Molly, squeaking mattress and springs), Brick then floats
off into a complex dream about Flora. At first, he's talking to
her on the telephone. It isn't Flora's voice, however, with its thick,
rolling *r*'s and singsong lilt, but the voice of Virginia Blaine,
and Virginia/Flora is begging him to fly—not walk, but fly—to
a certain corner in Buffalo, New York, where she'll be standing
naked under a transparent raincoat, holding a red umbrella in
one hand and a white tulip in the other. Brick begins to weep,
telling her that he doesn't know how to fly, at which point Vir-
ginia/Flora shouts angrily into the phone that she never wants
to see him again and hangs up. Stunned by her vehemence,
Brick shakes his head and mutters to himself: But I'm not in
Buffalo today, I'm in Worcester, Massachusetts. Then he's walking down a street in Jackson Heights, dressed in his Great Zavello costume with the long black cape, looking for his apartment
building. But the building is gone, and in its place there is a
one-story wooden cottage with a sign above the door that reads:

ALL-AMERICAN DENTAL CLINIC. He walks in, and there's Flora, the real Flora, dressed in a white nurse's uniform. I'm so glad you could come, Mr. Brick, she says, apparently not recognizing him, and then she's leading him into an office and gesturing for him to sit down in a dental chair. It's such a shame, she says, picking up a pair of large, gleaming pliers, it's such a shame, but it looks like we're going to have to pull out all your teeth. All of them? Brick asks, suddenly terrified. Yes, Flora answers, all of them. But don't worry. After we're done, the doctor will give you a new face.

The dream stops there. Someone is shaking Brick's shoulder and barking words at him in a loud voice, and as the groggy dreamer at last opens his eyes, he sees a large man with broad shoulders and muscular arms towering above him. One of those bodybuilder types, Brick thinks, Duke the boyfriend, the guy with the bad temper, dressed in a tight-fitting black T-shirt and blue boxer shorts, telling him to get the fuck out of the apartment.

I paid good money— Brick begins.

For one night, Duke shouts. The night's up now, and out you go.

Just a minute, just a minute, Brick says, raising his right hand as a sign of his peaceful intentions. Molly promised me breakfast. Coffee and toast. Just let me have some coffee, and then I'll be on my way.

No coffee. No toast. No nothing.

What if I paid you for it? A little extra, I mean.

Don't you understand English?

And with those words, Duke bends down, grabs hold of Brick's sweater, and yanks him to his feet. Now that he's standing, Brick has a clear view of the bedroom door, and the moment he catches sight of it, out comes Molly, securing the sash of her bathrobe and then running her hands through her hair.

Stop it, she says to Duke. You don't have to play rough.

Pipe down, he answers. You made this mess, and now I'm cleaning it up.

Molly shrugs, then looks at Brick with a small, apologetic smile. Sorry, she says. I guess you'd better be going now.

Slipping his feet into his shoes without bothering to tie the laces, then retrieving his leather jacket from the foot of the sofa and putting it on, Brick says to her: I don't get it. I give you all that money, and now you throw me out. It doesn't make sense.

Rather than answer him, Molly looks down at the floor and shrugs again. That apathetic gesture carries all the force of a defection, a betrayal. With no ally to stand up for him, Brick decides to leave without further protest. He bends down and picks up the green backpack from the floor, but no sooner does he turn to go than Duke snatches it out of his hands.

What's this? he asks.

My stuff, Brick says. Obviously.

Your stuff? Duke replies. I don't think so, funny man.

What are you talking about?

It's mine now.

Yours? You can't do that. Everything I own is in there.

Then try and get it back.

Brick understands that Duke is itching for a fight—and that

the bag is merely a pretext. He also knows that if he tangles with Molly's boyfriend, there is every chance he will be ripped apart. Or so his mind tells him the instant he hears Duke issue his challenge, but Brick is no longer thinking with his mind, for the outrage surging through him has overwhelmed all reason, and if he allows this bully to get his way without offering some form of resistance, he will lose whatever respect he still has for himself. So Brick takes his stand, unexpectedly wrenching the bag out of Duke's grasp, and immediately after that the drubbing begins, an assault so one-sided and short-lived that the big man floors Brick with just three blows: a left to the gut, a right to the face, and a knee to the balls. Pain floods into every corner of the magician's body, and as he rolls around on the tattered rug gasping for breath, one hand clutching his stomach and the other clamped over his scrotum, he sees blood dripping from the wound that has opened on his cheek, and then, lying in the gathering puddle of red, a fragment of a tooth—the lower half of one of his left incisors. He is only dimly aware of Molly's screams, which sound as if they are coming from ten blocks away. A moment after that, he is aware of nothing.

When he picks up the thread of his own story, Brick finds himself on his feet, maneuvering his body down the stairs as he clings to the banister with both hands, slowly descending to the ground floor, a single step at a time. The backpack is gone, which means that the gun and the bullets are also gone, not to speak of everything else that was in the bag, but as Brick pauses to reach into the right front pocket of his jeans, the trace of a smile flits across his bruised mouth—the bitter smile of the not quite vanquished. The money is still there. No longer the thousand that Tobak gave him the previous morning, but five hundred and sixty-five dollars is better than nothing, he thinks, more than enough to get him a room somewhere and a bite to eat. That's as far as his thoughts can take him now. To hide, to wash the blood off his face, to fill his stomach if and when his appetite returns.

However modest these plans might be, they are thwarted the moment he leaves the building and steps onto the sidewalk. Directly in front of him, standing with her arms folded and her back resting against the door of a military jeep, Virginia Blaine is eyeing Brick with a disgusted look on her face.

No monkey business, she says. You promised me.

Virginia, Brick replies, doing his best to play dumb, what are you doing here?

Ignoring his remark, the former queen of Miss Blunt's geometry class shakes her head and snaps back: We were supposed to meet at five-thirty yesterday afternoon. You stood me up.

Something happened, and I had to leave at the last minute.

You mean *I* happened, and you ran away.

Unable to think of an answer, Brick says nothing.

You don't look so good, Owen, Virginia continues.

No, I don't suppose I do. I just got the shit kicked out of me.

You should watch the company you keep. That Rothstein's a tough fellow.

Who's Rothstein?

Duke. Molly's boyfriend.

You know him?

He works with us. He's one of our best men.

He's an animal. A sadistic creep.

It was all an act, Owen. To teach you a lesson.

Oh? Brick snorts, indignation rising within him. And what lesson is that? The son of a bitch knocked out one of my teeth.

Just be glad it wasn't all of them.

Very nice, Brick mumbles, with a sarcastic edge to his voice, and then, all of a sudden, the final chapter of the dream comes rushing back to him: the All-American Dental Clinic, Flora and the pliers, the new face. Well, Brick thinks, as he touches the wound on his cheek, I got my new face, didn't I? Thanks to Rothstein's fist.

You can't win, Virginia says. Everywhere you go, someone is watching you. You'll never get away from us.

According to you, Brick says, not yet willing to give in, but knowing in his heart that Virginia is right.

Ergo, my dear Owen, this little interlude of dawdling and hide-and-seek has come to an end. Hop into the jeep. It's time for you to talk to Frisk.

No dice, Virginia. I can't hop, and I can't run, and I can't go anywhere yet. My face is bleeding, my balls are on fire, and every muscle in my stomach is torn to shreds. I have to patch myself up first. Then I'll talk to your man. But at least let me take a goddamn bath.

For the first time since the conversation began, Virginia smiles. Poor baby, she says, simpering with compassion, but whether this new concern for him is real or false is far from clear to Brick.

Are you with me or not? he asks.

Climb in, she says, patting the door of the jeep. Of course I'm with you. I'll take you back to my house, and we'll fix you up there. It's still early. Lou can wait a little while. As long as you see him before dark, we'll be okay.

With that reassurance, Brick hobbles over to the jeep and hoists his sorry carcass into the passenger seat as Virginia slips in behind the wheel. Once she starts the engine, she launches into a long, meandering account of the civil war, no doubt feeling an obligation to fill him in on the historical background of the conflict, but the problem is that Brick is in no condition to follow what she's saying, and as they lurch along over the pot-holed streets of Wellington, every jolt and bump sends a fresh attack of pain coursing through his body. To compound the trouble, the noise of the engine is so loud that it nearly swallows up Virginia's voice, and in order to hear anything at all, Brick must strain himself to the limit of his powers, which are diminished at best, if not entirely obliterated. Clutching the bottom of the seat with his two hands, pressing the soles of his shoes onto the floor to brace himself against the next bounce of the chassis, he keeps his eyes shut throughout the twenty-minute drive, and from the ten thousand facts that come tumbling down on him between Molly's apartment and Virginia's house, this is what he manages to retain:

The election of 2000 . . . just after the Supreme Court decision . . . protests . . . riots in the major cities . . . a movement to abolish the Electoral College . . . defeat of the bill in Congress . . . a new movement . . . led by the mayor and borough presidents of New York City . . . secession . . . passed by the state legislature in 2003 . . . Federal troops attack . . . Albany, Buffalo, Syracuse, Rochester . . . New York City bombed, eighty thousand dead . . . but the movement grows . . . in 2004, Maine, New Hampshire, Vermont, Massachusetts, Connecticut, New Jersey, and Pennsylvania join New York in the Independent States of America . . . later that year, California, Oregon, and Washington break off to form their own republic, Pacifica . . . in 2005, Ohio, Michigan, Illinois, Wisconsin, and Minnesota join the Independent States . . . the European Union recognizes the existence of the new country . . . diplomatic relations are established . . . then Mexico . . . then the countries of Central and South America . . . Russia follows, then Japan. . . . Meanwhile, the fighting continues, often horrendous, the toll of casualties steadily mounting . . . U.N. resolutions ignored by the Federals, but until now no nuclear weapons, which would mean death to everyone on both sides. . . . Foreign policy: no meddling anywhere. . . . Domestic policy: universal health insurance, no more oil, no more cars or planes, a fourfold increase in teachers' salaries (to attract the brightest students to the profession), strict gun control, free education and job training for the poor . . . all in the realm of fantasy for the moment, a dream of the future, since the war drags on, and the state of emergency is still in force.

The jeep slows down and gradually comes to a stop. As Virginia turns off the ignition, Brick opens his eyes and discovers that he is no longer in the heart of Wellington. They have come to a wealthy suburban street of large Tudor houses with pristine front lawns, tulip beds, forsythia and rhododendron bushes, the myriad trappings of the good life. As he climbs out of the jeep and looks down the block, however, he notices that several houses are standing in ruins: broken windows, charred walls, gaping holes in the facades, abandoned husks where people once lived. Brick assumes that the neighborhood was shelled during the war, but he doesn't ask any questions about it. Instead, pointing to the house they are about to enter, he blandly remarks: This is quite a place, Virginia. You seem to have done pretty well for yourself.

My husband was a corporate lawyer, she says flatly, in no mood to talk about the past. He made a lot of money.

Virginia opens the door with a key, and they walk into the house . . .

A warm bath, lying in water up to his neck for twenty minutes, thirty minutes, inert, tranquil, alone. After which he puts on the white terry-cloth robe of Virginia's dead husband, walks into the bedroom, and sits down in a chair as Virginia patiently applies an antibacterial astringent to the gash on his cheek and then covers the wound with a small bandage. Brick is beginning to feel somewhat better. The wonders of water, he says to himself, realizing that the pain in his stomach and nether parts has all but vanished. His cheek still smarts, but eventually that discomfort will abate as well. As for the broken tooth, there is nothing to be done until he can visit a dentist and have a cap put on it, but he doubts that will happen anytime soon. For now (as confirmed when he studied his face in the bathroom mirror), the effect is altogether repulsive. A few centimeters of missing enamel and he looks like a broken-down bum, a pea-brained yokel. Fortunately, the gap is visible only when he smiles, and in Brick's present state, the last thing he wants to do is smile. Unless the nightmare ends, he thinks, there's a good chance he'll never smile again for the rest of his life.

Twenty minutes later, now dressed and sitting in the kitchen with Virginia—who has prepared him toast and coffee, the same minimal breakfast that nearly cost him his life earlier that morning—Brick is answering the tenth question she has asked him about Flora. He finds her curiosity puzzling. If she is the person responsible for bringing him to this place, then it would seem likely that she already knows everything about him, including his marriage to Flora. But Virginia is insatiable, and now Brick begins to wonder if all this questioning isn't simply a ploy to hold him in the house, to make him lose track of the time so that he won't try to run off again before Frisk shows up. He wants to run, that's certain, but after the long soak in the tub and the terry-cloth robe and the gentleness of her fingers as she put the bandage on his face, something in him has begun to soften toward Virginia, and he can feel the old flames of his adolescence slowly igniting again.

I met her in Manhattan, he says. About three and a half years ago. A fancy birthday party for a kid on the Upper East Side. I was the magician, and she was one of the caterers.

Is she beautiful, Owen?

To me she is. Not beautiful in the way you are, Virginia, with your incredible face and long body. Flora's little, not even five-four, just a slip of a thing, really, but she has these big burning eyes and all this tangly dark hair and the best laugh I've ever heard.

Do you love her?

Of course.

And she loves you?

Yes. Most of the time, anyway. Flora has a huge temper, and she can fly off into these maniacal tirades. Whenever we fight, I begin to think the only reason she married me was because she wanted her American citizenship. But it doesn't happen very often. Nine days out of ten, we're good together. We really are.

What about babies?

They're on the agenda. We started trying a couple of months ago.

Don't give up. That was my mistake. I waited too long, and now look at me. No husband, no children, nothing.

You're still young. You're still the prettiest girl on the block. Someone else will come along, I'm sure of it.

Before Virginia can answer him, the doorbell rings. She stands up, muttering *Shit* under her breath as if she means it, as if she honestly resents the intrusion, but Brick knows that he's cornered now, and any chance of escape is gone. Before leaving the kitchen, Virginia turns to him and says: I called while you were taking your bath. I told him to come between four and five, but I guess he couldn't wait. I'm sorry, Owen. I wanted to have those hours with you and charm your pants off. I really did. I wanted to fuck your brains out. Just remember that when you go back.

Back? You mean I'm going back?

Lou will explain. That's his job. I'm just a personnel officer, a little cog in a big machine.

Lou Frisk turns out to be a dour-looking man in his early fifties, somewhat on the short side, with narrow shoulders, wire-rimmed glasses, and the marred skin of someone who once suffered from acne. He's dressed in a green V-neck sweater with a white shirt and plaid tie, and in his left hand he's carrying a black satchel that resembles a doctor's bag. The moment he enters the kitchen, he puts down the bag and says: You've been avoiding me, Corporal.

I'm not a corporal, Brick answers. You know that. I've never been a soldier in my life.

Not in your world, Frisk says, but in this world you're a corporal in the Massachusetts Seventh, a member of the armed forces of the Independent States of America.

Putting his head in his hands, Brick groans softly as another element of the dream comes back to him: Worcester, Massachusetts. He looks up, watches Frisk settle into a chair across from him at the table, and says: I'm in Massachusetts, then. Is that what you're telling me?

Wellington, Massachusetts, Frisk nods. Formerly known as Worcester.

Brick pounds his fist on the table, finally giving vent to the rage that has been building inside him. I don't like this! he shouts. Someone's inside my head. Not even my dreams belong to me. My whole life has been stolen. Then, turning to Frisk and looking him directly in the eye, he yells at the top of his voice: Who's doing this to me?

Take it easy, Frisk says, patting Brick on the hand. You have every right to be confused. That's why I'm here. I'm the one who explains it to you, who sets things straight. We don't want you to suffer. If you'd come to me when you were supposed to, you never would have had that dream. Do you understand what I'm trying to tell you?

Not really, Brick says, in a more subdued voice.

Through the walls of the house, he catches the faint sound of the jeep's engine being turned on, and then the distant squeal of shifting gears as Virginia drives away.

Virginia? he asks.

What about her?

She just left, didn't she?

She has a lot of work to do, and our business doesn't concern her.

She didn't even say good-bye, Brick adds, reluctant to drop the matter. There is hurt in his voice, as if he can't quite believe that she would ditch him in such an offhanded way.

Forget Virginia, Frisk says. We have more important things to talk about.

She said I was going back. Is that true?

Yes. But first I have to tell you why. Listen carefully, Brick, and then give me an honest answer. Putting his arms on the table, Frisk leans forward and says: Are we in the real world or not?

How should I know? Everything looks real. Everything sounds real. I'm sitting here in my own body, but at the same time I can't be here, can I? I belong somewhere else.

You're here, all right. And you belong somewhere else.

It can't be both. It has to be one or the other.

Is the name Giordano Bruno familiar to you?

No. Never heard of him.

A sixteenth-century Italian philosopher. He argued that if God is infinite, and if the powers of God are infinite, then there must be an infinite number of worlds.

I suppose that makes sense. Assuming you believe in God.

He was burned at the stake for that idea. But that doesn't mean he was wrong, does it?

Why ask me? I don't know the first thing about any of this. How can I have an opinion about something I don't understand?

Until you woke up in that hole the other day, your entire life had been spent in one world. But how could you be sure it was the only world?

Because . . . because it was the only world I ever knew.

But now you know another world. What does that suggest to you, Brick?

I don't follow.

There's no single reality, Corporal. There are many realities. There's no single world. There are many worlds, and they all run parallel to one another, worlds and anti-worlds, worlds and shadow-worlds, and each world is dreamed or imagined or written by someone in another world. Each world is the creation of a mind.

You're beginning to sound like Tobak. He said the war was in one man's head, and if that man was eliminated, the war would stop. That's about the most asinine thing I've ever heard.

Tobak might not be the brightest soldier in the army, but he was telling you the truth.

If you want me to believe a crazy thing like that, you'll have to prove it to me first.

All right, Frisk says, slapping his palms on the table, what about this? Without another word, he reaches under his sweater with his right hand and pulls out a three-by-five photograph from his shirt pocket. This is the culprit, he says, sliding the photo across the table to Brick.

Brick does no more than glance at the picture. It's a color snapshot of a man in his late sixties or early seventies sitting in a wheelchair in front of a white country house. A perfectly sympathetic-looking man, Brick notes, with spiky gray hair and a weathered face.

This doesn't prove anything, he says, thrusting the photo back at Frisk. It's just a man. Any man. For all I know, he could be your uncle.

His name is August Brill, Frisk begins, but Brick cuts him off before he can say anything else.

Not according to Tobak. He said his name was Blake.

Blank.

Whatever.

Tobak isn't up on the latest intelligence reports. For a long time, Blank was our leading suspect, but then we crossed him off the list. Brill is the one. We're sure of that now.

Then show me the story. Reach into that bag of yours and pull out his manuscript and point to a sentence where my name is mentioned.

That's the problem. Brill doesn't write anything down. He's telling himself the story in his head.

How can you possibly know that?

A military secret. But we know, Corporal. Trust me.

Bullshit.

You want to go back, don't you? Well, this is the only way. If you don't accept the job, you'll be stuck here forever.

All right. Just for the sake of argument, imagine I shoot this man . . . this Brill. Then what happens? If he created your world, then the moment he's dead, you won't exist anymore.

He didn't invent this world. He only invented the war. And he invented you, Brick. Don't you understand that? This is your story, not ours. The old man invented you in order to kill him.

So now it's a suicide.

In a roundabout way, yes.

Once again, Brick puts his head in his hands and begins to moan. It's all too much for him, and after struggling to hold his ground against Frisk's demented assertions, he can feel his mind dissolving, whirling madly through a universe of disconnected thoughts and amorphous dreads. Only one thing is clear to him: he wants to go back. He wants to be with Flora again and return to his old life. In order to do that, he must accept a command to murder someone he has never met, a total stranger. He will have to accept, but once he gets to the other side, what is to prevent him from refusing to carry out the job?

Still looking down at the table, he forces the words out of his mouth: Tell me something about the man.

Ah, that's better, Frisk says. Coming to our senses at last.

Don't patronize me, Frisk. Just tell me what I need to know.

A retired book critic, seventy-two years old, living outside Brattleboro, Vermont, with his forty-seven-year-old daughter and twenty-three-year-old granddaughter. His wife died last year. The daughter's husband left her five years ago. The granddaughter's boyfriend was killed. It's a house of grieving, wounded souls, and every night Brill lies awake in the dark, trying not to think about his past, making up stories about other worlds.

Why is he in a wheelchair?

A car accident. His left leg was shattered. They nearly had to amputate.

And if I agree to kill this man, you'll send me back.

That's the bargain. But don't try to wriggle out of it, Brick. If you break your promise, we'll come after you. Two bullets. One for you and one for Flora. Bang, bang. No more you. No more her.

But if you get rid of me, the war goes on.

Not necessarily. It's still just a hypothesis at this point, but some of us think that getting rid of you would produce the same result as eliminating Brill. The story would end, and the war would be over. Don't think we wouldn't be willing to take the risk.

How do I get back?

In your sleep.

But I've already gone to sleep here. Twice. And both times I woke up in the same place.

That's normal sleep. What I'm talking about is pharmacologically induced sleep. You'll be given an injection. The effect is similar to anesthesia—when they put a person under before surgery. The black void of oblivion, a nothingness as deep and dark as death.

Sounds like fun, Brick says, so unnerved by what is facing him that he can't help cracking a feeble joke.

Are you willing to give it a shot, Corporal?

Do I have a choice?

I feel a cough gathering in my chest, a faint rattle of phlegm buried deep in my bronchia, and before I can suppress it, the detonation comes blasting through my throat. Hack it up, propel the gunk northward, dislodge the slimy leftovers trapped in the tubes, but one try isn't enough, nor two, nor three, and here I am in a full-blown spasm, my whole body convulsing from the onslaught. It's my own fault. I stopped smoking fifteen years ago, but now that Katya is in the house with her ubiquitous American Spirits, I've begun to lapse into the old, dirty pleasures, cadging butts off her while we plunge through the entire corpus of world cinema, side by side on the sofa, blowing smoke in tandem, two locomotives chugging away from the loathsome, intolerable world, but without regret, I might add, without a second thought or single pang of remorse. It's the companionship that counts, the conspiratorial bond, the fuck-you solidarity of the damned.

Thinking about the films again, I realize that I have another example to add to Katya's list. I must remember to tell her first thing tomorrow morning—in the dining room over breakfast— since it's bound to please her, and if I can manage to coax a smile out of that glum face of hers, I'll consider it a worthy accomplishment.

The watch at the end of *Tokyo Story*. We saw the film a few days ago, the second time for both of us, but my first viewing goes decades back, the late sixties or early seventies, and other than remembering that I'd liked it, most of the story had vanished from my mind. Ozu, 1953, eight years after the Japanese defeat. A slow, stately film that tells the simplest of stories, but executed with such elegance and depth of feeling that I had tears in my eyes at the end. Some films are as good as books, as good as the best books (yes, Katya, I'll grant you that), and this is one of them, no question about it, a work as subtle and moving as a Tolstoy novella.

An aging couple travels to Tokyo to visit their grown-up children: a struggling doctor with a wife and children of his own, a married hairdresser who runs a beauty salon, and a daughter-in-law who was married to another son killed in the war, a young widow who lives alone and works in an office. From the beginning, it's clear that the son and daughter consider the presence of their old parents something of a burden, an inconvenience. They're busy with their jobs, with their families, and they don't have time to take proper care of them. Only the daughter-in-law goes out of her way to show them any kindness. Eventually, the parents leave Tokyo and return to the place where they live (never mentioned, I believe, or else I blinked and missed it), and some weeks after that, without warning, without any premonitory illness, the mother dies. The action of the film then shifts to the family house in that unnamed city or town. The

grown-up children from Tokyo come for the funeral, along with
the daughter-in-law, Norika or Noriko, I can't remember, but
let's say Noriko and stick with that. Then a second son shows up
from somewhere else, and finally there's the youngest child of
the group, who still lives at home, a woman in her early twenties
who works as an elementary school teacher. One quickly understands that not only does she adore and admire Noriko, she
prefers her to her own siblings. After the funeral, the family is
sitting around a table eating lunch, and once again the son and
daughter from Tokyo are busy, busy, busy, too wrapped up in
their own preoccupations to offer their father much support.
They begin looking at their watches and decide to return to Tokyo on the night express. The second brother decides to leave
as well. There is nothing overtly cruel about their behavior—
this should be emphasized; it's in fact the essential point Ozu is
making. They're merely distracted, caught up in the business of
their own lives, and other responsibilities are pulling them
away. But the gentle Noriko stays on, not wanting to abandon
her grieving father-in-law (a walled-off, stone-faced grief, to be
sure, but grief for all that), and on the last morning of her extended visit, she and the schoolteacher daughter have breakfast
together.

The girl is still irritated by the hasty departure of her brothers and sister. She says they should have stayed longer and calls
them selfish, but Noriko defends what they did (even if she
would never do it herself), explaining that all children drift
away from their parents in the end, that they have their own
lives to look after. The girl insists that she'll never be like that.

What's the point of a family if you act that way? she says. Noriko reiterates her previous comment, trying to comfort the girl by telling her that these things happen to children, that they can't be helped. A long pause follows, and then the girl looks at her sister-in-law and says: Life is disappointing, isn't it? Noriko looks back at the girl, and with a distant expression on her face, she answers: Yes, it is.

The teacher goes off to work, and Noriko begins straightening up the house (reminding me of the women in the other films Katya talked about tonight), and then comes the scene with the watch, the moment the entire film has been building up to. The old man walks into the house from the garden, and Noriko tells him she's leaving on the afternoon train. They sit down and talk, and if I can more or less remember the gist and flow of their conversation, it's because I asked Katya to play the scene again after the movie was finished. I was that impressed by it, and I wanted to study the dialogue more closely to see how Ozu managed to pull it off.

The old man begins by thanking her for everything she's done, but Noriko shakes her head and says she hasn't done anything. The old man presses on, telling her that she's been a great help and that his wife had talked to him about how kind she'd been to her. Again, Noriko resists the compliment, shrugging off her actions as unimportant, negligible. Not to be deterred, the old man says that his wife told him that being with Noriko was the happiest time she had in Tokyo. She was so worried about your future, he continues. You can't go on like this. You have to get married again. Forget about X (his son, her husband). He's dead.

Noriko is too upset to respond, but the old man isn't about to give up and let the conversation end. Referring to his wife again, he adds: She said you were the nicest woman she'd ever met. Noriko holds her ground, claiming that his wife overestimated her, but the old man bluntly tells her that she's wrong. Noriko is beginning to grow unhinged. I'm not the nice woman you think I am, she says. Really, I'm quite selfish. And then she explains that she isn't always thinking about the old man's son, that days go by and he doesn't even cross her mind once. After a little pause, she confesses how lonely she is and how, when she can't sleep at night, she lies in bed wondering what will become of her. My heart seems to be waiting for something, she says. I'm selfish.

OLD MAN: No, you're not.

NORIKO: Yes. I am.

OLD MAN: You're a good woman. An honest woman.

NORIKO: Not at all.

At that point, Noriko finally breaks down and begins to cry, sobbing into her hands as the floodgates open—this young woman who has suffered in silence for so long, this good woman who refuses to believe she's good, for only the good doubt their own goodness, which is what makes them good in the first place. The bad know they are good, but the good know nothing. They spend their lives forgiving others, but they can't forgive themselves.

The old man stands up, and a few seconds later he returns with the watch, an old-fashioned timepiece with a metal cover protecting the face. It belonged to his wife, he tells Noriko, and he wants her to have it. Accept it for her sake, he says. I'm sure she'd be glad.

Moved by the gesture, Noriko thanks him as the tears continue to roll down her cheeks. The old man studies her with a thoughtful look on his face, but those thoughts are impenetrable to us, since all his emotions are hidden behind a mask of somber neutrality. Watching Noriko cry, he then makes a simple declaration, delivering his words in such a forthright, unsentimental manner that they cause her to collapse in a fresh outburst of sobbing—prolonged, wrenching sobs, a cry of misery so deep and painful, it's as if the innermost core of her self has been cracked open.

I want you to be happy, the old man says.

One brief sentence, and Noriko falls apart, crushed by the weight of her own life. *I want you to be happy.* As she goes on crying, the father-in-law makes one more comment before the scene ends. It's strange, he says, almost in disbelief. We have children of our own, and yet you're the one who's done the most for us.

Cut to the school. We hear children singing, and a moment later we are in the daughter's classroom. The sound of a train is heard in the distance. The young woman looks at her watch and then walks to the window. A train roars by: the afternoon express, carrying her beloved sister-in-law back to Tokyo.

Cut to the train itself—and the thunderous noise of the wheels as they charge along the tracks. We are hurtling forward into the future.

A few moments after that, we are inside one of the carriages.

me as 4-F. No wars, then, but the time I came closest to something that resembled one, I happened to be with Betty and her second husband, Gilbert Ross. It was 1967, exactly forty years ago this summer, and the three of us were having dinner together on the Upper East Side, Lexington Avenue I think it was, Sixty-sixth or Sixty-seventh Street, in a long-gone Chinese restaurant called Sun Luck. Sonia had gone off to France to visit her parents outside Lyon with the seven-year-old Miriam. I was supposed to join them later, but for the time being I was holed up in our shoe box of an apartment off Riverside Drive, sweating out a long piece for *Harper's* on recent American poetry and fiction inspired by the Vietnam war—with no air conditioner, just a cheap plastic fan, scribbling and typing in my underwear as my pores gushed through another New York heat wave. Money was tight for us back then, but Betty was seven years older than I was and living comfortably, as they say, and therefore she was in a position to invite her kid brother out for a free dinner every now and then. After a bad first marriage that had lasted too long, she had married Gil about three years earlier. A wise choice, I felt—or at least it looked that way at the time. Gil earned his money as a labor lawyer and strike mediator, but he had also joined the Newark city government as corporation counsel in the early sixties, and when he and my sister came to New York that night forty years ago, he was driving a city car, which was equipped with a two-way radio. I can't remember a thing about the dinner itself, but when we walked back to the car and Gil started up the engine to drive me home, frantic voices came pouring through the radio—police calls, I presume, reporting that the Central Ward of Newark was in chaos. Without bothering to go uptown to drop me at my apartment, Gil headed straight for the Lincoln Tunnel, and that was how I came to witness one of the worst race riots in American history. More than twenty people killed, more than seven hundred people injured, more than fifteen hundred people arrested, more than ten million dollars in property damage. I remember these numbers because when Katya was in high school a few years ago, she wrote a paper on racism for her American history class, and she interviewed me about the riot. Odd that those figures should have stuck, but with so many other things slipping away from me now, I cling to them as proof that I'm not quite finished.

Driving into Newark that night was like entering one of the lower circles of hell. Buildings in flames, hordes of men running wildly through the streets, the noise of shattering glass as one store window after another was broken, the noise of sirens, the noise of gunshots. Gil drove to City Hall, and once the three of us were inside the building, we went directly to the mayor's office. Sitting at his desk was Hugh Addonizio, a bald, bulging, pear-shaped man in his mid-fifties, ex–war hero, six-time congressman, in his second term as mayor, and the big man was utterly lost, sitting at his desk with tears pouring down his face. What am I going to do? he said, looking up at Gil. What the hell am I going to do?

An indelible picture, undimmed after all these years: the sight of that pathetic figure paralyzed by the pressure of events, a man gone rigid with despair as the city exploded around him.

Meanwhile, Gil calmly went about his business, calling the governor in Trenton, calling the chief of police, doing his best to get a grip on the situation. At one point, he and I left the room and went downstairs to the jail on the bottom floor of the building. The cells were crammed with prisoners, every one of them a black man, and at least half of them stood there with their clothes torn, blood trickling from their heads, their faces swollen. It wasn't difficult to guess what had caused these wounds, but Gil asked the question anyway. Man by man, the answer never varied: each one had been beaten by the cops.

Not long after we returned to the mayor's office, in walked a member of the New Jersey State Police, a certain Colonel Brand or Brandt, a man of around forty with a razor-sharp crew cut, a square, clenched jaw, and the hard eyes of a marine about to embark on a commando mission. He shook hands with Addonizio, sat down in a chair, and then pronounced these words: We're going to hunt down every black bastard in this city. I probably shouldn't have been shocked, but I was. Not by the statement, perhaps, but by the chilling contempt of the voice that uttered it. Gil told him not to use that kind of language, but the colonel merely sighed and shook his head, dismissing my brother-in-law's remark as if he considered him to be an ignorant fool.

That was my war. Not a real war, perhaps, but once you witness violence on that scale, it isn't difficult to imagine something worse, and once your mind is capable of doing that, you understand that the worst possibilities of the imagination are the country you live in. Just think it, and chances are it will happen.

That fall, when Gil was put in the untenable position of having to defend the city of Newark against scores of lawsuits from shop-keepers whose businesses had been destroyed in the riot, he quit his post and never worked in government again. Fifteen years later, two months short of his fifty-third birthday, he was dead.

I want to think about Betty, but in order to do that I have to think about Gil, and to think about Gil I have to go back to the beginning. And yet, how much do I know? Not a lot, finally, no more than a few pertinent facts, gleaned from stories he and Betty told me. The first of three children born to a Newark sa-loonkeeper who supposedly could have passed as Babe Ruth's double. At some point, Dutch Schultz muscled in on Gil's father and stole the business, how or why I can't say, and a few years after that his father dropped dead of a heart attack. Gil was eleven at the time, and since his father died broke, the only thing he inherited from him was chronic high blood pressure and heart disease—which was first diagnosed at age eighteen and then blossomed into a full-blown coronary when he was just thirty-four, followed by another one two years later. Gil was a tall, powerful man, but he spent his whole life with a death sentence circulating in his veins.

His mother remarried when he was thirteen, and while his stepfather had no objections to raising the two younger kids, he wanted no part of Gil and kicked him out of the house—with the mother's consent. Talk about the unimaginable: to be exiled by your own mother and sent off to live with relatives in Florida for the rest of your childhood.

After high school, he came back north and started college at NYU, strapped for money, forced to work several part-time jobs to keep himself afloat. Once, when he was reminiscing about how hard up he was in those days, he described how he used to go to Ratner's, the old Jewish dairy restaurant on the Lower East Side, sit down at a table, and tell the waiter that he was expecting his girlfriend to show up at any minute. One of the chief lures of the place was the celebrated Ratner's dinner roll. The moment you took your seat, a waiter would come over and plunk down a basket of those rolls in front of you, accompanied by an ample supply of butter. Roll by buttered roll, Gil would eat his way through the basket, glancing at his watch from time to time, pretending to be upset by the lateness of his nonexistent girlfriend. Once the first basket was empty, it would automatically be replaced by a second, and then the second by a third. Finally, the girlfriend would fail to appear, and Gil would leave the restaurant with a disappointed look on his face. After a while, the waiters caught on to the trick, but not before Gil achieved a personal record of twenty-seven free rolls consumed at a single sitting.

Law school, followed by the start of a successful practice and a growing involvement with the Democratic Party. Idealistic, left-wing liberalism, a supporter of Stevenson for the 1960 presidential nomination, Eleanor Roosevelt's escort at the convention in Atlantic City, and later a photograph (which I've owned since Betty's death) of Gil shaking hands with John F. Kennedy during a visit to Newark in 1962 or 1963 as Kennedy said to him: We've been hearing great things about you. But all that turned sour after the Newark disaster, and once Gil left politics, he and Betty packed it in and moved to California. I didn't see much of them after that, but for the next six or seven years I gathered all was calm. Gil built up his law practice, my sister opened a store in Laguna Beach (kitchenware, table linens, top-quality grinders and gadgets), and even though Gil had to swallow more than twenty pills a day to keep himself alive, whenever they came east for family visits, he looked to be in good shape. Then his health turned. By the mid-seventies, a series of cardiac arrests and other debilitations made work all but impossible for him. I sent them whatever I could whenever I could, and with Betty working full-time to keep them going, Gil now spent most of his days alone in the house, reading books. My big sister and her dying husband, three thousand miles away from me. During those last years, Betty told me, Gil would plant love notes in the drawers of her bureau, hiding them among her bras and slips and panties, and every morning when she woke up and got dressed, she would find another billet-doux declaring that she was the most gorgeous woman in the world. Not bad, finally. Considering what they were up against, not bad at all.

I don't want to think about the end: the cancer, the final stay in the hospital, the obscene sunlight that flooded the cemetery on the morning of the funeral. I've already dredged up enough, but still, I can't let go of this without revisiting one last detail, one last ugly turn. By the time Gil died, Betty was so deeply in debt that paying for a burial plot was a genuine hardship. I was prepared to help, but she had already asked me for money so often that she couldn't bring herself to do it again. Rather than turn to me, she went to her mother-in-law, the infamous woman who had allowed Gil to be thrown out of the house when he was a boy. I can't remember her name (probably because I despised her so much), but by 1980 she was married to her third husband, a retired businessman who happened to be immensely rich. As for husband number two, I don't know if his departure was caused by death or divorce—but no matter. Rich husband number three owned a large family plot in a cemetery somewhere in southern Florida, and my sister managed to talk him into letting Gil be buried there. Less than a year after that, husband number three died, and a large, Balzacian inheritance war broke out between his children and Gil's mother. They took her to court, won their case, and in order for her to come out of the affair with any money at all, one of the conditions of the settlement required that Gil's remains be removed from the family plot. Imagine. The woman evicts her son from his house when he's a child, and then, for a bag of silver, evicts him from his grave after he's dead. When Betty called to tell me what had happened, she was sobbing. She had held up through Gil's death with a kind of grim, stoic grace, but this was too much for her, and she broke down and lost it completely. By the time Gil was exhumed and buried again, she was no longer the same person.

She lasted another four years. Living alone in a small apartment in the New Jersey suburbs, she grew fat, then very fat, and before long came down with diabetes, clogged arteries, and a thick dossier of other ailments. She held my hand when Oona left me and our catastrophic five-year marriage ended, applauded when Sonia and I got back together, saw her son whenever he and his wife flew in from Chicago, attended family events, watched television from morning to night, could still tell a decent joke when the spirit moved her, and turned into the saddest person I have ever known. One morning in the spring of 1987, her housekeeper called me in a state of quasi-hysteria. She had just entered Betty's apartment, using the key she had been given for her weekly cleaning chores, and had found my sister lying on the bed. I borrowed a car from a neighbor, drove out to New Jersey, and identified her body for the police. The shock of seeing her like that: so still, so far away, so terribly, terribly dead. When they asked me if I wanted the hospital to conduct an autopsy, I told them not to bother. There were only two possibilities. Either her body had given out on her or she had taken pills, and I didn't want to know the answer, for neither one of them would have told the real story. Betty died of a broken heart. Some people laugh when they hear that phrase, but that's because they don't know anything about the world. People die of broken hearts. It happens every day, and it will go on happening to the end of time.

No, I haven't forgotten. The cough sent me spinning into another zone, but I'm back now, and Brick is still with me. Through thick and thin, in spite of that dismal excursion into the past, but how to stop the mind from charging off wherever it wants to go? The mind has a mind of its own. Who said that? Someone, or else I just thought of it myself, not that it makes any difference. Coining phrases in the middle of the night, making up stories in the middle of the night—we're moving on, my little darlings, and agonizing as this mess can be, there's poetry in it, too, as long as you can find the words to express it, assuming those words exist. Yes, Miriam, life is disappointing. But I also want you to be happy.

Fret not. I'm treading water because I can see the story turning in any one of several directions, and I still haven't decided which path to take. Hope or no hope? Both options are available, and yet neither one is fully satisfying to me. Is there a middle way after such a beginning, after throwing Brick to the wolves and bending the poor sap's mind out of shape? Probably not. Think dark, then, and go down into it, see it through to the end.

The injection has already been given. Brick falls into the bottomless black of unconsciousness, and hours later he opens his eyes and discovers that he's in bed with Flora. It's early morning, seven-thirty or eight o'clock, and as Brick looks at the naked back of his sleeping wife, he wonders if he wasn't right all along, if the time he spent in Wellington wasn't part of some bad, nauseatingly vivid dream. But then, as he shifts his head on the pillow, he feels Virginia's bandage pressing into his cheek, and when he runs his tongue over the ragged edge of his chipped incisor, he has no choice but to face the facts: he was there, and everything that happened to him in that place was real. By now, there is only a single, improbable straw to clutch at: what if the two days that elapsed in Wellington were no more than a blink of the eyes in this world? What if Flora never knew he was gone? That would solve the problem of having to explain where he's been, for Brick knows the truth will be difficult to swallow, especially for a jealous woman like Flora, and yet even if the truth comes out sounding like a lie, he doesn't have the strength or the will to concoct a story that would seem more plausible, something that would appease her suspicions and make her understand that his two-day absence had nothing to do with another woman.

Unfortunately for Brick, the clocks in both worlds tell the same time. Flora knows that he's been missing, and when she turns over in her sleep and inadvertently touches his body, she is instantly jolted awake. His anxieties are stilled by the joy that comes rushing into her intense brown eyes, and suddenly he feels ashamed of himself, mortified that he ever could have doubted her love for him.

Owen? she asks, as if hardly daring to believe what has happened. Is it really you?

Yes, Flora, he says. I'm back.

She throws her arms around him, holding him tightly against her smooth, bare skin. I've been going *crazy,* she says, rolling the *r* with an emphatic trilling of her tongue. Just *crazy* out of my head. Then, as she sees the bandage on his cheek and the bruises around his lips, her expression changes to one of alarm. What happened? she asks. You're all beat up, baby.

It takes him over an hour to give a full account of his mysterious journey to the other America. The only thing he leaves out is Virginia's last remark about wanting to charm his pants off and fuck his brains out, but that is a minor detail, and he sees no point in riling up Flora with matters that have little bearing on the story. The most daunting part comes toward the end, when he tries to recapitulate his conversation with Frisk. It barely made sense to him at the time, and now that he's back in his own apartment, sitting in the kitchen and drinking coffee with his wife, all that talk about multiple realities and multiple worlds dreamed and imagined by other minds strikes him as out-and-out gibberish. He shakes his head, as if to apologize for making such a botch of it. But the injection was real, he says. And the order to shoot August Brill was real. And if he doesn't carry out the job, he and Flora will be in constant danger.

Until now, Flora has listened in silence, patiently watching her husband tell his absurd and ridiculous story, which she considers to be the largest mound of crap ever built by human hands. Under normal circumstances, she would fly into one of her rages and accuse him of two-timing her, but these are not normal circumstances, and Flora, who knows every one of Brick's faults, who has criticized him countless times during the three years of their marriage, has never once called him a liar, and in the face of the nonsense she has just been told, she finds herself stunned, at a loss for words.

I know it sounds incredible, Brick says. But it's all true, every word of it.

And you expect me to believe you, Owen?

I can hardly believe it myself. But it all happened, Flora, exactly as I told it to you.

Do you think I'm an idiot?

What are you talking about?

Either you think I'm an idiot or you've gone insane.

I don't think you're an idiot, and I haven't gone insane.

You sound like one of those crackpots. You know, one of those guys who's been abducted by aliens. What did the Martians look like, Owen? Did they have a big spaceship?

Stop it, Flora. That isn't funny.

Funny? Who's trying to be funny? I just want to know where you've been.

I've already told you. Don't think I wasn't tempted to make up another story. Some stupid thing about getting mugged and losing my memory for two days. Or being run over by a car. Or falling down the stairs in the subway. Some drek like that. But I decided to tell you the truth.

Maybe that's it. You got beat up, after all. Maybe you've been lying in an alley for the past two days, and you dreamed the whole thing.

Then why would I have this on my arm? A nurse put it there after they gave me the shot. It's the last thing I remember before I opened my eyes this morning.

Brick rolls up his left sleeve, points to a small flesh-colored bandage on his upper arm, and tears it off with his right hand. Look, he says. Do you see this little scab? That's the spot where the needle went into my skin.

It doesn't mean anything, Flora replies, dismissing the one piece of solid evidence Brick can offer. There are a million different ways you could have gotten that scab.

True. But the fact is it happened just one way, the way I told you. From Frisk's needle.

All right, Owen, Flora says, trying not to lose her temper, maybe we should stop talking about it now. You're home. That's the only thing that matters to me. Christ, baby, you don't know what it was like for those two days. I went nuts, I mean one hundred percent nuts. I thought you were dead. I thought you'd left me. I thought you were with another girl. And now you're back. It's like a miracle, and if you want to know the truth, I don't really care what happened. You were gone, and now you're back. End of story, okay?

No, Flora, it's not okay. I'm back, but the story isn't over. I have to go up to Vermont and shoot Brill. I don't know how much time I have, but I can't sit around and wait too long. If I don't do it, they're going to come after us. A bullet for you and a bullet for me. That's what Frisk said, and he wasn't joking.

Brill, Flora grunts, pronouncing the name as if it were an insult in some foreign language. I bet he doesn't even exist.

I saw his picture, remember?

A picture doesn't prove anything.

That's exactly what I said when Frisk showed it to me.

Well, there's one way to find out, isn't there? If he's some kind of hotshot writer, he has to be on the Internet. Let's turn on my computer and look him up.

Frisk said he won a Pulitzer Prize about twenty years ago. If his name isn't on the list, then we're home free. If it is, then watch out, little Flora. We're in for some big trouble.

It won't be, Owen. Count on it. Brill doesn't exist, so his name can't be there.

But it is there. August Brill, winner of the 1984 Pulitzer Prize for criticism. They look further, and within minutes they have uncovered vast amounts of information, including biographical data from *Who's Who in America* (born NYC, 1935; married Sonia Weil, 1957, divorced 1975; married Oona McNally, 1976, divorced 1981; daughter, Miriam, born 1960; B.A. from Columbia, 1957; honorary doctorates from Williams College and the Pratt Institute; member of the American Academy of Arts and Sciences; author of more than 1,500 articles, reviews, and columns for magazines and newspapers; book editor of the *Boston Globe*, 1972–1991), a Web site containing over four hundred of his pieces written between 1962 and 2003, as well as a number of photographs taken of Brill in his thirties, forties, and fifties, leaving no doubt that these are younger versions of the old man in the wheelchair parked in front of the white clapboard house in Vermont.

Brick and Flora are sitting side by side at a small desk in the bedroom, their eyes fixed on the screen in front of them, too afraid to look at each other as they watch their hopes turn to dust. At last, Flora switches off the laptop and says in a low, quavering voice: I guess I was wrong, huh?

Brick stands up and begins pacing around the room. Do you believe me now? he asks. This Brill, this goddamn August Brill . . . I'd never even heard of him until yesterday. How could I have made it up? I'm not smart enough to have thought of half the things I've told you, Flora. I'm just a guy who performs magic tricks for little kids. I don't read books, I don't know anything about book critics, and I'm not interested in politics. Don't ask me how, but I've just come from a place that's in the middle of a civil war. And now I have to kill a man.

He sits down on the edge of the bed, overwhelmed by the ferocity of his situation, by the sheer injustice of what has happened to him. Watching Brick with worried eyes, Flora walks across the room and sits down beside him. She puts her arms around her husband, leans her head against his shoulder, and says: You're not going to kill anyone.

I have to, Brick answers, staring down at the floor.

I don't know what to think or not to think, Owen, but I'm telling you now, you're not going to kill anyone. You're going to leave that man alone.

I can't.

Why do you think I married you? Because you're a sweet person, my love, a kind and honest person. I didn't marry a killer. I married you, my funny Owen Brick, and I'm not going to stand by and let you murder someone and spend the rest of your life in prison.

I'm not saying I want to do it. I just don't have any choice.

Don't talk like that. Everyone has a choice. And besides, what makes you think you'd be able to go through with it? Can you actually see yourself walking into that man's house, pointing a gun at his head, and shooting him in cold blood? Not in a hundred years, Owen. It's just not in you to do something like that. Thank God.

Brick knows that Flora is right. He could never kill an innocent stranger, not even if his own life depended on it—which it probably does. He lets out a long, shuddering breath, then runs his hand through Flora's hair and says: So what am I supposed to do?

Nothing.

What do you mean, *nothing*?

We start living again. You do your job, I do mine. We eat and sleep and pay the bills. We wash the dishes and vacuum the floor. We make a baby together. You put me in the bath and shampoo my hair. I rub your back. You learn new tricks. We visit your parents and listen to your mother complain about her health. We go on, baby, and live our little life. That's what I'm talking about. Nothing.

A month goes by. In the first week after Brick's return, Flora misses her period, and a home pregnancy test brings them the news that if all goes well, they will become parents by the following January. They celebrate the positive test result by going out to a fashionable Manhattan restaurant that is far beyond their means, consume an entire bottle of French champagne before placing their orders, and then gorge themselves on a gargantuan porterhouse for two, which Flora claims is almost as good as the meat in Argentina. The next day, on his second visit to the dentist, a cap is put on Brick's left incisor, and he resumes his career as the Great Zavello. Bolting around the city in his battered yellow Mazda, he dons his cape and performs at elementary school assemblies, retirement homes, community centers, and private parties, pulling doves and rabbits out of his top hat, making silk scarves disappear, snatching eggs out of thin air, and transforming dull newspapers into colorful bouquets of pansies, tulips, and roses. Flora, who left her catering job two years earlier and is now working as a receptionist at a doctor's office on Park Avenue, asks her boss for a twenty-dollar raise and is turned down. She explodes in a tantrum of injured pride and storms out of the building, but when she talks it over with Brick that evening, he persuades her to return the next morning and apologize to Dr. Sontag, which she does, and because the doctor doesn't want to lose such a competent, hardworking employee, he rewards her with a ten-dollar increase in salary, which is all she was hoping for in the first place. Money is nevertheless an issue, and with a child now on the way, Brick and Flora wonder if they will be able to feed that third mouth with what they are earning now. On a grim Sunday afternoon toward the end of the month, they even discuss the possibility of Brick going to work for his cousin Ralph, who owns a high-powered real estate agency in Park Slope. Magic would have to become a part-time occupation, little more than a hobby to be pursued on his days off, and Brick is reluctant to take such a drastic step, vowing to land some higher-paying jobs that will give them the breathing room they need. Meanwhile, he has not forgotten his visit to the other America. Wellington is still burning inside him, and not a day goes by when he doesn't think of Tobak, Molly Wald, Duke Rothstein, Frisk, and, most disturbingly of all, Virginia Blaine. He can't help himself. Flora has been so much more tender with him since his return, metamorphosing herself into the loving companion he always longed for, and while there is no question that he loves her back, Virginia is always there, lurking in a corner of his mind, gently putting the bandage on his face and telling him how much she wanted to charm his pants off. By way of compensation, perhaps, he begins reading Brill's old reviews on the Internet—always in secret, of course, since he doesn't want Flora to know that he's still thinking about the man he was instructed to kill—and every time he comes across an article about a book that sounds interesting, he checks it out of the library. He used to spend his evenings watching television with Flora on a sofa in the living room. Now he lies on the bed and reads books. So far, his most important discoveries have been Chekhov, Calvino, and Camus.

In this way Brick and Flora swim along in their conjugal nothing, the little life she lured him back to with the good sense of a woman who doesn't believe in other worlds, who knows there is only this world and that numbing routines and brief squabbles and financial worries are an essential part of it, that in spite of the aches and boredoms and disappointments, living in this world is the closest we will ever come to seeing paradise. After the horrific hours he spent in Wellington, Brick too wants only this, the jumbled grind of New York, the naked body of his little Floratina, his work as the Great Zavello, his unborn child growing invisibly as the days pass, and yet deep inside himself he knows that he has been contaminated by his visit to the other world and that sooner or later everything will come to an end. He contemplates driving up to Vermont and talking to Brill. Would it be possible to convince the old man to stop thinking about his story? He tries to imagine the conversation, tries to summon the words he would use to present his argument, but all he ever sees is Brill laughing at him, the incredulous laughter of a man who would take him for an imbecile, a mental defective, and promptly throw him out of the house. So Brick does nothing, and precisely one month after his return from Wellington, on the evening of May twenty-first, as he sits in the living room with Flora, demonstrating a new card trick to his laughing wife, someone knocks on the door. Without having to think about it, Brick already knows what has happened. He tells Flora not to open the door, to run into the bedroom and go down the fire escape as fast as she can, but willful, independent Flora, unaware of the fix they're in, scoffs at his panicked instructions and does exactly what he tells her not to do. Bounding off the sofa before he can grab her arm, she dances to the door with a mocking pirouette and yanks it open. Two men are standing on the threshold, Lou Frisk and Duke Rothstein, and since each one is holding a revolver in his hand and pointing it at Flora, Brick doesn't move from his spot on the sofa. Theoretically, he can still try to escape, but the moment he stood up, the mother of his child would be dead.

Who the fuck are you? Flora says, in a shrill, angry voice.

Sit down next to your husband, Frisk replies, waving his gun in the direction of the sofa. We have some business to discuss with him.

Turning to Brick with an anguished look on her face, Flora says: What's going on, baby?

Come here, Brick answers, patting the sofa with his right hand. Those guns aren't toys, and you have to do what they say.

For once, Flora doesn't resist, and as the two men enter the apartment and shut the door, she walks over to the sofa and sits down beside her husband.

These are my friends, Brick says to her. Duke Rothstein and Lou Frisk. Remember when I told you about them? Well, here they are.

Jesus holy Christ, Flora mutters, by now sick to death with fear.

Frisk and Rothstein settle into two chairs opposite the sofa. The cards that were used to demonstrate the trick are strewn across the surface of the coffee table in front of them. Taking hold of one of the cards and turning it over, Frisk says: I'm glad you remember us, Owen. We were beginning to have our doubts.

Don't worry, Brick says. I never forget a face.

How's the tooth? Rothstein asks, breaking into what looks like a cross between a grimace and a smile.

Much better, thank you, Brick says. I went to the dentist, and he put a cap on it.

I'm sorry I hit you so hard. But orders are orders, and I had to do my job. Scare tactics. I guess they didn't work too well, did they?

Have you ever had a gun pointed at you? Frisk asks.

Believe it or not, Brick says, this is the first time.

You seem to be handling it pretty well.

I've played it out in my head so often, I feel as if it's already happened.

Which means you've been expecting us.

Of course I've been expecting you. The only surprise is that you didn't show up sooner.

We figured we'd give you a month. It's a tough assignment, and it seemed only fair to give you a little time to work yourself up to it. But the month is over now, and we still haven't seen any results. Do you want to explain yourself?

I can't do it. That's all. I just can't do it.

While you've been twiddling your thumbs in Jackson Heights, the war has gone from bad to worse. The Federals launched a spring offensive, and nearly every town on the East Coast has been under attack. Operation Unity, they call it. A million and a half more dead while you sit here wrestling with your conscience. The Twin Cities were invaded three weeks ago, and half of Minnesota is under Federal control again. Huge parts of Idaho, Wyoming, and Nebraska have been turned into prison camps. Shall I go on?

No, no, I get the picture.

You have to do it, Brick.

I'm sorry. I just can't.

You remember the consequences, don't you?

Isn't that why you're here?

Not yet. We're giving you a deadline. One week from today. If Brill isn't taken care of by midnight on the twenty-eighth, Duke and I will be back, and next time our guns will be loaded. Do you hear me, Corporal? One week from today, or else you and your wife die for nothing.

I don't know what time it is. The hands on the alarm clock aren't illuminated, and I'm not about to switch on the lamp again and subject myself to the blinding rays of the bulb. I keep intending to ask Miriam to buy me one of those glow-in-the-dark jobs, but every time I wake up in the morning, I forget. The light erases the thought, and I don't remember it again until I'm back in bed, lying awake as I am now, staring up at the invisible ceiling in my invisible room. I can't be certain, but I would guess it's somewhere between one-thirty and two o'clock. Inching along, inching along . . .

The Web site was Miriam's idea. If I had known what she was up to, I would have told her not to waste her time, but she kept it a secret from me (in collusion with her mother, who had saved nearly every scrap of writing I'd ever published), and when she came to New York for my seventieth-birthday dinner, she took me into my study, turned on my laptop, and showed me what she had done. The articles were hardly worth the trouble, but the thought of my daughter spending untold hours typing up all those ancient pieces of mine—*for posterity*, as she put it— more or less undid me, and I didn't know what to say. My usual impulse is to deflect emotional scenes with a dry quip or wise-acre remark, but that night I simply put my arms around Miriam and said nothing. Sonia cried, of course. She always cried when she was happy, but on that occasion her tears were especially poignant and terrible to me, since her cancer had been detected only three days earlier and the prognosis was cloudy, touch-and-go at best. No one said a word about it, but all three of us knew that she might not be around for my next birthday. As it turned out, a year was too much to hope for.

I shouldn't be doing this. I promised myself not to fall into the trap of Sonia-thoughts and Sonia-memories, not to let myself go. I can't afford to break down now and sink into a despond of grief and self-recrimination. I might start howling and wake the girls upstairs—or else spend the next several hours thinking of ever more artful and devious ways to kill myself. That task has been reserved for Brick, the protagonist of tonight's story. Perhaps that explains why he and Flora turn on her computer and look at Miriam's Web site. It seems important that my hero should get to know me a bit, to learn what kind of man he's up against, and now that he's dipped into some of the books I've recommended, we've finally begun to establish a bond. It's turning into a rather complicated jig, I suppose, but the fact is that the Brill character wasn't in my original plan. The mind that created the war was going to belong to someone else, another invented character, as unreal as Brick and Flora and To-bak and all the rest, but the longer I went on, the more I understood how badly I was fooling myself. The story is about a man who must kill the person who created him, and why pretend that I am not that person? By putting myself into the story, the story becomes real. Or else I become unreal, yet one more figment of my own imagination. Either way, the effect is more satisfying, more in harmony with my mood—which is dark, my little ones, as dark as the obsidian night that surrounds me.

I'm blathering on, letting my thoughts fly helter-skelter to keep Sonia at bay, but in spite of my efforts, she's still there, the ever-present absent one, who spent so many nights in this bed with me, now lying in a grave in the Cimetière Montparnasse, my French wife of eighteen years, and then nine years apart, and then twenty-one more years together, thirty-nine years in all, forty-one counting the two years before our wedding, more than half my life, much more than half, and nothing left now but boxes of photographs and seven scratchy LPs, the recordings she made in the sixties and seventies, Schubert, Mozart, Bach, and the chance to listen to her voice again, that small but beautiful voice, so drenched in feeling, so much the essence of who she was. Photographs . . . and music . . . and Miriam. She left me our child, too, that mustn't be overlooked, the child who is no longer a child, and how strange to think that I'd be lost without her now, no doubt drunk every night, if not dead or on life support in some hospital. When she asked me to move in with her after the accident, I politely turned her down, explaining that she had enough burdens already without adding me to the list. She took hold of my hand and said: No, Dad, you don't get it. I need you. I'm so damned lonely in that house, I don't know how much longer I can take it. I need someone to talk to. I need someone to look at, to be there at dinner, to hold me every once in a while and tell me that I'm not an awful person.

Awful person must have come from Richard, an epithet that shot out of his mouth during an ugly row at the end of their marriage. People say the worst things in the flush of anger, and it pains me that Miriam allowed those words to stick to her like

the first thing to be done is to protect Flora by sending her as far away from him as possible.

Brick is calm, but it seems to have no effect on his wife, who is growing more and more agitated.

What are we going to do? she says. My God, Owen, we can't just sit around here and wait for them to come back. I don't want to die. It's too stupid to die when you're twenty-seven years old. I don't know . . . maybe we can run away and hide somewhere.

It wouldn't do any good. Wherever we went, they're bound to track us down.

Then maybe you have to kill that old man, after all.

We've already been through that. You were against it, remember?

I didn't know anything then. Now I know.

I don't see how that makes any difference. I can't do it, and even if I could, I'd only wind up in prison.

Who says you'll be caught? If you think of a good plan, maybe you'll get away with it.

Leave it alone, Flora. You don't want me to do it any more than I do.

Okay. Then we hire someone to do it for you.

Stop it. We're not killing anyone. Do you understand me?

What then? If we don't do something, we'll be dead one week from tonight.

I'm going to send you away. That's the first step. Back to your mother in Buenos Aires.

But you just said they'd find us wherever we go.

They're not interested in you. I'm the one they're after, and once we're apart, they're not going to bother with you.

What are you saying, Owen?

Just that I want you to be safe.

And what about you?

Don't worry. I'll think of something. I'm not going to let myself be killed by those two maniacs, I promise. You'll go down and visit your mother for a while, and when you come back, I'll be waiting for you in this apartment. Understood?

I don't like it, Owen.

You don't have to like it. You just have to do it. For me.

That evening they book a round-trip flight to Buenos Aires, and the next morning Brick drives Flora to the airport. He knows it is the last time he will ever see her, but he struggles to maintain his composure and gives no hint of the anguish roiling inside him. As he kisses her good-bye at the security entrance, surrounded by throngs of travelers and uniformed airport personnel, Flora suddenly begins to cry. Brick gathers her into his arms and strokes the top of her head, but now that he can feel her body convulsing against his, and now that her tears are seeping through his shirt and dampening his skin, he no longer knows what to say.

Don't make me go, Flora begs.

No tears, he whispers back to her. It's only ten days. By the time you come home, everything will be finished.

And so it will, he thinks, as he climbs into his car and drives home to Jackson Heights from the airport. At that point, he has every intention of keeping his word: to avoid another encounter

with Rothstein and Frisk, to be waiting for Flora in the apartment when she returns—but that doesn't mean he plans on being alive.

So now it's a suicide, he remembers saying to Frisk.

In a roundabout way, yes.

Brick is approaching his thirtieth birthday, and not once in
his life has he ever thought of killing himself. Now it has become his sole preoccupation, and for the next two days he sits in
the apartment trying to figure out the most painless and efficient
method of leaving this world. He considers buying a gun and
shooting himself in the head. He considers poison. He considers slitting his wrists. Yes, he says to himself, that's the old standard, isn't it? Drink half a bottle of vodka, pour twenty or thirty
sleeping pills down your throat, slip into a warm tub, and then
slash your veins with a carving knife. Rumor has it that you
barely feel a thing.

The conundrum is that there are still five more days to go,
and with each day that passes, the calm and certainty that descended over his mind as he looked into the barrel of Frisk's gun
loosen their hold on him by several more degrees. Death was a
foregone conclusion back then, a mere formality under the circumstances, but as his calm gradually turns into disquiet, and
his certainty melts away into doubt, he tries to imagine the vodka
and the pills, the warm bath and the blade of the knife, and suddenly the old fear returns, and once that happens, he understands that his resolve has vanished, that he will never find the
courage to go through with it.

How much time has passed by then? Four days—no, five

days—which means that only forty-eight hours are left. Brick
has yet to stir from his apartment and venture outside. He has
canceled all his Great Zavello performances for the week, claiming to be down with the flu, and has unplugged the phone from
the wall. He suspects that Flora has been trying to reach him, but
he can't bring himself to talk to her just now, knowing that the
sound of her voice would upset him so much that he might lose
control and start babbling inanities to her or, worse, start crying, which would only deepen her alarm. Nevertheless, on the
morning of May 27, he finally shaves, showers, and puts on a
fresh set of clothes. Sunlight is pouring through the windows,
the beckoning radiance of the New York spring, and he decides
that a walk in the air might do him some good. If his mind has
failed to solve his problems for him, perhaps he will find the
answer in his feet.

The instant he steps onto the sidewalk, however, he hears
someone calling his name. It's a woman's voice, and because no
other pedestrians are passing by at that moment, Brick is at a
loss to identify where the voice is coming from. He looks around,
the voice calls to him again, and behold, there is Virginia Blaine,
sitting behind the wheel of a car parked directly across the street.
In spite of himself, Brick is inordinately glad to see her, but as
he steps down from the curb and walks over to the woman who
has haunted him for the past month, a wave of apprehension flutters through him. By the time he reaches the white Mercedes
sedan, he can feel his pulse pounding inside his head.

Good morning, Owen, Virginia says. Do you have a minute?

I wasn't expecting to see you again, Brick replies, looking closely at her beautiful face, which is even more beautiful than he remembered, and her dark brown hair, which is shorter than it was the last time he saw her, and her delicate mouth with the red lipstick, and her blue eyes with the long lashes, and her thin, graceful hands resting on the wheel of the car.

I hope I'm not interrupting anything, she says.

Not at all. I was just going out for a walk.

Good. Let's make it a drive instead, okay?

Where to?

I'll tell you later. We have a lot to talk about first. By the time we get to where we're going, you'll understand why I took you there.

Brick hesitates, still uncertain whether Virginia can be trusted or not, but then he realizes that he doesn't care, that in all probability he's a dead man no matter what he does. If these are the last hours of his life, he thinks, then better to spend them with her than to wait it out alone.

So off they go into the brilliant May morning, leaving New York behind them and traveling along the southern rim of Connecticut on I-95, then veering onto 395 just before New London and heading north at seventy miles an hour. Brick pays little attention to the passing landscape, choosing instead to keep his eyes on Virginia, who is wearing a pale blue cashmere sweater and a pair of white linen slacks, sitting in her brown leather seat with an air of such confidence and self-sufficiency that he is reminded of her younger self, the one that used to leave him

stammering whenever he tried to talk to her. Things are different now, he tells himself. He grew up, and he isn't intimidated
by her anymore. He's a bit wary, perhaps, but not of Virginia
the woman—rather, of the *little cog in the big machine*, the
person in cahoots with Frisk.

You're looking a lot better, Owen, she begins. No more cuts,
no more bandages. And I see you've had your tooth fixed. The
miracles of dentistry, huh? From beat-up boxer to Mr. Handsome again.

The subject doesn't interest Brick, and instead of making
small talk about the condition of his face, he comes right to the
point. Did Frisk give you the injection? he asks.

It doesn't matter how I got here, she says. The important
thing is why I came.

To finish me off, I suppose.

You're wrong. I came because I was feeling guilty. I got you
into this mess, and now I want to try to get you out of it.

But you're Frisk's girl. If you work for him, then you're a part
of it, too.

But I don't work for him. That's only a cover.

What does that mean?

Do I have to spell it out?

You're a double agent?

Sort of.

You're not going to tell me you're with the Federals.

Of course not. I hate those murdering bastards.

Then who is it?

Patience, Owen. You have to give me some time. First things first, okay?

All right. I'm listening.

Yes, I was the one who suggested you for the job. But I didn't know what it was. Something big, they said, something vital to the outcome of the war, but they never gave me any details. I wasn't told until you were already on the other side. I swear, I had no idea they were going to order you to kill someone. And then, even after I found out, I had no idea Frisk was going to threaten to kill you if you didn't carry out the job. I only learned about that last night. That's why I came. Because I wanted to help.

I don't believe a word you're saying.

Why should you? If I were in your place, I wouldn't believe me either. But it's the truth.

The funny thing is, Virginia, it doesn't bother me anymore. When you lie, I mean. I like you too much to get worked up about it. You might be a fake, you might even be the person who winds up killing me, but I'll never stop liking you.

I like you, too, Owen.

You're a strange person. Did anyone ever tell you that?

All the time. Ever since I was a little girl.

How long has it been since you've been back on this side?

Fifteen years. This is my first trip. It wasn't even possible until about three months ago. You were the first one to go back and forth. Did you know that?

No one ever told me anything.

It's like stepping into a dream, isn't it? The same place, but entirely different. America without war. It's hard to digest. You get so used to the fighting, it kind of creeps into your bones, and after a while, you can't imagine a world without it.

America's at war, all right. We're just not fighting it here. Not yet, anyway.

How's your wife, Owen? It's stupid of me, but I can't remember her name.

Flora.

That's right, Flora. Do you want to call and let her know you'll be gone for a couple of days?

She isn't in New York. I sent her back to her mother in Argentina.

Smart thinking. You did the right thing.

She's pregnant, by the way. I thought you'd like to know that.

Good work, kid. Congratulations.

Flora's pregnant, I love her more than ever, I'd rather cut off my right arm than do anything to hurt her, and still, the only thing I really want right now is to go to bed with you. Does that make any sense?

Absolutely.

One last roll in the hay.

Don't talk like that. You're not going to die, Owen.

Well, what do you think? Does the idea appeal to you?

Do you remember what I said the last time you saw me?

How could I forget?

Then you already have your answer, don't you?

They cross the border into Massachusetts, and a few minutes later they stop to fill the tank with gas, visit the ladies' and men's, and eat a pair of wretched, microwaved hot dogs on soggy buns, which they wash down with gulps of bottled water. As they walk back to the car, Brick takes Virginia in his arms and kisses her, driving his tongue deep into her mouth. It is a delicious moment for him, fulfilling the dream of half a lifetime, but one also marked by shame and regret, for this small prelude to further pleasures with his old love is the first time he has touched another woman since marrying Flora. But Brick, who is nothing less than a soldier now, a man engaged in fighting a war, justifies his infidelity by reminding himself that he could well be dead by tomorrow.

Once they hit the highway again, he turns to Virginia and asks her the question he's been putting off for more than two hours: where are they going?

Two places, she says. The first one today, the next one tomorrow.

Well, that's a start, I guess. You wouldn't care to be a little more specific, would you?

I can't tell you about the first stop, because I want that to be a surprise. But tomorrow we're going to Vermont.

Vermont . . . That means Brill. You're taking me to Brill.

You catch on fast, Owen.

It won't do any good, Virginia. I've thought about going there a dozen times, but I have no idea what to say to him.

Just ask him to stop.

He'll never listen to me.

How do you know unless you try?

Because I do, that's all.

You're forgetting that I'll be with you.

What difference does that make?

I've already told you that I don't really work for Frisk. Who do you think I take my orders from?

How should I know?

Come on, Corporal. Think.

Not Brill.

Yes, Brill.

That's impossible. He's on this side, and you're on the other side. There's no way for you to communicate.

Did you ever hear of a telephone?

The phones don't work. I already tried to call when I was in Wellington. I dialed my apartment in Queens, and they said the number was out of service.

There are phones and there are phones, my friend. Given his part in all this, do you think Brill would have one that didn't work?

So you talk to him.

Constantly.

But you've never met.

No. Tomorrow is the big day.

And what about now? Why not go to him now?

Because the appointment is for tomorrow. And until then, you and I have other plans.

Your surprise . . .

Exactly.

How much longer to go?

Less than half an hour. In about two minutes, I'm going to

ask you to close your eyes. You can open them again after we get there.

Brick plays along with the game, gladly submitting to Virginia's puerile whims, and for the last minutes of the journey he sits in his seat without saying a word, trying to guess what prank she has in store for him. If he were better versed in geography, he might have found a solution long before their arrival, but Brick has no more than a fuzzy understanding of maps, and since he has never actually set foot in Worcester, Massachusetts (having imagined himself there only in a dream), when the car stops and Virginia tells him to open his eyes, he is convinced he's back in Wellington. The car has pulled up in front of the suburban house they entered last month, the same brick-and-stucco manor with the luxuriant front lawn, the flower beds, and the tall, blooming bushes. When he glances down the street, however, all the neighboring houses are intact. No charred walls, no collapsed roofs, no broken windows. The war has not touched the block, and as Brick slowly turns around in a circle, trying to absorb the familiar but altered setting, the illusion finally bursts, and he knows where he is. Not Wellington but Worcester, the former name of the city in the other world.

Isn't it wonderful? Virginia says, raising her arms and gesturing to the undamaged houses. Her eyes have lit up, and a smile is spreading across her face. This is the way it used to be, Owen. Before the guns . . . before the attacks . . . before Brill started tearing everything apart. I never thought I'd live to see it again.

Let Virginia Blaine have her brief moment of joy. Let Owen

Brick forget his little Flora and find comfort in the arms of Virginia Blaine. Let the man and the woman who met as children take mutual pleasure in their adult bodies. Let them climb into bed together and do what they will. Let them eat. Let them drink. Let them return to the bed and do what they will to every inch and orifice of their grown-up bodies. Life goes on, after all, even under the most painful circumstances, goes on until the end, and then it stops. And these lives will stop, since they must stop, since neither one of them can ever make it to Vermont to talk to Brill, for Brill might weaken then and give up, and Brill can never give up, since he must go on telling his story, the story of the war in that other world, which is also this world, and he can't allow anyone or anything to stop him.

It's the middle of the night. Virginia is lying under the covers asleep, her sated flesh expanding and contracting as the cool air enters and exits her lungs, dreaming God knows what in the dim moonlight that filters through the half-open window. Brick is on his side, his body curled around hers, one hand cupping her left breast, the other hand poised on the rounded area where her hip and buttock merge, but the corporal is restless, unaccountably wakeful, and after struggling to fall asleep for close to an hour, he slips out of bed to go downstairs and pour himself a drink, wondering if a shot of whiskey might not quell the tremors that are rising within him as he contemplates tomorrow's meeting with the old man. Dressed in the dead husband's terry-cloth robe, he walks into the kitchen and turns on the light. Confronted by the dazzle of that elegant space, with its sleek surfaces and costly appliances, Brick begins to think about Virginia's marriage. Her husband must have been a good deal older than she was, he muses, a sharp operator with the wherewithal to afford a house like this one, and because Virginia has yet to say a word about him (except to mention that he was rich), the not-so-well-off magician from Queens asks himself if she cared about her departed spouse or simply married him for his money. The idle thoughts of an insomniac, searching the cupboards for a clean glass and a bottle of scotch: the endless banalities that flit through the mind as one notion mutates into the next. So it goes with all of us, young and old, rich and poor, and then an unexpected event comes crashing down on us to jolt us out of our torpor.

Brick hears the low-flying planes in the distance, then the noise of a helicopter engine, and an instant after that, the keening blast of an explosion. The windows in the kitchen shatter to bits, the floor shakes under his bare feet and then begins to tilt, as if the entire foundation of the house were shifting position, and when Brick runs into the front hall to mount the stairs and check on Virginia, he is met by large, writhing spears of flame. Wooden shards and slate roof tiles are falling down from above. Brick turns his eyes upward, and after several seconds of confusion he understands that he is looking at the night sky through clouds of billowing smoke. The top half of the house is gone, which means that Virginia is also gone, and while he knows it will serve no purpose, he desperately wants to mount the stairs and look for her body. But the stairs are on fire now, and he will burn to death if he gets any closer.

He runs outside onto the lawn, and all around him howling

neighbors are pouring from their houses into the night. A contingent of Federal troops has massed in the middle of the street, fifty or sixty helmeted men, all of them armed with machine guns. Brick raises his hands in a gesture of surrender, but it doesn't do him any good. The first bullet hits him in the leg, and he falls down, clutching the wound as blood spurts onto his fingers. Before he can inspect the damage and see how badly he is hurt, a second bullet goes straight through his right eye and out the back of his head. And that is the end of Owen Brick, who leaves the world in silence, with no chance to say a last word or think a last thought.

Meanwhile, seventy-five miles to the northwest, in a white wooden house in southern Vermont, August Brill is awake, lying in bed and staring into the dark. And the war goes on.

Does it have to end that way? Yes, probably yes, although it wouldn't be difficult to think of a less brutal outcome. But what would be the point? My subject tonight is war, and now that war has entered this house, I feel I would be insulting Titus and Katya if I softened the blow. Peace on earth, good will toward men. Piss on earth, good will toward none. This is the heart of it, the black center of the dead of night, a good four hours still to burn and all hope for sleep utterly smashed. The only solution is to leave Brick behind me, make sure that he gets a decent burial, and then come up with another story. Something low to the ground this time, a counterweight to the fantastical machine I've just

only seventeen when she posed for the artist. We turned around and went into the restaurant, and over lunch he told us more about his connection to that woman. She was the one who made him fall in love with books, he said, because when he was her student he developed an intense crush on her, and that love wound up changing the direction of his life. When the Germans occupied Belgium in 1940, Jean-Luc was just fifteen, but he joined an underground resistance cell as a courier, attending school by day and running messages at night. His teacher joined the resistance as well, and one morning in 1942 the Germans marched into the lycée and arrested her. Shortly after that, Jean-Luc's cell was infiltrated and destroyed. He had to go into hiding, he said, and for the last eighteen months of the war he lived alone in an attic and did nothing but read books—all books, every book, from the ancient Greeks to the Renaissance to the twentieth century, consuming novels and plays, poetry and philosophy, understanding that he never could have done this without the influence of his teacher, who had been arrested before his eyes and for whom he prayed every night. When the war finally ended, he learned that she hadn't made it home from the camp, but no one could tell him how or when she had died. She had been blotted out, expunged from the face of the earth, and not a single person knew what had happened to her.

Some years after that (late forties? early fifties?), he was eating alone in a restaurant in Brussels and overheard two men talking at the next table. One of them had spent time in a concentration camp during the war, and as he told the other man a story about one of his fellow inmates, Jean-Luc became more and more convinced that he was referring to his teacher, the little water nymph sitting in the fountain at the end of the arcade. All the details seemed to fit: a Belgian girl in her twenties, red hair, small body, extremely beautiful, a left-wing troublemaker who had defied an order from one of the camp guards. To set an example for the other prisoners and demonstrate what happens to people who disobey the guards, the commandant decided to execute her in public, with the entire population of the camp on hand to witness the killing. Jean-Luc was expecting the man to say that they hanged her or stood her up against a wall and shot her, but it turned out that the commandant had something more traditional in mind, a method that had gone out of fashion several centuries earlier. Jean-Luc couldn't look at us when he spoke the words. He turned his head away and looked out the window, as if the execution were taking place just outside the restaurant, and in a quiet voice suddenly filled with emotion, he said: She was drawn and quartered. With long chains attached to both her wrists and both her ankles, she was led into the yard, made to stand at attention as the chains were attached to four jeeps pointing in four different directions, and then the commandant gave the order for the drivers to start their engines. According to the man at the next table, the woman didn't cry out, didn't make a sound as one limb after another was pulled off her body. Is such a thing possible? Jean-Luc was tempted to talk to the man, he said, but then he realized that he wasn't capable of talking. Fighting back tears, he stood up, tossed some money on the table, and left the restaurant.

———

Sonia and I returned to Paris, and within forty-eight hours I heard two more stories that hit me hard—not with the sickening violence of Jean-Luc's story, but hard enough to have left an enduring impact. The first one came from Alec Foyle, a British journalist who flew in from London to have dinner with us one night. Alec is in his late forties, a onetime boyfriend of Miriam's, and even if it's all water under the bridge now, Sonia and I were both a little surprised when our daughter chose Richard over him. We had been out of contact for a number of years, and there was a lot of catching up to do, which led to one of those hectic conversations that career abruptly from one subject to the next. At a certain point we started talking about families, and Alec told us about a recent conversation he'd had with a friend, a woman who covered the arts for the *Independent* or the *Guardian*, I forget which. He said to her: At one time or another, every family lives through extraordinary events— horrendous crimes, floods and earthquakes, bizarre accidents, miraculous strokes of luck, and there isn't a family in the world without secrets and skeletons, trunkfuls of hidden material that would make your jaw drop if the lid were ever opened. His friend disagreed with him. It's true for many families, she said, maybe for most families, but not all. Her family, for example. She couldn't think of a single interesting thing that had ever happened to any of them, not one exceptional event. Impossible, Alec said. Just concentrate for a moment, and you're bound to come up with something. So his friend thought for a while, and eventually she said: Well, maybe there's one thing. My grandmother told it to me not long before she died, and I suppose it's fairly unusual.

Alec smiled at us from across the table. Unusual, he said. My friend wouldn't have been born if this thing hadn't happened, and she called it *unusual*. As far as I'm concerned, it's bloody astonishing.

His friend's grandmother was born in Berlin in the early twenties, and when the Nazis took power in 1933, her Jewish family reacted in the same way so many others did: they believed that Hitler was nothing more than a passing upstart and made no effort to leave Germany. Even as conditions worsened, they went on hoping for the best and refused to budge. One day, when the grandmother was seventeen or eighteen, her parents received a letter signed by someone claiming to be a captain in the SS. Alec didn't mention what year it was, but 1938 would be a reasonable assumption, I think, perhaps a little earlier. According to Alec's friend, the letter read as follows: You don't know me, but I am well aware of you and your children. I could be court-martialed for writing this, but I feel it is my duty to warn you that you are in great danger. If you don't act soon, you will all be arrested and sent to a camp. Trust me, this is not idle speculation. I am willing to furnish you with exit visas that will allow you to escape to another country, but in exchange for my help, you must do me one important favor. I have fallen in love with your daughter. I have been watching her for some time now, and although we have never spoken, this love is unconditional. She is the person I have dreamed of all my life, and if this were a different world and we were ruled by different laws, I would propose marriage tomorrow. This is all I am asking: next Wednesday, at ten o'clock in the morning, your daughter will go to the park across the street from your house, sit down on her favorite bench, and stay there for two hours. I promise not to touch her, not to approach her, not to address a single word to her. I will remain hidden for the full two hours. At noon, she can stand up and return to your house. The reason for this request is no doubt evident to you by now. I need to see my darling girl one last time before I lose her forever . . .

It goes without saying that she did it. She had to do it, even though the family feared it was a hoax, not to mention the more dire possibilities of molestation, abduction, and rape. Alec's friend's grandmother was an inexperienced girl, and the fact that she had been turned into an adored Beatrice by some unknown Dante from the SS, that a stranger had been spying on her for the past several months, listening in on her conversations and following her around the city, threw her into an ever-mounting panic as she waited for Wednesday to come. Nevertheless, when the appointed hour arrived she did what she had to do and marched off to the park with her yellow star wrapped around the sleeve of her sweater, sat down on a bench, and opened the book she had carried along as a prop to still her nerves. For two straight hours, she didn't look up once. She was that scared, she told her granddaughter, and pretending to read was her only defense, the only thing that kept her from jumping up and running away. Impossible to calculate how long those two hours must have felt to her, but noon crept around at last, and she went home. The next day, the exit visas were slipped under the door as promised, and the family left for England.

The last story came from one of Sonia's nephews, the oldest son of the oldest of her three older brothers, Bertrand, the only other member of her family who had become a musician, and therefore someone special to her, a violinist in the orchestra of the Paris Opera, a colleague and a pal. The afternoon following our dinner with Alec, we met him for lunch at Allard, and midway through the meal he started talking about a cellist in the orchestra who was planning to retire at the end of the season. Everyone knew her story, he said, she talked about it openly, and so he didn't feel he would be breaking any confidence if he told it to us. Françoise Duclos. I have no idea why her name is still with me, but there it is—Françoise Duclos, the cellist. She married her husband in the mid-sixties, Bertrand said, gave birth to a daughter in the early seventies, and two years after that the husband vanished. Not such an uncommon occurrence, as the police told her when she reported him missing, but Françoise knew that her husband loved her, that he was crazy about their little girl, and, unless she was the blindest, most obtuse woman on earth, that he wasn't involved with another woman. He earned a decent salary, which meant that money wasn't an issue, he enjoyed his work, and he had never shown any penchant for gambling or risky investments. So what happened to him, and why did he disappear? No one knew.

Fifteen years went by. The husband was declared legally

dead, but Françoise never remarried or lived with another man. She raised her daughter on her own (with help from her parents), was hired by the orchestra, gave private lessons in her apartment, and that was it: a pared-down existence, with a handful of friends, summers in the country with her brother's family, and an unsolved mystery as her constant companion. Then, after all those years of silence, the telephone rang one day, and she was asked to go to the morgue to identify a body. The person who accompanied her into the room where the corpse was waiting warned her that she was in for a rough experience: the deceased had been pushed from a sixth-floor window and had died on contact with the pavement. Shattered as the body was, Françoise recognized it at once. He was twenty pounds heavier than he had been, his hair was thinner and had turned gray, but there was no question that she was looking at the corpse of her missing husband.

Before she could leave, a man entered the room, took Françoise by the arm, and said: Please come with me, Madame Duclos. I have something to tell you.

He led her outside, took her to his car, which was parked in front of a bakery on an adjacent street, and asked her to climb in. Rather than put the key in the ignition, the man rolled down the window and lit up a cigarette. Then, for the next hour, he told Françoise the story of the past fifteen years as she sat next to him in his little blue car, watching people walk out of the bakery carrying loaves of bread. That was one detail Bertrand remembered—the loaves of bread—but he couldn't tell us any-

thing about the man. His name, his age, what he looked like—
all a blank, but finally that's of scant importance.

Duclos was an agent for the DGSE, he told her. She couldn't
have known that, of course, since agents are under strict orders
not to talk about their work, and all those years when she
thought her husband was writing economic studies for the Ministry of Foreign Affairs, he was actually operating as a spy under the Direction Générale de la Sécurité Extérieure. Just after
the birth of their daughter seventeen years ago, he was given an
assignment that turned him into a double agent: ostensibly acting in support of the Soviets but in fact feeding information to
the French. After two years, the Russians found out what he
was up to and tried to kill him. Duclos managed to escape, but
from that point on returning home was no longer possible. The
Russians were keeping watch on Françoise and her daughter,
the phone in the apartment was tapped, and if Duclos tried
to call or visit, all three of them would have been murdered
instantly.

So he stayed away to protect his family, hidden by the French
for fifteen years as he moved from one Paris apartment to another, a hunted man, a haunted man, stealing out to catch an
occasional glimpse of his daughter, watching her grow up from
afar, never able to talk to her, to know her, observing his wife as
her youthful looks slowly vanished and she lapsed into middle
age, and then, because of carelessness, or because someone
informed on him, or because of sheer dumb luck, the Russians
finally caught up with Duclos. The capture . . . the blindfold . . .

the ropes around his wrists . . . the punches to his face and body . . . and then the plunge from the sixth-floor window. Death by defenestration. Another classic method, the execution of choice among spies and policemen for hundreds of years.

There were numerous gaps in Bertrand's account, but he couldn't answer any of the questions Sonia and I asked him. How had Duclos occupied himself during all those years? Did he live under a false name? Had he gone on working for the DGSE in some capacity or other? How often was he able to go out? Bertrand shook his head. He simply didn't know.

What year did Duclos die? I asked. You must remember that.

Nineteen eighty-nine. The spring of eighty-nine. I'm sure of it, because that's when I joined the orchestra, and the thing with Françoise happened just a few weeks later.

The spring of eighty-nine, I said. The Berlin Wall came down in November. The Eastern bloc threw out their governments, and then the Soviet Union fell apart. That makes Duclos one of the last casualties of the Cold War, doesn't it?

I clear my throat, and a second later I'm coughing again, retching up gobs of sputum as I cover my mouth to stifle the noise. I want to spit into my handkerchief, but when I reach out and search for it with my fingers, I brush against the alarm clock, which falls off the night table and clatters onto the floor. Still no handkerchief. Then I remember that all my handkerchiefs are in the wash, so I swallow hard and let the goo slide down my throat, telling myself for the fiftieth time in the past fifty days to stop smoking, which I know will never happen, but I say it anyway, just to torture myself with my own hypocrisy.

I start thinking about Duclos again, wondering if I might not be able to tease a story out of that awful business, not necessarily Duclos and Françoise, not the fifteen years of hiding and waiting, not what I already know, but something I can make up as I go along. The daughter, for instance, thrust forward from 1989 to 2007. What if she grows up to become a journalist or a novelist, a scribbler of some sort, and after her mother's death she decides to write a book about her parents? But the man who betrayed her father to the Russians is still alive, and when he gets wind of what she's up to, he tries to stop her—or even kill her . . .

That's as far as I get. A moment later, I hear footsteps on the second floor again, but this time they aren't heading for the bathroom, they're coming down the stairs, and as I imagine Miriam or Katya going into the kitchen to look for a drink or a cigarette or a snack from the refrigerator, I realize that the steps are coming in this direction, that someone is approaching my room. I hear a knock on the door—no, not exactly a knock, but a faint scratching of fingernails against the wood—and then Katya whispers, Are you awake?

I tell her to come in, and as the door opens I can make out her silhouette against the dim, bluish light behind her. She seems to be wearing her Red Sox T-shirt and gray sweatpants, and her long hair is tied back in a ponytail.

Are you all right? she asks. I heard something fall on the floor, and then a lot of terrible coughing.

I'm right as rain, I answer. Whatever that means.

Have you slept at all?

Not a wink. What about you?

In and out, but not much.

Why don't you close the door? It's better in here when it's completely dark. I'll give you one of my pillows, and you can lie down next to me.

The door shuts, I slide a pillow over to Sonia's old spot, and a few moments later Katya is stretched out on her back beside me.

It reminds me of when you were little, I say. When your grandmother and I came to visit, you always crawled into bed with us.

I miss her like crazy, you know. I still can't get it into my head that she isn't around anymore.

You and everyone else.

Why did you stop writing your book, Grandpa?

I decided it was more fun to watch movies with you.

That's recent. You stopped writing it a long time ago.

It got too sad. I enjoyed working on the early parts, but then I came to the bad times, and I started to struggle with it. I've done such stupid things in my life, I didn't have the heart to live through them again. Then Sonia got sick. After she died, the thought of going back to it revolted me.

You shouldn't be so hard on yourself.

I'm not. I'm just being honest.

The book was supposed to be for me, remember?

For you and your mother.

But she already knows everything. I don't. That's why I was looking forward to reading it so much.

You probably would have been bored.

You can be a real fathead sometimes, Grandpa. Did you know that?

Why do you still call me *Grandpa*? You stopped calling your mother *Mom* years ago. You must have been in high school, and suddenly *Mom* became *Mother*.

I didn't want to sound like a baby anymore.

I call you Katya. You could call me August.

I never liked that name very much. It looks good on paper, but it's hard to get it out of your mouth.

Something else, then. How about *Ed*?

Ed? Where did that come from?

I don't know, I say, doing my best to imitate a Cockney accent. It just popped into me little ole 'ed.

Katya lets out a brief, sarcastic groan.

I'm sorry, I continue. I can't help myself. I was born with the bad joke gene, and there's nothing I can do about it.

You never take anything seriously, do you?

I take everything seriously, my love. I just pretend not to.

August Brill, my grandfather, currently known as Ed. What did they call you when you were little?

Augie, mostly. On my good days I was Augie, but people called me a lot of other things, too.

It's hard to imagine it. You as a child, I mean. You must have been a weird kid. Reading books all the time, I'll bet.

That came later. Until I was fifteen, the only thing I cared about was baseball. We used to play it nonstop, all the way into November. Then it was football for a few months, but by the end of February we'd start in on baseball again. The old gang from Washington Heights. We were so nuts, we even played baseball in the snow.

What about girls? Do you remember the name of your first big love?

Of course. You never forget a thing like that.

Who was she?

Virginia Blaine. I fell for her when I was a sophomore in high school, and suddenly baseball didn't matter anymore. I started reading poetry, I took up smoking, and I fell in love with Virginia Blaine.

Did she love you back?

I was never sure. She went hot and cold on me for about six months, and then she skipped off with someone else. It felt like the end of the world, my first real heartbreak.

Then you met Grandma. You were only twenty, right? Younger than I am now.

You're asking a lot of questions . . .

If you're not going to finish your book, how else am I going to find out what I need to know?

Why the sudden interest?

It's not sudden. I've been thinking about it for a long time. When I heard you were awake just now, I said to myself, Here's my chance, and I came down and knocked on your door.

Scratched on my door.

All right, scratched. But here we are now, lying in the dark, and if you don't answer my questions, I'm not going to let you watch movies with me anymore.

Speaking of which, I came up with another example to support your theory.

Good. But we're not talking about films now. We're talking about you.

It's not such a pleasant story, Katya. There are a lot of depressing things in it.

I'm a big girl, Ed. I can handle anything you dish out.

I wonder.

As far as I know, the only depressing thing you're talking about is the fact that you cheated on your wife and left her for another woman. I'm sorry, chum, but that's pretty standard practice around here, isn't it? You think I can't handle that? I already have, with my own father and mother.

When did you speak to him last?

Who?

Your father.

Who?

Come on, Katya. Your father, Richard Furman, your mother's ex-husband, my ex-son-in-law. Talk to me a little, sweetheart. I promise to answer your questions, but just let me know when you last heard from your father.

About two weeks ago, I guess.

Did you make any arrangements to see each other?

He invited me to come to Chicago, but I told him I wasn't feeling up to it. When the semester's over next month, he said he'd come to New York for a weekend and we could stay at a hotel somewhere and eat lots of good food. I'll probably go, but I haven't decided yet. His wife's pregnant, by the way. Pretty Suzie Woozy is with child.

Does your mother know?

I didn't tell her. I thought she might be upset.

She's bound to find out eventually.

I know. But she seems to be doing a little better now, and I didn't want to rock the boat.

You're one tough cookie, kid.

No, I'm not. I'm a big soft jelly doughnut. All ooze and mush.

I take hold of Katya's hand, and for the next half minute or so we look up into the dark without saying a word. I wonder if she might not drift off to sleep if I don't resume the conversation, but a moment after I think that thought she breaks the silence by asking me another question:

When was the first time you saw her?

April fourth, nineteen fifty-five—at two-thirty in the afternoon.

For real?

For real.

Where were you?

Broadway. Broadway and One Hundred-fifteenth Street, walking uptown on my way to Butler Library. Sonia went to Juilliard, which was near Columbia at the time, and she was walking downtown. I must have spotted her about half a block away, probably because she was wearing a red coat—red jumps out at you, especially on a city street, with nothing but drab bricks and stones in the background. So I catch sight of the red

coat coming toward me, and then I see that the person wearing
the coat is a short girl with dark hair. Quite promising from a
distance, but still too far away to be sure of anything. That's how
it is with boys, you know that. Always looking at girls, always
sizing them up, always hoping to run into the knockout beauty
who will suck the breath out of you and make your heart stop
beating. So I've seen the red coat, and I've seen that it's worn by
a girl with short dark hair who stands approximately five feet
five inches tall, and the next thing I notice is that her head is
bobbing around a little bit, as if she's humming to herself, and
that there's a certain bounce to her step, a lightness in the way
she moves, and I say to myself, This girl is happy, happy to be
alive and walking down the street in the crisp, sun-drenched
air of early spring. A few seconds later, her face begins to ac-
quire more definition, and I see that she's wearing bright red
lipstick, and then, as the distance between us continues to narrow, I simultaneously absorb two important facts. One: that she
is indeed humming to herself—a Mozart aria, I think, but can't
be certain—and not only is she humming, she has the voice of
a real singer. Two: that she's sublimely attractive, perhaps even
beautiful, and that my heart is about to stop beating. By now,
she's only four or five feet away, and I, who have never stopped
to talk to an unknown girl on the street, who have never in my
life had the audacity to address a good-looking stranger in public, open my mouth and say hello, and because I'm smiling at
her, no doubt smiling in a way that carries no threat or hint of
aggression, she stops humming, smiles back at me, and returns
my greeting with one of her own. And that's it. I'm too nervous

Fate, luck, whatever you want to call it.

Where did it happen?

On the subway. The Seventh Avenue IRT. Heading down-town on the evening on April twenty-seventh, nineteen fifty-five. The car was crowded, but the seat next to mine was empty. We stopped at Sixty-sixth Street, the doors opened, and in she walked. Since there were no other seats available, she sat down beside me.

Did she remember you?

A vague recollection. I reminded her of our little encounter on Broadway earlier that month, and then it came back to her. We didn't have much time. I was on my way to the Village to meet some friends, but Sonia was getting off at Forty-second Street, so we were together for only three stops. We managed to introduce ourselves and exchange phone numbers. I learned that she was studying at Juilliard. I learned that she was French but had spent the first twelve years of her life in America. Her English was perfect, no accent at all. When I tried out some of my mediocre French on her, her French turned out to be perfect as well. We probably talked for seven minutes, ten minutes at the most. Then she got off, and I knew that something monumental had happened. For me, in any case. I couldn't know what Sonia was thinking or feeling, but after those seven or ten minutes, I knew that I had met the one.

First date. First kiss. First . . . you know what.

I called her the next afternoon. Trembling hands . . . I must have picked up the receiver and put it down three or four times before I found the courage to dial. An Italian restaurant in the West Village, I can't remember the name anymore. Inexpensive, I didn't have much money, and this was the first time—it's hard to believe—the first time I'd ever asked a girl out to *dinner.* I can't see myself. I have no idea what kind of impression I made, but I can see her sitting across from me in her white blouse, her steady green eyes, watchful, alert, amused, and that superb mouth with the rounded lips, smiling, smiling often, and her low voice, a resonant voice that came from somewhere deep in her diaphragm, an extremely sexy voice, I found, always did, and then her laugh, which was much higher, almost squeaky at times, a laugh that seemed to emerge from her throat, even her head, and whenever something tickled her funny bone—I'm talking about later now, not that night—she would go into these wild giggling fits, laughing so hard that tears would come streaming from her eyes.

I remember. I never saw anyone laugh like her. When I was little, I sometimes got scared by it. She would go on for so long, I thought it would never stop, that she would actually die laughing. Then I grew to love it.

So there we were, two twenty-year-old kids in that restaurant on Bank Street, Perry Street, wherever it was, out on our first date. We talked about a lot of things, most of which I've forgotten, but I remember how taken I was when she told me about her family, her background. My own story seemed so dull by comparison, with my furniture-salesman father and fourth-grade schoolteacher mother, the Brills of upper Manhattan, who had never gone anywhere or done anything but work and pay the rent. Sonia's father was a research biologist, a professor, one of the top scientists in Europe. Alexandre Weil—a distant relative of the composer—born in Strasbourg, a Jew (as you already know), and therefore what a fortunate turn when Princeton offered him a job in 1935 and he had the good sense to accept it. If the family had stayed in France during the war, who knows what would have happened to them? Sonia's mother, Marie-Claude, was born in Lyon. I forget what her father did, but both of her grandfathers were Protestant ministers, which means that Sonia was hardly your typical French girl. No Catholics anywhere in sight, no Hail Marys, no visits to the confession box. Marie-Claude met Alexandre when they were students in Paris, and the marriage took place sometime in the early twenties. Four kids in all: three boys and then, five years after the last one was born, along came Sonia, the baby of the bunch, the little princess, who was only one month old when the family left for America. They didn't go back to Paris until nineteen forty-seven. Alexandre was given an important position at the Pasteur Institute—*directeur* was his title, I think—and Sonia wound up going to the Lycée Fénelon. She had already made up her mind to become a singer and didn't want to finish her *bac,* but her parents insisted. That's why she went to Juilliard instead of the conservatory in Paris. She was pissed off at her parents for bearing down on her so hard and more or less ran away. But all was forgiven in the end, and by the time I met Sonia, peace had broken out among the Weils. The family welcomed me in. I think they were touched by the fact that I came from a mixed family, too—in my case a Jewish mother and an Episcopalian father—and so, mind. The middle road, then, which I improvised as follows: I put my hands on her shoulders, leaned forward and down (down because she was shorter than I was), and pressed my lips against hers—rather hard. No tongue involved, no enveloping hug, but a good solid buss for all that. I heard a quiet rumbling in Sonia's throat, a low-pitched *m*-sound, mmmm, and then a slight catch to her breath, a drop to another register, and something that resembled a laugh. I backed away, saw that she was smiling, and put my arms around her. An instant later, her arms were around me, and then I dove in for a real kiss, a French kiss, a French kiss with the French girl who was suddenly the only person who counted anymore. Just one, but a long one, and then, not wanting to overplay my hand, I said good night and headed for the stairs.

Pas mal, mon ami.

A kiss for the ages.

Now I need a sociology lesson. We're talking about nineteen fifty-five, and from all I've heard and read, the fifties weren't the best time for young people. I'm talking about young people and sex. These days, most kids start screwing in their teens, and by the time they've hit twenty, they're old pros at it. So there you are at twenty. Your first date with Sonia has just ended with a triumphant, slobbering kiss. You clearly have the hots for each other. But the prevailing wisdom of the period says: no sex before marriage, at least if you're a girl. You didn't get married until nineteen fifty-seven. You're not going to tell me you held back for two years, are you?

Of course not.

That's a relief.

Horniness is a human constant, the engine that drives the world, and even back then, in the dark age of the mid-twentieth century, students were fucking like rabbits.

Such language, Grandpa.

I thought you'd appreciate it.

That's just it. I do.

On the other hand, I'm not going to pretend there weren't a lot of girls who believed in the myth of the virgin bride, middle-class girls mostly, the so-called good girls, but we mustn't exaggerate either. The obstetrician who delivered your mother in nineteen sixty had been a doctor for almost twenty years. As she was stitching up Sonia's episiotomy after Miriam was born, she assured me that she was going to do a terrific job. She was an expert with the needle, she said, because she'd had so much practice: sewing up girls for their wedding nights to make the husbands think they'd married a virgin.

The things I never knew . . .

That was the fifties. Sex everywhere, but people closed their eyes and made believe it wasn't happening. In America anyway. What made things different for me and your grandmother was the fact that she was French. There are countless hypocrisies in French life, but sex isn't one of them. Sonia moved back to Paris when she was twelve and stayed there until she was nineteen. Her education was far more advanced than mine, and she was prepared to do things that would have sent most American girls shrieking from the bed.

Such as?

Use your imagination, Katya.

You're not going to shock me, you know. I went to Sarah Lawrence, remember? The sex capital of the Western world. I've been all around the block, believe me.

The body has a limited number of orifices. Let's just say that we explored every one of them.

In other words, Grandma was good in bed.

That's a blunt way of putting it, but yes, she was good. Uninhibited, comfortable in her body, sensitive to the shifts and swerves of her own feelings. Every time we did it, it seemed to be different from the time before. Fierce and dramatic one day, slow and languid the next, the surprise of it all, the endless nuances . . .

I remember her hands, the gentleness of her hands when she touched me.

Gentle hands, yes. But strong hands, too. Wise hands. That's how I used to think of them. Hands that could speak.

Did you live together before you were married?

No, no, that was out of the question. We had to sneak around a lot. It had its exciting aspects, but most of the time it was frustrating. I was still living with my parents in Washington Heights, so I didn't have a place of my own. And Sonia had her two roommates. We'd go there whenever they were gone, but that didn't happen often enough to satisfy us.

What about hotels?

Off-limits. Even if we could have afforded them, it was too dangerous. There were laws in New York that made it illegal for unmarried couples to be alone together in the same room. Every hotel had a detective—the house dick—and if he caught you, you'd be thrown in jail.

Lovely.

So what to do? Sonia had lived in Princeton as a child, and she still had friends there. There was one couple—the Gontorskis, I'll never forget them—a physics professor and his wife, refugees from Poland who loved Sonia and didn't give a damn about American sexual customs. They let us stay in their guest room on the weekends. And then there was the outdoor sex, the warm-weather sex in fields and meadows outside the city. A large element of risk. Someone finally found us naked in the bushes, and we got cold feet after that and stopped taking chances. Without the Gontorskis, we would have been in hell.

Why didn't you just get married? Right then, while you were still students.

The draft. The minute I graduated from college, I was going to be called up for my physical, and we figured I'd have to spend two years in the army. Sonia was already singing professionally by my senior year, and what if they shipped me off to West Germany or Greenland or South Korea? I couldn't have asked her to follow me. It wouldn't have been fair.

But you never were in the army, were you? Not if you were married in nineteen fifty-seven.

I flunked the exam. A false diagnosis, as it turned out—but no matter, I was free, and a month later we were married. We didn't have much money, of course, but the situation wasn't quite desperate. Sonia had dropped out of Juilliard and started her going through her head at those moments, she smiled at me and said, Nothing. It was as if her whole being would empty out, and she'd lose contact with herself and the world. All her instincts and impulses about other people were deep, uncannily deep, but her relation to herself was strangely shallow. She had a good mind, but essentially she was uneducated, and she had trouble following a train of thought, couldn't concentrate on anything for very long. Except her music, which was the most important thing in her life. She believed in her talent, but at the same time she knew her limits and refused to tackle pieces she felt were beyond her ability to perform well. I admired her honesty, but there was also something sad about it, as if she thought of herself as second-rate, doomed always to be a notch or two below the best. That's why she never did any opera. Lieder, ensemble work in choral pieces, undemanding solo cantatas—but she never pushed herself beyond that. Did we fight? Of course we fought. All couples fight, but she was never vicious or cruel when we argued. Most of the time, I have to admit, her criticisms of me were spot-on. For a Frenchwoman, she turned out to be a rather lousy cook, but she liked good food, so we ate in restaurants fairly often. An indifferent housekeeper, absolutely no interest in possessions—I say that as a compliment—and even though she was a beautiful young woman with an adorable body, she didn't dress very well. She loved clothes, but she never seemed to choose the right ones. To be frank, I sometimes felt lonely with her, lonely in my work, since all my time was spent reading and writing about books, and she didn't read much, and what she did read she found difficult to talk about.

I'm getting the impression that you felt disappointed.

No, not disappointed. Far from it. Two newlyweds gradually adjusting to each other's foibles, the revelations of intimacy. All in all, it was a happy time for me, for both of us, with no serious complaints on either side, and then the dam in Africa was finished, and we went back to New York with Sonia three months pregnant.

Where did you live?

I thought you weren't interested in real estate.

That's right, I'm not. Question withdrawn.

Several places over the years. But when your mother was born, our apartment was on West Eighty-fourth Street, just off Riverside Drive. One of the windiest streets in the city.

What kind of baby was she?

Easy and difficult. Screaming and laughing. Great fun and a terrible pain in the ass.

In other words, a baby.

No. The baby of babies. Because she was *our* baby, and *our* baby was like no other baby in the world.

How long did Grandma wait until she went back to performing?

She took a year off from traveling, but she was singing in New York again when Miriam was just three months old. You know what a good mother she was—your own mother must have told you that a hundred times—but she also had her work. It was what she was born to do, and I never would have dreamed of trying to hold her back. Still, she had her doubts, especially in the beginning. One day, when Miriam was about six months old, I walked into the bedroom, and there was Sonia on her knees by the bed, hands together, head raised, murmuring to herself in French. My French was quite good by then, and I understood everything she said. To my astonishment, it turned out that she was praying. Dear God, give me a sign and tell me what to do about my little girl. Dear God, fill the emptiness inside me and teach me how to love, to forbear, to give myself to others. She looked and sounded like a child, a small, simpleminded child, and I have to say that I was a little thrown by it—but also moved, deeply, deeply moved. It was as if a door had opened, and I was looking at a new Sonia, a different person from the one I'd known for the past five years. When she realized I was in the room, she turned around and gave me an embarrassed smile. I'm sorry, she said, I didn't want you to know. I walked over to the bed and sat down. Don't be sorry, I told her. I'm just a little puzzled, that's all. We had a long talk after that, at least an hour, the two of us sitting side by side on the bed, discussing the mysteries of her soul. Sonia explained that it started toward the end of her pregnancy, in the middle of the seventh month. She was walking down the street one afternoon on her way home, when all of a sudden a feeling of joy rose up inside her, an inexplicable, overwhelming joy. It was as if the entire universe were rushing into her body, she said, and in that instant she understood that everything was connected to everything else, that everyone in the world was connected to everyone else in the world, and this binding force, this power that held everything and everyone together, was God. That was the only word she could think of. God. Not a Jewish or Christian God, not the God of any religion, but God as the presence that animates all life. She started talking to him after that, she said, convinced that he could hear what she was saying, and these monologues, these prayers, these supplications—whatever you wanted to call them—always comforted her, always put her on an even keel with herself again. It had been going on for months now, but she didn't want to tell me because she was afraid I would think she was stupid. I was so much smarter than she was, so superior to her when it came to intellectual matters—her words, not mine—and she was worried that I'd burst out laughing at my ignorant wife when she told me that she'd found God. I didn't laugh. Heathen that I am, I didn't laugh. Sonia had her own way of thinking and her own way of doing things, and who was I to make fun of her?

I knew her all my life, but she never spoke to me about God, not once.

That's because she stopped believing. When our marriage broke up, she felt that God had abandoned her. That was a long time ago, angel, long before you were born.

Poor Grandma.

Yes, poor Grandma.

I have a theory about your marriage. Mother and I have talked about it, and she tends to go along with me, but I need confirmation, the inside dope from the horse's mouth. How would you respond if I said: You and Grandma got divorced because of her career?

My answer would be: Nonsense.

All right, not her career per se. The fact that she traveled so much.

I would say you were getting warmer—but only as an indi-
rect cause, a secondary factor.

Mother says she used to hate it when Grandma went on tour.
She'd break down and cry, she'd scream, she'd beg her not to go.
Hysterical scenes . . . unadulterated anguish . . . separation af-
ter separation . . .

That happened once or twice, but I wouldn't make too big
an issue of it. When Miriam was very young, say from one to
six, Sonia never left for more than a week at a time. My mother
would move in with us to take care of her, and things went
rather smoothly. Your great-grandmother had a knack with little
kids, she adored Miriam—who was her only granddaughter—
and Miriam couldn't wait for her to show up. It all comes back
to me now . . . the funny things your mother used to do. When
she was three or four, she became fascinated by her grandmother's breasts. They were quite huge, I have to say, since my
mother had grown into a fairly chunky broad by then. Sonia was
small on top, with little adolescent breasts that filled out only
when she was nursing Miriam, but after your mother was weaned,
they got even smaller than they'd been before the pregnancy.
The contrast was utterly stark, and Miriam couldn't help noticing. My mother had a voluminous chest, twenty times the size of
Sonia's. One Saturday morning, she and Miriam were sitting on
the sofa together watching cartoons. A commercial for pizza
came on, which ended with the words: Now, that's a pizza! A
moment later, your mother turned to my mother, clamped her
mouth on her grandmother's right breast, and then came up
shouting: Now, *that's* a pizza! My mother laughed so hard, she

let out a fart, a gigantic trumpet blast of a fart. That got Miriam
laughing so wildly, she peed in her pants. She jumped off the
sofa and started running around the room, yelling at the top of
her lungs: Fart-pee, fart-pee, *oui, oui, oui!*

You're making this up.

No, it really happened, I swear it did. The only reason I mention it is to show you that it wasn't all gloom in the house when
Sonia was gone. Miriam didn't mope around feeling like some
neglected Oliver Twist. She was mostly fine.

And what about you?

I learned to live with it.

That sounds like an evasive answer.

There were different periods, different stages, and each one
had its own texture. In the beginning, Sonia was relatively unknown. She'd done a little singing in New York before we moved
to Paris, but she had to start all over again in France, and then,
just when things seemed to be taking off a bit, we came back to
America, and she had to make another start. In the end, it all
worked to her advantage, since she was known both here and
in Europe. But it took time for her to develop a reputation. The
turning point came in sixty-seven or sixty-eight, when she
signed the contract to make those records with Nonesuch,
but until then she didn't go away that often. I was torn down the
middle. On the one hand, I was happy for her whenever she got
a booking to perform in a new city. On the other hand—just
like your mother—I hated to see her go. The only choice was to
learn to live with it. That's not an evasion, it's a fact.

You were faithful . . .

Totally.

And when did you start to slip?

Stray is probably the word to use in this context.

Or *lapse*. There's a spiritual connotation to it that seems fitting.

All right, lapse. Around nineteen seventy, I suppose. But there was nothing spiritual about it. It was all about sex, sex pure and simple. Summer came, and Sonia went off on a three-month tour of Europe—with your mother, by the way—and there I was by myself, still just thirty-five years old, hormones roaring at full tilt, womanless in New York. I worked hard every day, but the nights were empty, colorless, stagnant. I began hanging out with a bunch of sportswriters, most of them heavy drinkers, playing poker until three in the morning, going out to bars, not because I especially liked any of them, but it was something to do, and I needed a little company after being alone all day. One night, after another boozy session in a bar, I was walking home from midtown to the Upper West Side, and I spotted a prostitute standing in the doorway of a building. A very attractive girl, as it happened, and I was drunk enough to accept her offer of a good time. Am I upsetting you?

A little.

I wasn't planning to give you any details. Just the general drift.

That's okay. It's my fault. I've turned this into Truth Night at Castle Despair, and now that we've started, we might as well go all the way.

Onward, then?

Yes, keep telling the story.

So I had my good time, which wasn't a good time at all, but after fifteen years of sleeping with the same woman I found it fascinating to touch another body, to feel flesh that was different from the flesh I knew. That was the discovery of that night. The novelty of being with another woman.

Did you feel guilty?

No. I considered it an experiment. A lesson learned, so to speak.

So my theory is right. If Grandma had been home in New York, you never would have paid that girl to sleep with you.

In that particular case, yes. But there was more to our downfall than infidelity, more to it than Sonia's absences. I've thought about this for years, and the only half-reasonable explanation I've ever come up with is that there's something wrong with me, a flaw in the mechanism, a damaged part gumming up the works. I'm not talking about moral weakness. I'm talking about my mind, my mental makeup. I'm somewhat better now, I think, the problem seemed to diminish as I grew older, but back then, at thirty-five, thirty-eight, forty, I walked around with a feeling that my life had never truly belonged to me, that I had never truly inhabited myself, that I had never been real. And because I wasn't real, I didn't understand the effect I had on others, the damage I could cause, the hurt I could inflict on the people who loved me. Sonia was my ground, my one solid connection to the world. Being with her made me better than I actually was—healthier, stronger, saner—and because we started living to-gether when we were so young, the flaw was masked for all those years, and I assumed I was just like everyone else. But I wasn't. The moment I began to wander away from her, the bandage dropped off my wound, and then the bleeding wouldn't stop. I went after other women because I felt I'd missed out on something and had to make up for lost time. I'm talking about sex now, nothing but sex, but you can't run around and act the way I did and expect your marriage to hold together. I deceived myself into thinking it would.

Don't hate yourself so much, Grandpa. She took you back, remember?

I know . . . but all those wasted years. It makes me sick to think about them. My dumb-ass flings and dalliances. What did they add up to? A few cheap thrills, nothing of any importance—but there's no question that they laid the groundwork for what happened next.

Oona McNally.

Sonia was so trusting, and I was so discreet, our life went on together without any crucial disturbances. She didn't know, and I didn't tell, and not for one second did I ever think of leaving her. Then, in nineteen seventy-four, I wrote a favorable review of a first novel by a young American author. *Anticipation*, by the aforementioned O.M. It was a startling book, I felt, highly original and written with great command, a strong, promising debut. I didn't know anything about the writer—only that she was twenty-six years old and lived in New York. I read the book in galleys, and since galleys didn't have author photos on them in the seventies, I didn't even know what she looked like. About four months later, I went to a poetry reading at the Gotham

Book Mart (without Sonia, who was at home with Miriam), and when the reading was over and we all started walking down the stairs, someone grabbed me by the arm. Oona McNally. She wanted to thank me for the nice review I'd given her novel. That was the extent of it, but I was so impressed by her looks—tall and lithe, an exquisite face, the second coming of Virginia Blaine—that I asked her out for a drink. How many times had I betrayed Sonia by then? Three or four one-night stands, and one mini-affair that lasted roughly two weeks. Not such a gruesome catalogue when compared to some men, but enough to have taught me that I was prepared to seize opportunities whenever they presented themselves. But this girl was different. You didn't sleep with Oona McNally and say good-bye to her the next morning—you fell in love with her, you wanted her to be part of your life. I won't bore you with the tawdry incidentals. The clandestine dinners, the long talks in out-of-the-way bars, the slow mutual seduction. She didn't jump into my arms immediately. I had to go after her, win her confidence, persuade her that it was possible for a man to be in love with two women at the same time. I still had no intention of leaving Sonia, you understand. I wanted both of them. My wife of seventeen years, my comrade, my innermost heart, the mother of my only child— and this ferocious young woman with the burning intelligence, this new erotic charm, a woman I could finally share my work with and talk to about books and ideas. I began to resemble a character in a nineteenth-century novel: solid marriage in one box, lively mistress in another box, and I, the master magician, standing between them, with the skill and cunning never to

too much a part of me, and even after the divorce, she was still there, still talking to me in my head—the ever-present absent one, as I sometimes call her now. We were in contact, of course, we had to be because of Miriam, the logistics of shared custody, the weekend arrangements, the summer holidays, the high school and college events, and as we slowly adjusted to our new circumstances, I felt her anger against me turn to a kind of pity. Poor August, the champion of fools. She had men. That goes without saying, *n'est-ce pas?* She was only forty when I walked out on her, still radiant, still the same shining girl she'd always been, and one of her entanglements became quite serious, I think, although your mother probably knows more about it than I do. When Oona waltzed off with her German painter, I was shattered. Your tactful reference to *a bad period* doesn't begin to describe how bad it was. I'm not going to delve into those days now, I promise, but even then, at a time when I was absolutely alone, it never occurred to me to reach out to Sonia. That was nineteen eighty-one. In nineteen eighty-two, a couple of months before your parents' wedding, she wrote me a letter. Not about us, but about your mother, worried that Miriam was too young to be rushing into marriage, that she was about to make the same mistake we did in our early twenties. Very prescient, of course, but your grandmother always had a nose for such things. I wrote back and said she was probably right, but even if she was right, there was nothing we could do about it. You can't meddle with other people's feelings, least of all your own child's, and the truth is that kids learn nothing from their parents' mistakes. We have to leave them alone and let them thrash out into the world to make their own mistakes. That was my answer, and then I concluded the letter with a rather trite remark: The only thing we can do is hope for the best. On the day of the wedding, Sonia walked up to me and said: I'm hoping for the best. If I had to pinpoint the moment when our reconciliation began, I would choose that one, the moment when your grandmother said those words to me. It was an important day for both of us—our daughter's wedding—and there was a lot of emotion in the air—happiness, anxiety, nostalgia, a whole range of feeling—and neither one of us was in a mood for bearing grudges. I was still a wreck at that point, by no means fully recovered from the Oona debacle, but Sonia was going through a hard time as well. She'd retired from singing earlier that year, and as I later found out from your mother (Sonia never shared any secrets with me about her private life), she had recently parted ways with a man. So, on top of everything else, we were both at a low ebb that day, and seeing each other somehow had a consoling effect. Two veterans who'd fought in the same war, watching their child march off to a new war of her own. We danced together, we talked about the old days, and for a few moments we even held hands. Then the party was over, and everyone went home, but I remember thinking when I was back in New York that being with her that day was the best thing that had happened to me in a long time. I never made a conscious decision about it, but one morning about a month later, I woke up and realized that I wanted to see her again. No, more than that. I wanted to win her back. I knew my chances were probably nil, but I also knew that I had to give it a try. So I called.

Just like that? You just picked up the phone and called?

Not without trepidation. Not without a lump in my throat and a knot in my stomach. It was an exact reprise of the first time I'd called her—twenty-seven years before. I was twenty again, a jittery, lovesick juvenile plucking up his courage to call his dream girl and ask her out on a date. I must have stared at the phone for ten minutes, but when I dialed the number at last, Sonia wasn't in. The answering machine clicked on, and I was so rattled by the sound of her voice that I hung up. Relax, I said to myself, you're behaving like an idiot, so I dialed the number again and left a message. Nothing elaborate. Just that I wanted to talk to her about something, that I hoped she was well, and that I would be in all day.

Did she call back—or did you have to try again?

She called. But that didn't prove anything. She had no idea what I wanted to talk about. For all she knew, it might have been about Miriam—or some trivial, practical matter. In any case, her voice sounded calm, a little reserved, but with no edge to it. I told her that I'd been thinking about her and wanted to know how she was. Hanging in there, she said, or words to that effect. It was good to see you at the wedding, I said. Yes, she answered, it was a remarkable day, she'd had a wonderful time. Back and forth we went, a bit tentatively on both sides, polite and cautious, not daring to say much of anything. Then I popped the question: would she have dinner with me one night that week. *Dinner?* As she repeated the word, I could hear the disbelief in her voice. There was a long pause after that, and then she said she wasn't sure, she'd have to think it over. I didn't insist. The important thing was not to come on too strong. I knew her too well, and if I started to push, the odds were that she'd start pushing back. That's how we left it. I told her to take care of herself and said good-bye.

Not such a promising start.

No. But it could have been worse. She hadn't turned down the invitation, she just didn't know if she should accept it or not. Half an hour later, the phone rang again. Of course I'll have dinner with you, Sonia said. She apologized for having hesitated, but I'd caught her with her guard down, and she'd been entirely flustered. So we made our dinner date, and that was the beginning of a long and delicate dance, a minuet of desire, fear, and surrender that went on for more than eighteen months. It took that much time before we started living together, but even though we made it through another twenty-one years, Sonia refused to marry me again. I don't know if you were aware of that. Your grandmother and I lived in sin until the day she died. Marriage would have jinxed us, she said. We'd tried it once, and look what happened to us, so why not take another approach? After struggling so hard to get her back, I was happy to abide by her rules. I proposed to her every year on her birthday, but those declarations were no more than encrypted messages, a sign that she could trust me again, that she could go on trusting me for the duration. There was so much I never understood about her, so much she didn't understand about herself. That second courtship was a tough business, a man wooing his ex-wife, and the ex-wife playing hard to get, not giving an inch, not knowing what she wanted, going back and forth between temptation and revulsion until she finally gave in. It took half a year before we wound up in bed. The first time we made love, she laughed when it was over, collapsing into one of those crazy giggling jags of hers that went on so long I began to grow frightened. The second time we made love, she cried, sobbing into the pillow for more than an hour. So many things had changed for her. Her voice had lost the indefinable quality that had made it her voice, that fragile, crystalline ache of unbridled feeling, the hidden god who had spoken through her—all that was gone now, and she knew it, but giving up her career had been a difficult blow, and she was still coming to terms with it. She taught now, giving private singing lessons in her apartment, and there were many days when she had no interest in seeing me. Other days, she would call in a fit of desperation: Come now, I have to see you now. We were lovers again, probably closer to each other than we'd ever been the first time around, but she wanted to keep our lives separate. I wanted more, but she wouldn't give in. That was the line she wouldn't cross and then, after a year and a half, something happened, and it all suddenly changed.

What was it?

You.

Me? What do you mean, *me*?

You were born. Your grandmother and I took the train to New Haven, and we were there when your mother went into labor. I don't want to exaggerate or sound overly sentimental about it, but when Sonia held you in her arms for the first time, she glanced over at me, and when I saw her face—I'm stumbling here, groping for the right words—her face . . . was illuminated. Tears were rolling down her cheeks. She was smiling, smiling and laughing, and it looked as if she'd been filled with light. A few hours later, after we'd gone back to our hotel, we were lying in bed in the dark. She took hold of my hand and said: I want you to move in with me, August. As soon as we get back to New York, I want you to move in and stay with me forever.

I did it.

You did it. You were the one who got us together again.

Well, at least I've accomplished one thing in my life. Too bad I was only five minutes old and didn't know what I was doing.

The first of many great deeds, with many more to come.

Why is life so horrible, Grandpa?

Because it is, that's all. It just is.

All those bad times with you and Grandma. All the bad times with my mother and father. But at least you loved each other and had your second chance. At least my mother loved my father enough to marry him. I've never loved anyone.

What are you talking about?

I tried to love Titus, but I couldn't. He loved me, but I couldn't love him back. Why do you think he joined that stupid company and went away?

To make money. He was going to put in a year and earn close to a hundred thousand dollars. That's an awful lot of cash for a twenty-four-year-old kid. I had a long talk with him before he left. He knew he was taking a risk, but he thought it was worth it.

He left because of me. Don't you understand that? I told him

I didn't want to see him anymore, and so he went off and got himself killed. He died because of me.

You can't think that way. He died because he was in the wrong place at the wrong time.

And I put him there.

You had nothing to do with it. Stop beating yourself up, Katya. It's gone on long enough.

I can't help it.

You've been stuck here for nine months now, and it isn't doing you any good. I think it's time for a change.

I don't want anything to change.

Have you thought about going back to school in the fall?

Off and on. I'm just not sure I'm ready.

It doesn't start for another four months.

I know. But if I want to go back, I have to tell them by next week.

Tell them. If you're not feeling up to it, you can always change your mind at the last minute.

We'll see.

In the meantime, we have to shake things up around here. Does the thought of a trip interest you?

Where would we go?

Anywhere you like, for as long as you like.

What about Mother? We can't just leave her alone.

Her classes end next month. The three of us could go together.

But she's working on her book. She wanted to finish it this summer.

She can write while we're on the road.

The road? You can't ride around in a car. Your leg would hurt too much.

I was thinking more along the lines of a camper. I have no idea what those things cost, but I have a nice chunk of money in the bank. The proceeds from the sale of my New York apartment. I'm sure I could afford one. If not new, then secondhand.

What are you saying? That the three of us drive around in a camper all summer?

That's right. Miriam works on her book, and every day the two of us go off on a quest.

What are we looking for?

I don't know. Anything. The best hamburger in America. We make a list of the top hamburger restaurants in the country and then go around from one to the next and rate them according to a complex list of criteria. Taste, juiciness, size, the quality of the bun, and so on.

If you ate a hamburger every day, you'd probably have a heart attack.

Fish, then. We'll look for the best fish joint in the Lower Forty-eight.

You're pulling my leg, right?

I don't pull legs. Men with bad legs don't do that. It's against our religion.

A camper would be pretty crowded. And besides, you're forgetting one important thing.

What's that?

You snore.

Ah. So I do, so I do. All right, we'll scrap the camper. What about going to Paris? You can see your cousins, practice your French, and gain a new perspective on life.

No thanks. I'd rather stay here and watch my movies.

They're turning into a drug, you know. I think we should cut down, maybe even stop for a while.

I can't do that. I need the images. I need the distraction of watching other things.

Other things? I don't follow. Other than what?

Don't be so dense.

I know I'm dumb, but I just don't get it.

Titus.

But we looked at that video only once—more than nine months ago.

Have you forgotten it?

No, of course not. I think about it twenty times a day.

That's my point. If I hadn't seen it, everything would be different. People go off to war, and sometimes they die. You get a telegram or a phone call, and someone tells you that your son or your husband or your ex-boyfriend has been killed. But you don't see how it happened. You make up pictures in your mind, but you don't know the real facts. Even if you're told the story by someone who was there, what you're left with is words, and words are vague, open to interpretation. We saw it. We saw how they murdered him, and unless I blot out that video with other images, it's the only thing I ever see. I can't get rid of it.

We'll never get rid of it. You have to accept that, Katya. Accept it, and try to start living again.

I'm doing my best.

You haven't stirred a muscle in close to a year. There are other distractions besides watching movies all day. Work, for one thing. A project, something to sink your teeth into.

Like what?

Don't laugh at me, but after looking at all those films with you, I've been thinking that maybe we should write one of our own.

I'm not a writer. I don't know how to make up stories.

What do you think I've been doing tonight?

I don't know. Thinking. Remembering.

As little as possible. I'm better off if I reserve my thinking and remembering for the daytime. Mostly, I've been telling myself a story. That's what I do when I can't sleep. I lie in the dark and tell myself stories. I must have a few dozen of them by now. We could turn them into films. Co-writers, co-creators. Instead of looking at other people's images, why not make up our own?

What kind of stories?

All kinds. Farces, tragedies, sequels to books I've liked, historical dramas, every kind of story you can imagine. But if you accept my offer, I think we should start with a comedy.

I'm not much into laughs these days.

Exactly. That's why we should work on something light—a frothy bagatelle, as frivolous and diverting as possible. If we really put our minds to it, we might have some fun.

Who wants fun?

I do. And you do, too, my love. We've turned into a couple of sad sacks, you and I, and what I'm proposing is a cure, a remedy to ward off the blues.

———

I launch into a story I sketched out last week—the romantic adventures of Dot and Dash, a chubby waitress and a grizzled short-order cook who work in a New York City diner—but less than five minutes into it, Katya falls asleep, and our conversation comes to an end. I listen to her slow, regular breathing, glad that she's finally managed to conk out, and wonder what time it is. Well past four, probably, perhaps even five. An hour or so until dawn, that incomprehensible moment when the blackness starts to thin out and the vireo who lives in the tree beside my window delivers his first chirp of the day. As I mull over the various things Katya has said to me, my thoughts gradually turn to Titus, and before long I'm inside his story again, reliving the disaster I've been struggling to avoid all night.

Katya blames herself for what happened, falsely linking herself to the chain of cause and effect that ultimately led to his murder. One mustn't allow oneself to think that way, but if I succumbed to her faulty logic, then Sonia and I would be responsible as well, since we were the ones who introduced her to Titus in the first place. Thanksgiving dinner five years ago, just after her parents' divorce. She and Miriam drove down to New York to spend the long weekend with us, and on Thursday Sonia and I cooked turkey for twelve people. Among the guests were Titus and his parents, David Small and Elizabeth Blackman, both painters, both old friends of ours. The nineteen-year-old Titus and the eighteen-year-old Katya seemed to hit it off. Did he die because he fell in love with our granddaughter? Follow that thought through to the end, and you could just as easily blame his parents. If David and Liz hadn't met, Titus never would have been born.

He was a bright boy, I thought, an open-hearted, undisciplined boy with wild red hair, long legs, and big feet. I met him when he was four, and since Sonia and I visited his parents' place fairly often, he felt comfortable around us, treating us not as family friends so much as a surrogate aunt and uncle. I liked him because he read books, a rare kid with a hunger for literature, and when he started writing short stories in his mid-teens, he would send them to me and ask for my comments. They weren't very good, but I was touched that he had turned to me for advice, and after a while he began coming to our apartment about once a month to talk about his latest efforts. I would suggest books for him to read, which he would plow through diligently with a kind of lunging, scattershot enthusiasm. His work gradually improved somewhat, but every month it was different, bearing the marks of whatever writer he happened to be reading at the moment—a normal trait in beginners, a sign of development. Flashes of talent began to glimmer through his ornate, overwritten prose, but it was still too early to judge whether he had any genuine promise. When he was a senior in high school and announced that he wanted to stay in the city to attend college at Columbia, I wrote a letter of recommendation for him. I don't know if that letter made any difference, but my alma mater accepted him, and his monthly visits continued.

He was in his second year when he showed up at that Thanksgiving dinner and met Katya. They made an odd and fetching duo, I thought. The floppy, grinning, arm-waving Titus and the small, slender, dark-haired daughter of my daughter. Sarah Lawrence was in Bronxville, just a short train ride into the city, and Katya stayed with us quite often during her undergraduate days, most weekends in fact, escaping dormitory life for a comfortable bed in her grandparents' apartment and nights out in New York. She now claims that she didn't love Titus, but all during the years they were together, there were dozens upon dozens of dinners at our place, usually just the four of us, and I never felt anything but affection between them. Maybe I was blind. Maybe I took too much for granted, but except for an occasional intellectual disagreement and one breakup that lasted under a month, they struck me as a happy, thriving couple. When Titus came to see me on his own, he never hinted at any trouble with Katya, and Titus was a garrulous boy, a person who spoke whatever was on his mind, and if Katya had called it quits with him, surely he would have mentioned it to me. Or maybe not. It could be that I didn't know him as well as I thought I did.

When he started talking about going off to work in Iraq, his parents went into a tailspin of panic. David, normally the gentlest and most tolerant of men, screamed at his son and called him pathologically disturbed, a know-nothing dilettante, a suicidal maniac. Liz wept, took to her bed, and started gorging herself with heavy doses of tranquilizers. That was in February last year. Sonia had died the previous November, and I was in awful shape just then, drinking myself into oblivion every night, not fit for human contact, out of my mind with grief, but David was so distraught, he called me anyway and asked if I would talk some sense into the boy. I couldn't refuse. I had known Titus for too long, and the fact was that I felt concerned for him as well. So I pulled myself together and did the best I could—which was nothing, nothing at all.

I had lost touch with Titus after Sonia became ill, and he seemed to have changed in the intervening months. The talkative, goofy optimist had turned sullen, almost belligerent, and I knew from the start that my words would have no effect on him. At the same time, I don't think he was unhappy to see me, and when he spoke about Sonia and her death, there was true compassion in his voice. I thanked him for his words, poured us two glasses of neat scotch, and then led him into the living room, where we had had so many conversations in the past.

I'm not going to sit here and argue with you, I began. It's just that I'm a little confused, and I'd like you to clarify some things for me. Okay?

Okay, Titus said. No problem.

The war has been going on for close to three years now, I said. When the invasion started, you told me you were against it. *Appalled* was the word you used, I think. You said it was a phony, trumped-up war, the worst political mistake in American history. Am I right, or have I mixed you up with someone else?

You're dead-on. That's exactly how I felt.

We haven't seen much of each other lately, but the last time you were here, I remember you said that Bush should be thrown in jail—along with Cheney, Rumsfeld, and the whole gang of fascist crooks who were running the country. When was that? Eight months ago? Ten months ago?

Last spring. April or May, I can't remember.

Have you changed your thinking since then?

No.

Not at all?

Not one bit.

Then why on earth do you want to go to Iraq? Why participate in a war you detest?

I'm not going there to help America. I'm going for myself.

The money. Is that it? Titus Small, mercenary-at-large.

I'm not a mercenary. Mercenaries carry weapons and kill people. I'm going to drive a truck, that's all. Transporting supplies from one place to another. Sheets and towels, soap, candy bars, dirty laundry. It's a shit job, but the pay is enormous. BRK— that's the name of the company. You sign up for a year, and you come home with ninety or a hundred thousand dollars in your pocket.

But you'll be supporting something you're opposed to. How can you justify that to yourself?

I don't look at it that way. For me, it's not a moral decision. It's about learning something, about starting a new kind of education. I know how horrible and dangerous it is over there, but that's just why I want to go. The more horrible, the better.

You're not making sense.

All my life, I've wanted to be a writer. You know that, August. I've been showing you my wretched little stories for years, and you've been kind enough to read them and give me your comments. You've encouraged me, and I'm very grateful to you for that, but we both know I'm no good. My stuff is dry and heavy and dull. Crap. Every word I've written so far is crap. I've been out of college for close to two years now, and I spend my days sitting in an office, answering the phone for a literary agent. What kind of life is that? It's so fucking safe, so fucking dreary, I can't stand it anymore. I don't *know* anything, August. I haven't *done* anything. That's why I'm going away. To experience something that isn't about me. To be out in the big rotten world and discover what it feels like to be part of history.

Going off to war isn't going to turn you into a writer. You're thinking like a schoolboy, Titus. At best, you'll come back with your head full of unbearable memories. At worst, you won't come back at all.

I know there's a risk. But I have to take it. I have to change my life—*right now.*

Two weeks after that conversation, I climbed into a rented Toyota Corolla and set off for Vermont to spend some time with Miriam. The trip ended with the crash that put me in the hospital, and by the time I was released, Titus had already left for Iraq. There was no chance to say good-bye to him or wish him luck or beg him to reconsider his decision one last time. Such romantic claptrap . . . such childish drivel . . . but the kid was in despair over his ruined ambitions, facing up to the fact that he didn't have it in him to do the one thing he had always wanted to do, and he ran off in an impulsive attempt to redeem himself in his own eyes.

I moved in with Miriam in early April. Three months later, Katya called from New York, sobbing into the phone. Turn on the television, she said, and there was Titus on the evening news, sitting in a chair in some unidentified room with cinder-block walls, surrounded by four men with hoods over their heads and rifles in their hands. The quality of the video was poor, and it was difficult to read the expression on Titus's face. He looked more stunned than terrified, I felt, but apparently he had been beaten, for I could dimly make out what appeared to be a large bruise on his forehead. There was no sound, but over the images the newscaster was reading his prepared text, which went more or less as follows: *Twenty-four-year-old New Yorker Titus Small, a truck driver for the contracting company BRK, was abducted this morning en route to Baghdad. His captors, who have yet to identify themselves with any known terrorist organization, are demanding ten million dollars for his release, as well as the immediate cessation of all BRK activities in Iraq. They have vowed to execute their prisoner if these demands are not met within seventy-two hours. George Reynolds, a spokesman for BRK, said his company is doing everything in its power to ensure Mr. Small's safety.*

Katya arrived at her mother's house the following day, and two nights after that we switched on her laptop and looked at the second and last video shot by the kidnappers, the one that could be seen only on the Internet. We already knew that Titus was dead. BRK had made a substantial offer on his behalf, but as expected (why think the unthinkable when profits are at stake?), they had refused to shut down their operations in Iraq. The slaughter was carried out as promised, precisely seventy-two hours after Titus was torn from his truck and thrown into that room with the cinder-block walls. I still don't understand why the three of us felt driven to watch the tape—as if it were an obligation, a sacred duty. We all knew it would go on haunting us for the rest of our lives, and yet somehow we felt we had to be there with Titus, to keep our eyes open to the horror for his sake, to breathe him into us and hold him there—in us, that lonely, miserable death, in us, the cruelty that was visited on him in those last moments, in us and no one else, so as not to abandon him to the pitiless dark that swallowed him up.

Mercifully, there is no sound.

Mercifully, a hood has been placed over his head.

He is sitting in a chair with his hands tied behind him, motionless, making no attempt to break free. The four men from the previous video are standing around him, three holding rifles, the fourth with a hatchet in his right hand. Without any signal or gesture from the others, the fourth man suddenly brings the blade down on Titus's neck. Titus jerks to his right, his upper body squirms, and then blood starts seeping through the hood. Another blow from the hatchet, this one from behind. Titus's head lolls forward, and by now blood is streaming down all over him. More blows: front and back, right and left, the dull blade chopping long past the moment of death.

One of the men puts down his rifle and clamps Titus's head firmly in his two hands to prop it up as the man with the hatchet continues to go about his business. They are both covered in blood.

When the head is finally severed from the body, the executioner lets the hatchet fall to the floor. The other man removes the hood from Titus's head, and then a third man takes hold of Titus's long red hair and carries the head closer to the camera. Blood is dripping everywhere. Titus is no longer quite human. He has become the idea of a person, a person and not a person, a dead bleeding thing: *une nature morte.*

The man holding the head backs away from the camera, and a fourth man approaches with a knife. One by one, working with great speed and precision, he stabs out the boy's eyes.

The camera rolls for a few more seconds, and then the screen goes black.

Impossible to know how long it has lasted. Fifteen minutes. A thousand years.

I hear the alarm clock ticking on the floor. For the first time in hours, I close my eyes, wondering if it might not be possible to sleep after all. Katya stirs, lets out a little groan, and then rolls onto her side. I consider putting my hand on her back and stroking it for a few seconds but then give up the idea. Sleep is such a rare commodity in this house, I don't want to risk disturbing her. Invisible stars, invisible sky, invisible world. I see Sonia's hands on the keyboard. She's playing something by Haydn, but I can't hear anything, the notes make no sound, and then she swivels around on the stool and Miriam runs into her arms, a three-year-old Miriam, an image from the distant past, perhaps real, perhaps imagined, I can barely tell the difference anymore. The real and the imagined are one. Thoughts are real, even thoughts of unreal things. Invisible stars, invisible sky. The sound of my breath, the sound of Katya's breath. Bedtime prayers, the rituals of childhood, the gravity of childhood. *If I should die before I wake.* How fast it all goes. Yesterday a child, today an old man, and from then until now, how many beats of the heart, how many breaths, how many words spoken and heard? Touch me, someone. Put your hand on my face and talk to me . . .

I can't be sure, but I think I might have dozed off for a while. No more than a few minutes, perhaps only seconds, but suddenly I've been interrupted by something, a sound, I believe, yes, several sounds in fact, a knocking on the door, a faint and persistent knocking, and then I open my eyes and tell Miriam to come in. As the door opens, I can see her face with a certain clarity, and I understand that it's no longer night, that we've come to the cusp of dawn. The world inside my room is gray now. Miriam has already put on some clothes (blue jeans and a baggy white sweater), and the moment she shuts the door behind her, the vireo lets out his first chirp of the day.

What a relief, she whispers, looking at the sleeping Katya. I just checked in on her, and when she wasn't in her bed, I got a little scared.

She came down a few hours ago, I whisper back to her. Another rough night, so we lay in the dark and talked.

Miriam walks over to the bed, plants a kiss on my cheek, and sits down beside me. Are you hungry? she asks.

A little.

Maybe I should start the coffee.

No, sit here and talk to me for a while. There's something I need to know.

About what?

Katya and Titus. She told me she broke up with him before he went away. Is that true? She seems to think he left because of her.

You had so many other things on your mind, I didn't want to bother you with it. Mommy's cancer . . . all those months . . . and then the car accident. But yes, they broke up.

When?

Let me think. . . . Your seventieth birthday was in February, February two thousand and five. Mommy was already sick then. It was just a few months after that. Late spring or early summer.

But Titus didn't leave until the following February, two thousand and six.

Eight or nine months after they broke up.

So Katya is wrong. He didn't go to Iraq because of her.

She's punishing herself. That's what this is all about. She wants to implicate herself in what happened to him, but she really had nothing to do with it. You talked to him before he left. He explained his reasons to you.

And he didn't mention Katya's name. Not once.

You see?

It makes me feel a little better. And also a little worse.

She's coming along now. I can smell it. Bit by bit by bit. The next step is to talk her into going back to school.

She says she's considering it.

Which was out of the question just two months ago.

I grab hold of Miriam's hand and say, I almost forgot. I read some more of your manuscript last night . . .

And?

I think you've nailed it. No more doubts, all right? You're doing a first-rate job.

Are you sure?

I've told a lot of fibs in my day, but I never lie about books.

Miriam grins, aware of the two hundred and fifty-nine secret references buried in that remark, and I grin back at her. Keep on smiling, I say. You look beautiful when you smile.

Only when I smile?

All the time. Every minute of every day.

Another one of your fibs, but I'll take it. She pats me on the cheek and says: Coffee and toast?

No, not today. I think we should go all out this morning. Scrambled eggs and bacon, French toast, pancakes, the whole works.

A farmer's breakfast.

That's it, a farmer's breakfast.

I'll get your crutch, she says, standing up and walking over to the hook on the wall beside my bed.

I follow her with my eyes for a moment, and then I say: Rose Hawthorne wasn't much of a poet, was she?

No. Pretty awful, in fact.

But there's one line . . . one great line. I think it's as good as anything I've ever read.

Which one? she asks, turning to look at me.

As the weird world rolls on.

Miriam breaks into another big smile. I knew it, she says. When I was typing up the quote, I said to myself, He's going to like this one. It could have been written for him.

The weird world rolls on, Miriam.

Crutch in hand, she walks back to the bed and sits down beside me. Yes, Dad, she says, studying her daughter with a worried look in her eyes, the weird world rolls on.